About

Stevyn Colgan is the author of nine books and is a popular speaker at UK and international events and festivals. He has appeared on numerous podcasts and radio shows including *Freakonomics*, *Saturday Live*, *Do The Right Thing*, *Eat Sleep Work Repeat*, *No Such Thing As A Fish*, Josie Long's *Short Cuts* and many more.

For more than a decade he was one of the 'elves' that research and write the multi award-winning TV series *QI* and he was part of the writing team that won the Rose d'Or for BBC Radio 4's *The Museum of Curiosity*. In his previous career, he was a police officer in London for thirty years.

His first novel, *A Murder to Die For*, was shortlisted for the Penguin Books Dead Good Reader Awards and longlisted for the *Guardian*'s Not the Booker prize 2018.

He lives on the Buckinghamshire/Oxfordshire border and can't afford to live in the Cotswolds.

Also by Stevyn Colgan

Joined-Up Thinking
Henhwedhlow: The Clotted Cream of Cornish Folktales
(with Tony Hak)
Constable Colgan's Connectoscope
The Third Condiment
Colgeroons
Saving Bletchley Park (with Dr Sue Black OBE)
One Step Ahead: Notes from the Problem Solving Unit
A Murder to Die For
The Nearly Invisible Man and Other Stories

AS A CONTRIBUTOR

I Remember: Reflections on Fishing and Childhood
(ed. Joe Cowley)
Ottakar's Local History: High Wycombe (ed. Roger Cole)
The QI 'F' Annual
The QI 'G' Annual
The QI 'H' Annual
The 'EFG' Bumper Book of QI Annuals
Subject Verb Object (ed. Dane Cobain)

Praise for *A Murder to Die For*

'Stevyn Colgan bestrides the territory of English rural comedy, one foot on the throat of Joanna Trollope, the other knocking the bonnet of Miss Marple off her silver head. Divine black village comedy.'

– Stephen Fry

'Only the British can mix humour and homicide so charmingly.'

– Sandi Toksvig

'Delightful witty fun. A joy for any fan of the great English murder-mystery. It's a literary cream tea with a glass of fizz.'

– Neil Dudgeon, DCI Barnaby of *Midsomer Murders*

'The jokes come thick and fast, from the outrageous to the sly, with some wonderful observations on the fans who attend murder-mystery festivals.'

– Mike Ripley (*Shots* Magazine)

'Joyfully plays up the tropes and themes of murder-mystery stories … truly remarkable, funny, sharp.'

– Fell From Fiction

'This book is very, very funny, playing with the cosy murder-mystery stereotype and – despite mentions of mobile phones etc. – you could well imagine the setting to be timeless.'

– It Takes A Woman

The Diabolical Club

The Diabolical Club

Stevyn Colgan

unbound

This edition first published in 2019

Unbound
6th Floor Mutual House, 70 Conduit Street, London W1S 2GF
www.unbound.com

ISBN (eBook): 978-1-78965-040-2
ISBN (Paperback): 978-1-78965-039-6

Cover design by Mecob

Printed and bound in Great Britain by Clays Ltd, Elcograf S.p.A.

*Dedicated to the unique and magical Cottage
Bookshop in Penn, Buckinghamshire (1951–2018)
and to the ladies who worked there – Liz, Paula, Sue
and the two Barbaras.*

You are sorely and deeply missed.

'The only way to save a rhinoceros is to save the environment in which it lives. Because there's a mutual dependency between it and millions of other species.'

– *Sir David Attenborough*

KILLER OF AWARD-WINNING
AUTHOR JAILED

By Verity Hyman-Lightstone, Court Reporter

There were unprecedented scenes at Bowcester Crown Court yesterday when hundreds of book fans arrived for the sentencing of the man found guilty of murdering popular author Shirley Pomerance last May. In his summing up, Mr Justice Catermoul described Fireball Savidge (54), of Beller Row, Milverton, as 'a troubled, volatile and dangerous man' who should be imprisoned for a minimum of thirty years and undergo psychiatric evaluation. The news brought loud cheers from the crowds outside. The judge also praised retired police detective Frank Shunter (56), whose 'public-spirited investigation' identified the killer.

Miss Pomerance (73), author of the Trupenie Prize-winning novel *Dali Plays Golf*, was beaten to death and then stabbed multiple times during last year's Agnes Crabbe Murder-Mystery Festival in Nasely, South Herewardshire. The annual event celebrates the life and works of the reclusive author, who died in 1944. Miss Pomerance was a guest at the event because it was recently discovered that she was Agnes Crabbe's grand-daughter. She was also united with a half-sister, Brenda Tradescant (71, now writing under the name of Brenda Crabbe), of whom she had been previously unaware. Neither of the women had known that the illustrious author was their grandmother as their own mother had been given up for adoption as a baby.

Savidge was also charged with the abduction and assault of three people that he took hostage: Mrs Esme Handibode, solicitor Andrew Tremens and journalist Pamela Dallimore.

Savidge will serve his sentence in the maximum security wing of HM Prison Pickthall, near Jarnton.

DIARY FIND GIVES NEW HOPE TO CRABBE FANS

By Aliffe Levinshulme, Arts Correspondent

The celebrated murder-mystery author Agnes Crabbe may have written a book that has been 'lost' for more than half a century. That's the claim being made by Mr Andrew Tremens, the solicitor who manages the Crabbe estate. He says that new evidence has emerged to support the idea.

'Two years ago we found diaries belonging to Iris Gobbelin, Agnes's best friend and the only person who saw her during her self-imposed years of seclusion. Those diaries led us to the discovery that Agnes had given birth to a daughter in secret,' he said, while speaking at the Sprittlethorpe Crime Fiction Festival. 'And now we have found a third diary, which strongly suggests that Crabbe wrote a novel, possibly called *Wallowing in the Mire*, that has yet to be found.'

HOPE

After losing her husband, Daniel, her father, John Brock, and her brother, Tom, in the First World War, Agnes Crabbe withdrew from village life and remained a recluse until she died aged forty-nine. But in that time, she penned twenty-one novels, along with short stories, plays and poems. She never submitted any of her work for publication and her manuscripts were only discovered in 2000. Since then her books have become bestsellers and have been turned into award-winning TV adaptations, starring Helen Greeley as amateur sleuth Miss Millicent Cutter.

Mr Tremens says that a new Crabbe novel would be a fantastic find. 'A previously unpublished twenty-second novel would delight millions of Agnes Crabbe fans all over the world,' he told festival goers. 'And I'm one of them.' The discovery of a new book is likely to result in a six- or seven-figure bidding war among publishers.

Chapter 1

Joan Bultitude's poodles were noisy, prone to biting and indiscriminate in their toilet habits, which meant that they were disliked by almost everyone who had ever had the misfortune of encountering them. She acknowledged that this was entirely her fault; despite her best intentions, her busy work schedule meant she had never found enough free time to devote to their training and she firmly believed that there were no bad dogs, only bad owners. It was therefore guilt, as much as anything else, that had led to her walking them early in the mornings in remote locations far away from judgemental eyes and the temptation offered by joggers' ankles.

Black Dog Wood consisted of 120 acres of land that spooned two sides of the Harpax Grange School estate in a loose L-shape. A number of time-worn paths snaked their various ways through the densely crowded trees and intersected at places of interest. One such was at the boundary of the school's playing fields by an ancient oak known as the Knicker Tree. It had become a tradition for the boarders to hang an item of underwear among its branches on their last day of school and the practice had been going on for over fifty years. Consequently, the foibles and fancies of late twentieth- and early twenty-first-century fashion could be seen among the panties, bras and occasional suspender belts and girdles that festooned its branches. Miss Bultitude frowned at the latest crop of lingerie, recently donated by the outgoing Sixth Form. Every year the underwear seemed to get flimsier and flimsier.

She set off along a path that wound its way around the edge of the wood to Gertie's Plash, a large man-made pond fed and refreshed by a small tributary of the nearby River Gew. The Plash was a popular local beauty spot and a favourite with picnickers and birdwatchers. However, it was currently cordoned off as it was due to be drained in the coming week and long, fat orange hoses lay on the muddy shore like spray-tanned anacondas, awaiting the arrival of the pumping machinery. Giving the Plash and the river a wide berth so that her dogs didn't harass the waterfowl, Miss Bultitude made her way briskly along another path towards Monty's Folly, the tall stone obelisk that marked the location of the Whorne family mausoleum. Built by Sir Montgomery in the 1790s, the building occupied a clearing at the furthest point in the woods from Harpax Grange. Thrusting up from its centre, the obelisk was topped by a golden pig that represented the source of the Whorne's once sizeable fortune. The fact that the family's historic seat was now a private girls' school was a blunt reminder that their star had since descended to Earth with a resounding thump.

'What do you have there, Teasel?'

The little dog trotted forward and Miss Bultitude wrestled an object from its mouth.

'Good heavens. It looks like a collarbone,' she said, examining the item closely. 'Where on earth did you find it?'

The dog looked at her blankly and yapped for the return of its trophy.

'No, no, this is not for you,' scolded Miss Bultitude as a

2

sudden terrible thought struck her. 'Oh my. I do hope it's not one of the Whornes.'

A bank of cloud smothered the low sun and a chill settled over the woods as she stepped off the path and kicked her way through the deep litter of crisp autumn leaves in the direction from which Teasel had come. A creeping dread began to gnaw at her insides. Like most local people, she'd first been told the story of the Shaggy Beast of Black Dog Wood when she was a young child, and remembrance of her parents' warnings to 'Stay on the path!' now made her imagine that feral eyes were watching and that hungry, knife-fanged monsters lurked in the bosky places between the trees. It surely didn't help that there had been several alleged sightings of the fabled creature in recent years. But Joan Bultitude was an educated and intelligent woman, the headmistress of this prestigious private girls' school, and not the sort of person to be rattled by old folk tales. She took a deep breath and shrugged off her sense of unease. It was just the sudden drop in temperature to blame for her discomfort, she reasoned, nothing more. There were no such things as monsters.

The sun emerged from the clouds, casting a watery, anaemic light over a patch of open ground upon which Teasel suddenly halted and began pawing at the dewy loam. Miss Bultitude stepped in and began sweeping away the leaves and topsoil with her booted foot. And all of a sudden she found herself looking at the unmistakeable creamy-coloured dome of a human skull.

Chapter 2

'And lastly, so that we may remind ourselves that the dead reside not in the grave but in the hearts and minds of the living, I'd like you all to take a few minutes to reflect upon your fondest memories of our dear departed friend Hugh while we play a piece of music that I'm told he was particularly fond of. Mr Wyngarde, if you'd be so kind?'

The aged verger of St Probyn's rose unsteadily to his feet, shuffled his way to a table and pressed the play button on a portable CD player. As heavy urban beats began to rattle the chandeliers and rapper Earl Grey T explained how his homies were 'strapping up to fight for their flow' in Downtown LA, the Reverend Dudley Tirbett's luxuriant eyebrows knitted together above his keel of a nose. He turned to his colleague and shrugged in a way that invited an explanation.

'I'm so sorry,' whispered the verger. 'I borrowed the player from that young Ginger fellow at the café. I must have forgotten to change the record.'

At the front of the congregation, the newly widowed Mrs Gladys Brockhole sat in dignified silence while her three middle-aged daughters struggled to maintain their composure. As emotions ranged from grief to embarrassment to the urge to laugh out loud, their eyes streamed and their noses ran; a situation made all the worse by the fact that none of their husbands had remembered to bring along a packet of tissues, as they'd been instructed to do. Consequently, all they had at their disposal was a single paper napkin that one of them had found in the bottom of her handbag. As it passed from sister to sister and back again, it quickly began to take on all of the more unpleasant physical properties of raw egg.

'I thought they were going to play "Our Last Song Together",' said Gerry Waxleigh, sitting several pews behind the grieving Brockholes. 'This isn't Neil Sedaka.'

'It isn't even music,' moaned Len Youlden. 'I can't sit here and listen to this.'

'We're pall-bearers, Len. We have to.'

'Bloody bugger,' said Youlden, pushing his fingers deeper into his enormous hairy ears.

Following the service, the family and friends of Hugh Donelan Brockhole gathered at the graveside to say their final farewells. Someone had suggested that his sister and family in New Zealand should be part of his send-off by way of mobile phone but Gladys hadn't yet recovered from her late husband's unexpected rap tribute and didn't feel up to it. Nor, for that matter, did any of her dishevelled daughters or their chastised and apologetic husbands. Therefore, Mr Wyngarde had volunteered to provide a blow-by-blow account of the committal by way of an apology for his earlier blunder.

As the Reverend Tirbett began his final blessing, the weather seemed to sense the mood and heavy grey clouds, pregnant with rain, gathered over the churchyard.

'In sure and certain hope of the resurrection to eternal life through our Lord Jesus Christ, we commend to Almighty God our brother Hugh. We commit his body to the ground...'

'They're lowering him in now,' shouted the verger into the phone at a volume he considered necessary for speaking to people half a world away. 'Oh, what a shame, it's started to rain.'

'Earth to earth, ashes to ashes, dust to dust...'

'The casket is at the bottom now and— Oh dear. I've dropped my umbrella. Hang on...'

'The Lord bless him and keep him, the Lord make his face to shine upon him and be gracious to him...'

'I'll just reach...'

'The Lord lift up his countenance upon him and— What on earth are you doing down there, Mr Wyngarde?'

In nearby Sacker Street, Barry Chetwynd looked at his watch and growled. He had intended to be at the funeral as Hugh Brockhole had been a regular customer, with a particular penchant for offal. It had seemed only right to pay his last respects and to say thank you for his kidney-heavy custom. However, sometime during the night, the main display window of his shop had been vandalised with spray paint and he'd had to miss the service to wait for the arrival of a specialist cleaning firm. They were now over half an hour late and it had begun to spit with rain. He folded his beefy arms and swore.

'I say. That's a nuisance,' said Charlie Barnfather, appearing at his side. 'I can't remember the last time we had graffiti in the village. During the Thatcher years as I recall. Something about cruise missiles?'

'Hmf,' grunted Chetwynd.

'What have they written there? *Nando's is the neo-opiate of the masses.* What's that supposed to mean?'

'Damned if I know,' growled Chetwynd. 'Little bastards did it overnight.'

'What a nuisance,' said Barnfather again.

'When I was a kid, at least the graffiti made some kind of sense. *No Nukes. Eat the Rich. M. Kahn is Bent.* Not pseudo-intellectual bollocks like this. So, how did the funeral go?'

Charlie Barnfather scratched at the large white sideburns that didn't quite cover his pock-marked cheeks. Flecks of dandruff littered his dark suit and black tie like unpleasant little stars in a polyester firmament.

'They played the wrong music during the service. Then the verger fell into the grave during the committal.'

'You're kidding me.'

'I'm not.'

'The doddery old sod should retire before he gets himself killed,' said the butcher. 'This isn't the first time he's had an accident. Good turn-out, though?'

'Not bad. Hugh was a popular chap. Oh, Sid Munsun told me to tell you that there was a fresh sighting up at Black Dog Wood last night.'

'Really?'

'Apparently. Young Jessica Tremblett came into the mini-market first thing this morning boasting that she'd seen a big hairy thing in the woods.'

Chetwynd laughed lewdly.

'Behave yourself,' said Barnfather.

'You could have phrased it better,' said Chetwynd. 'So what else did Sid say?'

'That was it. You'd best speak to him if you want more details,' said Barnfather. 'Or to young Jessie herself. I'm just passing on the news.'

'Thanks, Charlie. I'll do that. I've always said that there's something in those woods.'

'Magic mushrooms,' said Barnfather, tapping his nose. 'The fields are full of them this time of year, and you know what youngsters are like. I reckon Jessie and some beau of hers heard a couple of amorous foxes and the drugs did the rest. They make a heck of a noise when mating.'

'Who? Jessie or the foxes?'

Charlie Barnfather waved an admonishing finger and headed off to his chemist's shop on the High Street.

'The Shaggy Beast is real,' said Chetwynd. 'And one day I'll prove it.'

He looked once again at the message scrawled across his shop window and cursed sulphurously.

'Best funeral I've been to in ages,' mused Gerry Waxleigh. 'It's gone straight in at Number Four in my Top Ten.'

'Remember when old Wyngarde tried to scatter Henry Gawkrodger's ashes during a gale?' chuckled Len Youlden. 'He swallowed half of him, I reckon. And he was sick as a dog afterwards.'

'Wasn't there a debate about whether they should bury the sick as it was mostly composed of Henry?' asked pub landlord Vic Sallow.

'That's Number Three,' said Waxleigh. 'Our verger is going for gold.'

Youlden hiccupped and grinned, his puny tolerance for alcohol already being sorely tested after just a couple of pints. The two old friends were enjoying a post-funeral drink in the saloon bar of the curiously named Happy Onion, Nasely's only pub. Waxleigh was tall and gaunt, the result of a lifetime of hard work on the farm. A floss of frizzy grey hair covered him everywhere except for the crown of his head. Youlden was shorter and paunchier and sported a cruel scar that ploughed a furrow across his lower lip and badly shaven chin. He whistled as he spoke due to a missing incisor.

'You have a Top Ten of funerals?' asked Vic. 'Isn't that in poor taste?'

'Not at all,' said Waxleigh. 'Most send-offs are completely unmemorable. A good one is worth celebrating, surely?'

'OK. So what's your Number One?'

'Has to be the Cheesemans,' said Waxleigh.

'When the marquee came down and everyone got trapped inside?'

'That's the one.'

'And Mrs Martensen choked to death on a falafel?'

'Yes indeed.'

'And that stable boy got clonked on the head and went doolally and set fire to all those hay bales?'

'More of an unstable boy, I'd say,' said Waxleigh. 'But yes, what a corker of a funeral that was, eh?'

'Three people died and fifteen were hospitalised, Gerry.'

'Ah, memories,' said Waxleigh, with a nostalgic smile.

'It's Gladys I feel sorry for,' slurred Youlden. 'Loses her husband and then some bloody bugger paints a cock and balls on the side wall of her cottage.'

'So I saw,' said Vic.

'A foot long it is, I reckon,' said Youlden. 'It's a disgrace.'

'Must have come as a shock to her.'

'I'll say. They were childhood sweethearts and Hugh was the only man she ever slept with,' said Waxleigh. 'She probably doesn't know that they come bigger than a Chantenay carrot.'

Len Youlden choked on his beer.

'Have some respect, Gerry,' said Vic. 'You just buried the man.'

'Ah, he'd have laughed along with us,' said Waxleigh, smiling. 'He had a rare sense of humour, did Hugh. Knew every dirty joke in the book, and a few more besides. If he'd been at his own funeral he'd have wet himself. I know I did. And so did old Miss Shelmerdine, incidentally. She really needs to see Dr Meissen about that. Anyhow, here's to Hugh.'

'To Hugh,' said Youlden.

The two men clinked their glasses together and looked expectantly at Vic, who lifted the empty glass he was wiping dry in solidarity.

'Two more?' he asked.

'Go on then,' said Waxleigh, downing the last of his pint. 'For Hugh.'

'The little sods spray-painted on Barry Chetwynd's shop window too,' said Vic as he pulled their pints. 'He reckons it's animal rights protesters.'

'Those scruffy herberts who are always waving placards outside the abattoir?'

'Could be,' said Vic. 'I didn't understand a bloody word of what they wrote, mind.'

'Bloody buggers. How do they expect to have bacon sandwiches without killing pigs?'

'I don't think they're the kind of people who eat bacon sandwiches, Len,' said Waxleigh. 'That's the point they're making; that none of us should be eating meat.'

'They'll have to pry my morning fry-up from my cold dead hands.'

'That'll be sooner rather than later,' said Waxleigh. 'You might just as well be hooked up to a cholesterol drip.'

'The thing is, I can understand protests at the abattoir. And at a butcher's shop,' said Vic. 'But what have they got against Gladys Brockhole?'

'Indeed. The last thing a newly widowed woman wants is a big cock on her side wall,' said Waxleigh. 'Ah, good morning, Frank.'

10

Frank Shunter had appeared in the pub doorway. He wiped his shoes on the doormat.

'Good morning, gents.'

'Hello, stranger,' said Vic.

'Stranger? It's only been a week.'

'A week is a long time in this trade,' said Vic. 'Pubs are closing at a rate of six a day.'

'Then I'll do my bit to keep you afloat. Pint of the Cockering IPA please, Vic.'

'Didn't see you at the funeral,' said Youlden.

'No, you didn't,' said Shunter. 'I've buried too many colleagues over the years and I avoid them if I can. Plus, I hardly know the Brockholes. How was it?'

'Hilarious,' said Waxleigh. 'Straight in at Number Four.'

'That high? Maybe I should have gone after all.'

'So you know about this Top Ten business too?' asked Vic, handing over Shunter's pint.

'Only because Gerry and I were talking the other day about what happened at Pernilla Stashwick's funeral. Remember? Just after she was buried, her estranged twin sister unexpectedly turned up and terrified half the villagers, who thought Pernilla had turned into a zombie.'

'That's Number Two,' said Waxleigh.

'So what do you reckon about this sudden epidemic of graffiti in the village?' asked Vic.

'Does writing pretentious twaddle on the butcher's shop window constitute an epidemic?' said Shunter.

'Have you not seen Gladys Brockhole's cock and balls?' asked Waxleigh.

'No. But it sounds like I might need a drink before I do,' said Shunter, sipping at his ale. The froth caught in his neatly clipped grey moustache and he sucked it away noisily.

'Animal rights protesters, we reckon,' said Vic.

'Bloody buggers,' said Youlden.

'Sounds likely. Though it's unlike them to be so brazen,' said Shunter. 'Perhaps they're building up to something. Protesting at the public meeting tomorrow, perhaps?'

'Waste of their time that'll be. The Plash has got to be drained. It's a done deal,' said Waxleigh, popping his tweed cap on his head. 'Fancy a gasper, Len?'

'Aye.'

The two men made their way outside to the beer garden and smoking area.

Chapter 3

On the riverside terrace of Westminster Palace, Sir Giles Luscott-Whorne, MP for South Herewardshire (South), stood looking down at the Thames, his thoughts as dark and murky as the swirling waters below.

Sir Giles was a very wealthy man. While his father, and his grandfather before him, had been content to earn a decent living from the family's pig farms, Giles had wanted more than just 'decent'. And, having noted the steady increase in the number of TV food programmes throughout the 1990s, he had decided to push the family business onto the fine dining bandwagon. The gamble had paid off handsomely and, thanks to a combination of classy packaging, clever marketing and the endorsements of several *en vogue* celebrity chefs, his range of organic free-range pork products had quickly become the preferred choice of the discerning carnivore. In the two decades since, he had supplied the top hotels and restaurants, won countless awards for quality and taste, and been applauded worldwide for his commitment to animal welfare and his 'nose-to-tail' philosophy to reduce waste. His company's marketing blurb proudly proclaimed '*We use everything but the oink!*', which was more or less true. Leftover cuts and offal were passed on to a subsidiary company, which produced children's favourites such as Piggystix and Hoglogz – products so popular and delicious that most parents were happy to turn a blind eye to the listed ingredients and not to dwell on the question of which parts of the 'nose-to-tail' had been used to make them. Giles had made his first million by the age of thirty and his tenth before his fortieth. Now in his mid-fifties and knighted for his services to the food industry, he was a very rich man. But he remained frustrated and unfulfilled.

As a child, he had been constantly drip-fed stories of his illustrious ancestors – those worthy men and stalwart women whose bones and ashes now resided in the family mausoleum at Harpax. Before circumstance had forced the Whorne family to become farmers themselves, they had been landed gentry, lording it over the southern parishes of South Herewardshire for four hundred years and growing fat on the profits generated by their farms and the rents from their hard-working tenants. But the march of time had not been kind and they had lost everything after the wars, including Harpax Grange, the family seat. The sale had marked the beginning of the family's fall from grace and by the time Giles had arrived, screaming, into the world in 1962, the Whornes had been relegated to the respectable but ubiquitous middle classes. These days, the name was associated mostly with tasty bangers and dubious pig-shaped things covered in savoury breadcrumbs.

Sir Giles dreamed of restoring the Whorne name to the elevated position in society that it had once enjoyed, but he knew that wealth didn't automatically provide you with a ticket to the nobility. Many dukes and duchesses were strapped for cash while hordes of lowly born and barely sentient footballers and reality TV stars were multi-millionaires. You had to have breeding and class and a family seat with some history. Therefore, Sir Giles's first step towards returning the Whornes to the upper classes had been to marry into them.

The Luscotts of Milverton could trace their lineage back to Domesday but Lady Tilly Luscott was flat broke, widowed, terminally ill and Proutt House was falling down around her ears. There were sufficient numbers of well-placed relatives to ensure that she was taken care of and that the Luscott name remained firmly anchored in the aristocracy, but none of them wanted to take on the money pit that was Proutt. She had therefore cast her jaded eye over the county's society pages in search of a suitably rich husband for her 'difficult' only child, Cecily, to marry and a likely suitor had soon presented himself. Meat magnate Sir Giles Whorne had money to burn and had recently entered the world of politics, winning the seat of South Herewardshire (South). He had just the right amount of determination to rise to the top, thought Lady Tilly, and, from what she had heard, he had made no secret of the fact that he was desperate for the sort of leg-up on the social ladder that her family could provide.

And so Giles and Cecily had been gently nudged towards the idea of marriage and, to the majority of observers, it appeared that love had brought two great English dynasties together. The truth was a somewhat different story. Quite apart from the fact that Giles was twenty years older than Cecily, the couple were not at all suited to each other's company and spent much of their time avoiding it. They didn't laugh at the same things, they didn't share any interests or hobbies, and their tastes in art, music, film and theatre were almost polar opposites. The only thing they had in common at all was that Giles enjoyed the company of women, and so did Cecily.

Initially, their lavender marriage had suited their needs very well; Cecily had acceded to her mother's dying wishes and, in doing so, had seen the restoration of her family home. It had also allowed her the use of her husband's expansive bank accounts to pursue her love of the dramatic arts. Meanwhile, Giles had reaped the benefits of the Luscotts' extraordinary network of influence to advance himself in the party and, with a general election looming, he stood a very good chance of being offered a post in the new cabinet.

However, things had quickly taken a turn for the worse. The Luscotts had begun to advise Giles which way he should vote during important parliamentary debates. And Cecily's spending had rapidly increased; in recent months she'd even purchased an ailing local theatre in the sure knowledge that Giles wouldn't complain for fear of rocking the marital boat. In short, he realised that he had entered into a contract in which he had a great deal more to lose than his wife did. The threat of divorce was all the Luscotts needed to keep him in thrall; if the tabloids got their teeth into him, he'd be ridiculed as a man and chastised for entering into a marriage of convenience solely to further his ambitions. He would have to say goodbye to Proutt House – thanks to a prenuptial agreement – and a significant proportion of his personal fortune as settlement. But, worst of all, as his public standing withered and died, the Whornes would once again be relegated to the ranks of the hoi polloi. That was the very last thing he wanted.

And, as if that weren't enough to contend with, there was the constant irritation of Harpax Grange. Despite several substantial offers – the most recent far in excess of the building's actual value – he had failed to persuade the redoubtable headmistress to sell, and Joan Bultitude was not easily cowed or bullied. After her first refusal, she had explained that she was deeply and sentimentally attached to the school, having lived there for most of her life, first as a boarder, then as a teacher and now as headmistress. Sir Giles had assumed that it was all bluff and that she was holding out for a higher offer but

Miss Bultitude genuinely seemed to have no interest in money beyond what was needed to pay the bills. And, to Sir Giles's further annoyance, the term fees she charged appeared to see to that very comfortably. The school seemed to be rolling in cash, in fact.

He watched as some unidentifiable piece of garbage swirled around in an eddy created by two buoys, unable to break free and return to the flow of the river. That was how he felt, he mused; trapped and powerless to escape his situation. And what made it worse was knowing that it was a trap into which he had willingly walked. What had seemed to be a sensible business arrangement was now a prison of his own making – a loveless marriage in which he had to submit to his wife's every impulse and fancy, and a political career in which he was little more than a puppet for the Luscotts. He had no choice but to present to the outside world a pretence of marital bliss while, behind closed doors, he and Cecily conducted their private lives in separate bedrooms and in a careful and clandestine manner. The alternative was derision and professional suicide.

His stomach rumbled, reminding him that he had skipped breakfast. He made his way to his office to inform his parliamentary assistant that he would be going out to his club for lunch.

Chapter 4

Detective Sergeant Clifford Jaine parked his car on the gravel forecourt of Harpax Grange School and set the handbrake with a loud wrench. It was a beautiful building, he noted; a fine eighteenth-century three-storey mansion house clad in Bath stone, with tall sash windows and a balustraded roof terrace. Ivy and wisteria climbed the walls and two rampant stone boars guarded the entrance. A third – transfixed by a long spear – formed part of a coat of arms carved into the keystone of the arch above the impressively tall front doors. Jaine stepped out of the car and attempted to tidy himself up. While he had never met the headmistress, Miss Bultitude's reputation as a stickler for good manners and smartness of appearance preceded her. Jaine was long in the body and short in the leg and developing a beer belly in his thirties had simply made matters worse by forcing his waistline lower. His trousers were baggy at the knees, his shirts bulged where they weren't designed to, and he looked untidy in almost anything he wore, no matter how new or well-pressed his clothes were. He tucked himself in, straightened his ketchup-stained tie, and then tucked himself in again as the action of raising his hands to his collar had pulled out his shirt tails. He sighed and hoped for the best as he walked towards the building.

At an upstairs window, Phoebe Kingshaw watched his approach. 'It could be a police car, I suppose,' she said. 'But there are no blue lights or anything.'

'I insisted on a plain clothes officer,' said Miss Bultitude.

'Plain clothes is what you've got,' said Phoebe, smiling. 'I haven't seen a mustard corduroy jacket in years. Will you be needing me?'

'I don't think so. You can finish off those timetables, if you don't mind.'

'No problem. I've got the hang of the spreadsheets now.'

Phoebe watched the headmistress leave and then sat down at her desk. She opened a file on her laptop and sighed as she stared at the screen. Preparing the timetables for the coming term was a boring, repetitive job and far below her level of skill, but it wouldn't do to complain. She was already under close scrutiny by the weasel-like deputy head. Miss Deak was overseeing her probationary period as school secretary and she had no intention of giving the sly old bat any rope with which to hang her. Not when she had such an important job to do.

Len Youlden and Gerry Waxleigh re-entered the pub, trailing the smell of cheap rolling tobacco behind them.

'Sid Munsun just told us there's been another Shaggy Beast sighting up at Black Dog Wood,' said Waxleigh. 'Young Jessie Tremblett says she saw it. That's the fourth sighting in three months.'

'Any photos?' asked Vic.

'Are there ever?' said Waxleigh.

'Everyone has a camera in their phone these days,' said Vic.

'Seems to me that the more cameras there are, the fewer photos.'

'Didn't I read somewhere that the Loch Ness Monster hasn't put in an appearance for over a year?' said Waxleigh.

'The tourist office is claiming that she's camera shy,' said Shunter.

Waxleigh laughed.

'The Shaggy Beast is a spirit,' said Youlden, as he attempted to climb onto a high bar stool and failed. 'You can't capture a spirit on film.'

'Spirit?' said Shunter.

'Film?' said Waxleigh.

'Are you saying that it's a ghost?' said Shunter. 'I thought it was some kind of werewolf.'

'It all began with Sir Veryard Whorne…' said Youlden.

'Bloody hell. Here we go again,' sighed Vic. 'If you want me, I'll be in the cellar.'

As Vic disappeared through a trap door in the floor, Len Youlden gave up on his attempt to mount the stool, spread his feet and gripped the place where his lapels would be if he had lapels on his anorak. He swayed unsteadily on his booted feet and cleared his throat. 'Sir Veryard had a prize hunting hound,' he began. 'A great black brute it was, as fierce as a bear, as strong as an ox, and so fleet of foot that it could keep pace with the fastest horse. He named it Shax and it's said that he and Old Shaxy killed a thousand boars between them.' He took a moment to gulp hungrily on his pint and then launched back into his narrative.

'But one animal eluded them. A monster of a pig, twice the size of a prize Herewardshire Hog and with tusks as long and as sharp as kitchen knives. Many a hunter had tried to kill the Boar King and many a hunter had died. Sir Veryard became obsessed with vanquishing the beast. But his pride was his undoing, for instead of taking a party of hunting men with him, he chose to face the beast alone with only Shax at his side. For hours they fought, but the outcome was inevitable. Both Sir Veryard and his beloved dog were killed, their hearts pierced by the Boar King's tusks.'

'What a load of old cobblers,' said a disembodied voice from the cellar.

'You should have a bit more pride in your heritage,' snapped Youlden.

'Maybe I would if I didn't have to listen to you spouting the same old guff every time you're drunk and you spot a bunch of gullible tourists.'

Youlden harrumphed and continued his story.

'Sir Veryard's sons were stricken with grief and called together the finest hunters in the county to track down the Boar King and kill it. And so they did, even though the beast took half of their number to the grave with it. They celebrated with a great roast and the boar gave so much meat that every person in the parish had a full belly. And then they hung its head over the fireplace at Harpax as a trophy and added a skewered boar to the Whorne family coat of arms. But then, a year to the day after Sir Veryard's death, a terrible apparition began to haunt the forest, a shaggy beast with scything claws and burning red eyes and—'

'Hang on,' said Shunter. 'Are you saying that the Shaggy Beast is the ghost of Shax? Or Sir Veryard?'

'Sir Veryard made a pact with the Devil. In return for his immortal soul, he begged that he and Shax be returned to Earth to take their revenge upon the Boar King. But the Devil is a trickster and he merged their two spirits into one body and created a monster. And because the Boar King was already dead, Sir Veryard and Old Shaxy were cheated of their revenge. Which is why the Shaggy Beast is doomed to roam what's left of the ancient forest for all eternity and with no hope of redemption.'

'Where do you get this stuff from?' asked Vic, emerging from the cellar.

'From Mad Connie. She's the expert.'

'Mad Connie?' said Shunter.

'Old Constance Tremblett,' explained Waxleigh. 'Matriarch of that odd family over Ordon way. Her lift may not go all the way to the top floor, but she does know her local folklore.'

'I remember her from when I was a lad,' said Youlden. 'A real looker she was. Long brown hair and an eye as blue as a whetstone.'

'Eye?' said Shunter. 'Singular?'

'Never stopped her being popular with the boys,' said Youlden. 'A right raver she was. Her looks have all gone now, mind.'

'Turns stomachs more often than heads these days,' added Waxleigh.

'The Trembletts keep themselves to themselves,' said Youlden.

'Except young Jessie, that is,' said Waxleigh. 'She takes after her gran.'

'So, have you finished now?' asked Vic.

Len Youlden sank the last of his pint and burped indignantly.

'If that's your attitude, I'll bugger off,' he said. 'I won't stay where I'm not wanted.'

'I'll walk with you,' said Waxleigh. 'We can take another look at Gladys Brockhole's cock on the way, if you like. It's no Banksy, I'll grant you. But it does have a naive charm.'

'More Wanksy than Banksy, eh?' said Shunter.

'Ha! Very good. You coming, Len?'

But Len Youlden wasn't listening. He'd spotted a group of

young adults who were settling around a table at the far end of the bar. His mouth set into a sneer and he pointed a drunken accusatory finger at them.

'Oi, you lot!' he barked.

'Are you talking to us?' asked a thin youth dressed in a cheap black suit jacket that was too big for him. His lapels bore badges for various animal welfare and conservation charities.

'You're that Cheeseman lad, aren't you?' said Youlden.

'So what if I am?' asked the youth.

'Did your lot graffiti the butcher's shop window?'

'Why would you automatically assume it was us?' asked Colin Cheeseman. 'Not everyone under the age of twenty-five fits your prejudiced view of the world, old man.'

'But you aren't denying it, are you?' said the tipsy farmer. His gaze settled upon the other members of the group. 'You're them animal rights protesters, aren't you?'

'Which animal rights protesters do you mean?' asked a good-looking young man with curly blond hair and piercing blue eyes. 'PETA? WWF? ALF? Greenpeace? It would help if you could be more specific.'

'Don't you be cheeky to your elders!'

'Cheeky? No. I'm just seeking some clarity,' said the blond man with a winning smile. 'But let's, for the moment, say that we are "them animal rights protesters", as you suggest. Would we be wrong to want animals to live long and happy lives free of pain and suffering?'

'Did you paint a cock and balls on Gladys Brockhole's side wall?' snarled Youlden.

'The law says that we're innocent until proven guilty,' said Cheeseman angrily. 'Come on, guys. Let's get out of this dump.'

The group stood up and several of them looked daggers at the bar.

'Fascists,' growled a large youth in a 'Frankie Says Relax' T-shirt.

'We'll be sure to tell everyone about your hospitality,' said Cheeseman. He slammed the pub door as they left.

'Bloody buggers,' said Youlden.

'Well, that's one bunch of customers I won't get back,' said Vic, frowning. 'I wouldn't mind but that Cheeseman lad is worth a few bob since his parents died.'

'Best funeral ever,' said Waxleigh, chuckling. 'Right, we're off. See you later, Vic.'

'I'm going to head off too,' said Shunter. 'Lots to do.'

'I thought you were retired?' said Vic. 'You're hardly ever in here these days.'

'I'm a retired cop, not a retired husband,' said Shunter. 'We had builders in to extend the cottage but I'm doing all of the internal DIY work myself. And I've taken a bit of a shine to it, to be honest. You sweat the pounds off while saving the pennies.'

'I thought you were looking a bit trimmer than when I last saw you. But I didn't like to say anything. In case you had cancer or something. Like old Hugh Brockhole. He went downhill very quickly once everyone knew.'

'What a sensitive friend you are, Vic,' said Shunter.

DS Jaine waited outside the reception office and passed the time by reading the school noticeboard. Girls of various ages from eleven to seventeen were milling about in the corridor, whispering to each other and giggling as they walked between classes in their distinctive green blazers, grey skirts and long white socks. He smiled in a way that he hoped wouldn't be seen as creepy.

'Sergeant Jaine?'

He turned and found himself looking up at a tall, broad-shouldered woman in her mid-forties, although her austere hairstyle and woollen skirt-and-jacket ensemble made her look older. Her hair was gathered into a bun and scraped back so tightly that it gave her a slight squint. She extended a hand like a striking cobra.

'Joan Bultitude. Headmistress.'

'How do you do,' he said. Her grip was surprisingly firm. 'DS Cliff Jaine, Bowcester CID.'

'Sorry to have kept you waiting.'

'That's fine. I was just admiring the school's coat of arms,' said Jaine, pointing to a painted wooden shield above the notices. It portrayed a wise-looking and clearly female owl perched upon a book. 'Much nicer than the one you have over the front door. The one with the pig being speared.'

'That is the Whorne family coat of arms and, sadly, we can't have it removed as this is a listed building,' said Miss Bultitude. 'But yes, we much prefer ours. That's our motto there, on the scroll beneath. *Puellae veniunt primum.* Girls come first.'

'It's a fine motto,' said Jaine, with a smile.

Miss Bultitude smiled back but not with her eyes.

'If you'll follow me to the staff room, I've organised some tea.'

She set off at a brisk march down a hallway lined with framed photographs. As Jaine huffed and puffed to keep up with her, Miss Bultitude proudly regaled him with a potted history of the school.

'Is it your first visit to Harpax Grange?'

'It is. This is quite a place you have here.'

'As you know, the house used to belong to the Whorne family,' she said, pointing to a sepia-toned photograph of the building with a family group in the foreground. As the image flashed by, Jaine caught a glimpse of flamboyant hats, luxuriant moustaches and the faces of long-dead Whornes staring joylessly at the camera.

'The history of this building is testament to what happens when you underestimate women or take them for granted. When the Whorne men went to war in 1914, the wives were left in charge of the family businesses. In the modern age they would undoubtedly have had the opportunity to show how smart and canny they were, but that was not the case back then. Like so many women of noble birth, their education was meagre and did not include lessons on finance and business practice. That was deemed man's work. Consequently, they were easy prey for unscrupulous business rivals.'

'That's … huff … unfortunate.'

'And barely had the… Rita Delores Palmer!'

The headmistress came to an abrupt halt and the object of her attention, a plump, mousy-haired girl with a mouth full of metal, grimaced. Her eyes bulged like blisters.

'Y-yes, Miss Bultitude?'

'Since when has school uniform included the wearing of pink socks?'

'I'm sorry, Miss. Something red must have got into the washing machine when I was—'

'Report to Matron in the laundry room after supper tonight. After you've loaded a few dozen machines you might start to appreciate the importance of separating your whites from your coloureds. Now run along with you.'

'Yes, Miss Bultitude,' said the startled child, and quickly scuttled away.

'Discipline is paramount,' explained the headmistress. 'Now, where were we? Ah yes…'

She set off at a sprightly canter once again, with a somewhat intimidated Cliff Jaine trotting behind.

'Barely had the surviving male Whornes come to terms

with the loss of their assets when another war came along in which most of them were either killed or seriously injured,' she continued. 'Those who remained were then hit by crippling taxes and death duties and by the late 1940s, the family was living in near penury. All because of warmongering, male ego and insecurity. That's when the family was forced to sell the house to our founder, Blaise Millerick.'

She stopped and pointed to a portrait of a stern-looking matron with intelligence shining brightly in her eyes. 'This was painted in 1911 by my grandfather. I think he captured her personality perfectly. Miss Millerick was an extraordinary woman. Bold but benevolent, strong but caring. She believed that women could shape the future if they were empowered to do so and she set the school upon a path that we still follow to this day – to equip our girls with the skills they need to ensure they will never fall into the same traps that the Whorne women did. Our girls leave here with the confidence and sure knowledge that they can do anything a man can do, and probably better.'

She indicated a door to the right of the portrait. 'The staff room. Do go in.'

A breathless Jaine opened the door and stepped through into a warm space panelled in rich coffee-coloured wood. A fire burned in the hearth and the air was smoky and scented with old leather and older books. A tray with a Brown Betty teapot, milk jug and crockery stood on a table next to a distressed armchair in which a wiry lady was sipping tea from a china cup and reading a copy of *The Pit and the Pendulum*.

'Jemima Deak, my deputy,' explained Miss Bultitude. 'And this is Detective Sergeant Jaine. Would you be mother, Tiggy?'

Miss Deak nodded and blew gently on her own cup of hot tea. The pursing of her thin lips gave her a sour look that barely softened when she spoke.

'Milk and sugar, officer?'

'Just a drop of milk, please.'

'We can speak freely in here,' said Miss Bultitude. 'Miss Deak and I have no secrets when it comes to school business.'

'You reported that there had been an incident of some kind that requires a CID officer,' said Jaine, collecting his cup and saucer.

'Well, it's not really an incident as such but I didn't know what else to call it. You see, I've found a body.'

'A what?' said Jaine, startled.

'A dead body. A corpse,' said Miss Bultitude matter-of-factly.

'Not one of the girls?'

'Good gracious me, no. It's quite old. Just a skeleton, in fact. Teasel found it this morning on our dog walk.'

Seeing the puzzlement on the detective's face, she picked up the collarbone from a nearby desk and handed it to him.

'My apologies for the teeth marks. Teasel is one of my poodles and, well, dogs will be dogs. The grave is in the woods, about a ten-minute walk from here and not far from the Whorne family mausoleum. I assume you'll need to cast an eye over the spot?'

'Yes, I will.'

'Then I'll take you there after we've had our tea. Biscuit?'

'Not for me, thanks. Near the mausoleum, you say?'

'Yes.'

'There's a public car park there, off the A113 Larock Road, isn't there?'

'There is.'

'Good. I'll ask the SOCO – the Scene of Crime Officer – to meet us there.'

'That would be good,' said Miss Bultitude. 'I'd rather not have police vehicles at the school unless it's absolutely necessary.'

'I completely understand,' said Jaine, glaring at his phone. 'Damn. No signal. Do you mind if I borrow your landline?'

Upstairs in the headmistress's office, Phoebe Kingshaw rooted through her employer's desk, checking the contents of tins, boxes, folders and envelopes. When she didn't find what she was looking for, she quickly returned everything to its place, checking for accuracy against a series of reference photos that she had taken on her phone prior to her rummage. She then walked back to her desk in the outer office and continued with her timetabling work.

Miss Bultitude would not suspect a thing.

Chapter 5

'I'm just popping out to Titters for lunch,' said Sir Giles. 'Can you take my calls for an hour or so?'

'That is your secretary's job,' said Raif Clyst, icily. He was sulking, as he had been for nearly a fortnight.

'Yes, I know, but—'

'And yet, here I am, opening your mail while she's off on some secret business that I'm not deemed trustworthy enough to know about.' He sliced angrily through an envelope with a letter opener.

'As I've already told you, what she is doing for me is nothing for you to be concerned about, and—'

'Of course I should be concerned!' snapped Clyst. 'I am your parliamentary assistant and diary manager. It's my job to keep you safe from scandal, gossip and rumour. How do you expect me to be able to refute allegations that you're doing something you shouldn't be doing if I don't know what that something is?'

'Yes, but on this occasio—'

'If you don't think I'm trustworthy enough, there are plenty of other ministers who would snap me up in an instant.'

'I don't doubt that. And I do trust you, Raif. Of course I do.

It's just that it's a personal matter. It has nothing to do with parliamentary business.'

'You're an MP. She's your secretary. She works for you and, incidentally, for me. There is no "personal" involving the two of you that I shouldn't be aware of.'

'I'm not sure that that's entirel—'

'You are putting me in a very awkward position and I am not happy about it. Not happy at all.'

'You've made that very clear,' said Sir Giles. He grabbed his overcoat and left.

A fat raindrop spattered on his shoulder as he walked out into Parliament Square and hailed a black cab. And as he sat, half-listening to the driver's opinion on the state of US politics, his phone rang and a photo of Phoebe Kingshaw appeared on his screen. It was a formal portrait – unsmiling, bespectacled and dressed in a sombre and unflattering business suit – but it couldn't disguise what an attractive woman his secretary was. It was a very different photo from most of the others that Giles had stored on his phone. He let the call go to voicemail. He wasn't in the mood for talking.

His taxi arrived in Jermyn Street and he paid the driver. Titters was one of the few remaining gentlemen's clubs that didn't allow women through its doors. Younger members, who had grown up in more enlightened times, had been pushing for change in recent years but the club elders remained obdurate. The Titterton Club was, they said, one of the last remaining bastions of male-only privilege and the protection of that privilege was at the very core of the club's constitution. Sir Giles knew they were on a hiding to nothing and suspected that they knew it too. It was inevitable that women would eventually be allowed in and, personally, he was all in favour of it. A bit of glamour would be a welcome alternative to the fatty jowls, rheumy eyes and dangling wattles that adorned the liver-spotted faces of the older members. However, there were days, like today, when being able to escape from the fairer sex was just what he needed. Plus, the club's chef made one of the best bouillabaisses in London and he had a hankering for it.

His stew arrived and he was savouring his first mouthful when his phone buzzed to indicate a text message. He glanced at the screen and nearly choked. It was from Phoebe and it said:

'You're obviously too busy to talk to me right now. All I wanted to say is that I've thought about this a lot and I'm ready for us to take the next step. I love you and want to be with you. And if you love me, you'll want to be with me too. Talk later. P.'

Giles dabbed the sweat from his forehead as a mild panic swept over him.

Phoebe Kingshaw had been his mistress for over a year and had proved herself to be a trustworthy and loyal companion as well as an exciting sexual partner. He had therefore recently asked her to carry out, for want of a better description, a 'secret mission' at Harpax Grange School on his behalf. And things had been going well. Until now, that is.

What on earth was he to do? Cecily had always turned a blind eye to his affairs, just as he had done for her. But that was because the women he'd been with were no threat to the status quo. But this was different. He was fond of Phoebe, to be sure, but not so fond that he was willing to sacrifice everything for her. But how was she likely to react once he told her that? In using her loyalty and affection for him to push her to do some of his dirty work, he'd made himself vulnerable; she had more than enough dirt on him to sink his political career if she chose to do so. And once their affair became public knowledge Cecily would almost certainly be pressurised by her family to sue for divorce, and then the awful truth about his sham life would all come out. Therefore, he couldn't risk ending his affair with Phoebe, but nor could he 'take the next step'. Either course would lead him down a path towards professional ruin.

He mopped at his brow again. With just one text message, Phoebe Kingshaw had destabilised his entire life and he had no idea how to deal with the situation. He needed to speak to his PA. Clyst had been right: he shouldn't have kept secrets from his chief confidant and advisor. The man was brilliantly devious. He'd surely know how to fix things.

'The SOCO will be there in about fifteen minutes,' said Jaine, hanging up the phone. 'Now, you said that it's a skeleton you found?'

'Yes. It looked to me like it was buried decades ago, certainly long before the school was here,' said Miss Bultitude. 'So it might be worth you interviewing one of the Whornes, I imagine. Sir Giles, for instance?' She said his name with undisguised contempt. 'He might be able to shed some light on that poor soul's identity.'

'What poor soul is that?' asked Phoebe, entering the staff room.

'This is Miss Kingshaw, my secretary,' explained Miss Bultitude. 'This is Detective Sergeant Jaine from Bowcester Police Station. He's here about the body.'

'Oh, right,' said Phoebe. 'Pleased to meet you.'

'Likewise,' said Jaine, sweeping back his hair and failing to pull in his stomach. Chestnut-haired and excitingly curvy, Phoebe Kingshaw ticked all of the boxes on his 'what I look for in a woman' card.

'I suspect it'll turn out to be some poor scullery maid who threatened to kiss and tell, or something like that,' said Miss Deak. 'The Whorne men have always been philanderers. It's in their nature. You just have to look at their family history.'

'I came to say that I've finished the timetables,' said Phoebe. 'Is there anything else that needs doing?'

'No, I don't think so, thank you,' said Miss Bultitude. 'Will you be able to lock up the office and the staff room after school today? Miss Deak has to go to the bank in Bowcester and won't be back in time. I have to show Sergeant Jaine where the body is and then take the dogs for a groom at 4 p.m.'

'Of course, no problem,' said Phoebe. 'Nice to meet you, Sergeant.'

'You too,' said Jaine.

Miss Deak narrowed her eyes and pursed her thin lips as the secretary turned to leave the room.

'Shall we view the body?' suggested Miss Bultitude.

'I'd love to,' said Jaine, his eyes still lingering on Phoebe Kingshaw.

Sir Giles was sitting in the members' lounge when Phoebe rang again. Although his phone was set to silent, the vibrating buzz was loud enough to cause several of the older members to glare at him or to tut and grumble from behind their broadsheets. A steward gestured towards the door of the lounge with an obsequious smile. Sir Giles stood up, smoothed the creases from his trousers and walked out into the hallway to take the call. Phoebe wasn't happy.

'I've been trying to get hold of you for ages,' she chided. 'I have some important news.'

'I'm sorry. I'm at Titters and they're a bit old-fashioned about mobile phones in here, and—'

'The police are here.'

'What? Why?' said Sir Giles, a note of alarm in his voice. 'You haven't been—'

'Been what? Careless? Give me some credit, Giles. No, it's

something else. Miss Bultitude has found a body buried in the woods.'

'A body? Good Lord. It's too much to hope that she's killed someone, I suppose.'

'She'd hardly inform the police if she had.'

'A clever double bluff?'

'Not everyone is as Machiavellian as you are,' said Phoebe. 'And, besides, it's apparently from ages ago. They'll probably want to speak to you about it.'

'Me? Why me?'

'Because it was buried back in the days when the land belonged to your family. And you hold all of the Whorne family records. There's a detective sergeant here from Bowcester so I figured I should give you the heads-up. There's likely to be a police presence at the school for a few days so I may not be able to do much snooping for you.'

'This is a damned nuisance.'

'So I thought I might come and see you in London.'

'I won't be in London. I have to come home for this pond-drainage business. I'll be at Proutt for the weekend.'

'Even better. Saves me a drive. You can come to me. We have some things to discuss, don't we?'

'Er… but you're living at the school, aren't you? Didn't you say that the deputy head is watching you and—'

'I'm not suggesting you come to the school, you idiot. Book a hotel or a guest house or something. Somewhere nice with a big bed, Egyptian cotton sheets and a decent full English breakfast.'

'OK. It's just that th—'

'You don't sound very pleased about the prospect of seeing me,' said Phoebe, with just a hint of menace.

'What? No, nothing of the sort,' spluttered Sir Giles. 'It's just not very convenient at the moment, that's all. There's a public meeting I have to attend tomorrow in Nasely and I have county archaeologists braying in one ear and animal rights people in the other, and all of this on top of preparing for a general election and—'

'And all of that is more important than spending a few hours with me, is it?'

'No, of course not. But th—'

'Then I'll see you at the weekend. Love you!' said Phoebe, and she hung up.

Sir Giles stared at his phone and frowned.

'Anything I can help you with?' asked a passing steward.

'Not unless you know an inexpensive hit man,' grumbled Sir Giles. The steward appeared to be about to speak but Giles cut him off. 'No, don't answer that. I bet you bloody do, don't you?'

He left Titters and jumped into a black cab to take him back to Westminster.

Chapter 6

On Nasely village green, a group of angry youths took turns to swig from a two-litre bottle of cloudy cider that one of them had bought from Munsun's Mini-Market.

'I live in this village and, believe me, they're all like that old git in the pub,' said Colin Cheeseman, still smarting from his confrontation with Len Youlden. 'Closed-minded little Englanders to a man.'

'Or woman,' said a lady called June.

'Fascists,' growled Willy Tremblett, scratching at something under his 'Frankie Says Relax' T-shirt.

'To be fair to the chap, he had every right to be angry about what I did to the butcher's shop window,' said the blond man. 'Nasely is a very pretty little village. I'd be cross if I lived here.'

'I painted a cock,' said Willy, grinning.

There was a ripple of laughter.

'I must point out that Bron and Willy's actions were not authorised by me,' said Cheeseman. 'And, as such, must be considered acts of individual free expression and not official protests by FLAN.'

'Fine with me,' said Bron.

'Why did you paint a cock?' asked a big man called Terry.

'I couldn't remember what Bron told me to paint,' said Willy.

'Willy's good at drawing animals,' explained Bron. 'So I asked him to paint some cows and chickens with speech bubbles saying things like "Animals are not ingredients" and "Don't have a cow, man" and "Wings are for flying not frying".'

'See? How was I supposed to remember all that?' said Willy.

Oberon and Wylstan Tremblett were twins, but non-identical in almost every way. Bron was tanned, good-looking and habitually well dressed, while Willy was dark-haired, heavy-featured and wore old frayed jeans and shapeless T-shirts. Bron had read history at university. Willy had read the same copy of *The Beano* four times without noticing any repetition. The only thing they truly shared was a passion for protecting animals, but even in this their viewpoints differed. Willy favoured direct action while Bron preferred a more subtle approach, championing the use of discourse and intelligent protest. Overnight, he had written a message on the butcher's shop window to highlight the fact that chickens' lives were considered to be little more than a commodity. Willy hadn't really understood what his twin had written and would have preferred to simply smash the window, but Bron had insisted that his message was a subtler attack on the 'languor of the proletariat'. Willy had no idea what two of those words meant – although he suspected that a languor was a type of monkey – so he'd painted a cock and balls on the side wall of Gladys Brockhole's cottage and been content with that instead.

'You could have picked a better wall,' said June. 'The poor woman's just lost her husband.'

'I didn't know that,' said Willy, his brows furrowing. 'I just picked the blank wall next door to the shop. I thought the cottage might belong to the butcher. I wouldn't have done it there if I'd known.'

'Look, we're getting off track,' moaned Cheeseman. 'This is a special meeting of FLAN to discuss the draining of Gertie's Plash. And I'll start by officially welcoming our new members, Bhavin and Maisie. May the minutes be noted as such?'

'Sorry. I wasn't ready,' said a man known as Onions, who, curiously, always smelled of onions. 'What came after getting off track?'

'Why do you insist on keeping minutes, Colin?' asked Bron. 'Surely writing things down only provides the police with evidence against us?'

'He has a point,' said Terry.

'Fine,' said Cheeseman, feeling undermined and slightly discomfited. 'The first item on... I mean, this meeting is to discuss how we are going to respond to the drainage plan. Firstly, we need to make our voices heard at the public meeting. I say we start a leaflet campaign to—'

'Talking's no good,' said Willy. 'We should smash the pumps. That'll stop them.'

'While I appreciate your enthusiasm, Willy, we'd need to discuss the pros and cons before we could consider any form of direct action,' said Cheeseman. 'We'd have to complete a risk assessment and a—'

'Heaven forbid we take some action that the authorities don't expect,' interrupted Bron. He regarded the state of his fingernails. 'Very unsporting.'

There were chuckles from the group, much to Cheeseman's annoyance.

'What exactly would we be up against if things did get violent?' asked Terry. He looked altogether too excited by the prospect.

'Well, we don't have to worry about the law,' said Cheeseman.

'Fascists,' said Willy.

'Why not?' asked Maisie, a curvy Goth from Tingwell.

'Because nothing ever happens around here,' said Cheeseman. 'That's why there's no police station.'

'There was a murder here two years ago,' said Onions.

'And the hotel got blown up,' said June.

'Admittedly, but—'

'And there was a police shoot-out,' said Onions.

'Yes! But those were very unusual circumstances,' snapped Cheeseman.

'But won't they send officers from Bowcester?' asked Bhavin.

'They will. But there's only a skeleton crew on the night shift and it would take them, on average, around ten to fifteen minutes to get to Black Dog Wood,' said Bron. 'I had ample time to spray a slogan right across the butcher's window last night without a copper in sight. Police cutbacks, eh? The Tories got something right.'

Maisie smiled at Bron and it was not missed by Cheeseman.

'We're getting off topic again,' he said. 'The Plash is our priority. It is a unique local environment and draining it just to solve some damp problem at a private school is an outrage. The bourgeoisie only ever think of themselves, and—'

'What's a boar's wazee?' asked Willy.

'Another name for its cock,' said Bron.

'No it isn't!' snapped Cheeseman.

'What is it then?' asked Willy.

'The bourgeoisie are the comfortable, well-off middle classes with their materialistic values and conventional attitudes.'

'Like people who inherit their houses, are mortgage-free and who have enough in the bank to ensure that they never have to work?' said Bron pointedly.

Cheeseman shot daggers at him, which pleased Bron immensely.

'Rich people are all the bloody same,' snapped Willy. 'Whatever big words you use to describe them. So what if their posh school falls down? They can afford to rebuild it.'

'Exactly. But you can't rebuild a duck... er...' stuttered Cheeseman.

'You can't rebuild a duck?' said Bron.

'Let me finish!' flustered Cheeseman. 'You can't rebuild a duck-friendly... you know, the environment that encourages them to visit the Plash... habitat! That's the word. You can't rebuild a duck-friendly habitat. It will be destroyed. Just to save a girls' school.'

'Harpax Grange isn't just a girls' school. It's a Grade II listed building and a national treasure,' said Bron. 'You can't let a piece of English heritage like that be destroyed by damp.'

'Oh? And what do you suggest?'

'A third way,' said Bron. 'An alternative plan that saves the school but doesn't involve draining the pond and killing off half the wildlife. We force the school governors and our pompous prig of an MP to have a rethink.'

'Or we smash the pumps,' reiterated Willy.

'How safe will we be going into the woods at night?' asked Bhavin. 'The man at the mini-market told me that strange things have been going on up there.'

'You mean the Shaggy Beast?' said Willy.

'Stay on the path!' said Onions, waggling his fingers spookily.

'Rubbish. There's no such thing,' said Cheeseman.

'I don't know about that,' said Willy. 'I've heard stories.'

'Well, you've certainly never read any,' said Bron.

Cliff Jaine had offered to drive Miss Bultitude from the school to the mausoleum car park but she had insisted on them walking through the woods as it would be good for their cardiovascular systems. Jaine found himself unable to argue and as they'd passed out through the main doors, he'd looked up and concluded that perhaps the old Whorne heraldic crest wasn't so wrong for the school after all. No male chauvinist pig would ever get the better of Miss Bultitude.

They arrived at the burial site to find that the SOCO and his assistant were already hard at work. The skeleton was partly exposed from skull to ribcage and seemed to be buried under no more than a couple of feet of soil.

'What have we got, Topsy?' asked Jaine breathlessly. 'Man or woman?'

Bob Turvey winced at the nickname. It was what he'd been called at school and even though he'd since tried to modify it to 'Autopsy' Turvey, it had stuck with him throughout adult life too.

'A man, judging by the skull. We'll know for sure when we get to the pelvis.'

'There goes the serving wench theory then,' said Jaine.

Turvey placed a collarbone, the twin of the one found by Miss Bultitude's poodle, on a tarpaulin next to a small pile of neck vertebrae. The grinning skull was there too, bound with a faded and tattered length of green cloth. Deep scars were carved into the cheekbones and forehead. A woodlouse bimbled over the bridge of the nose and ducked into an eye socket. 'There's some evidence of animal interference,' he said. 'It's what brought the skull to the surface, I imagine. A fox maybe?'

'Probably one of my dogs,' said Miss Bultitude, passing him the bone that she'd found that morning. 'Terribly sorry.'

'One bone is the same as any other to them, I guess,' said Turvey.

'A fox did that much damage to his skull?' said Jaine.

'I doubt that,' said Turvey. 'It looks more like shrapnel wounds.'

'Shrapnel? Like in a war? How long do you reckon he's been here?'

'I'd say around a hundred years. Maybe a bit less.'

'Shit,' said Jaine.

'Language,' said Miss Bultitude.

Jaine looked at her in surprise.

'I'm so sorry,' said the headmistress. 'Force of habit.'

'I was hoping for something Roman or medieval,' said Jaine. 'The archaeologists could have had it then.'

'Sorry. Definitely twentieth-century,' said Turvey. 'Apart from the shrapnel wounds, he has modern fillings in his teeth. I'll be able to give you a more precise date once I'm back at the lab but I reckon 1920s? Thirties? Somewhere around then, anyway.'

'Too early to guess at a cause of death, I suppose?'

'Nothing obvious yet,' said Turvey. 'There is one odd thing, though. I think he was blindfolded.'

He pointed to the strip of green fabric wrapped around the skull.

'You mean by a firing squad?' said Miss Bultitude. 'That adds a macabre flavour to things, doesn't it?'

'As I said, it's too early to make any assumptions yet. I need to exhume the whole skeleton,' said Turvey. 'Who's going to be the officer in charge of this one if we call it a homicide?'

'Kipper McNabb,' said Jaine gloomily.

'Oh fu— bad luck.'

'Is that a bad thing?' asked Miss Bultitude.

'The worst,' said Jaine.

Sir Giles collected his briefcase from his office and, having run the gauntlet of Clyst's withering glare, decided that today was not the day to ask for the man's advice. He'd take him out for a good lunch next week, once he'd had a chance to simmer down. Besides, he had a busy weekend ahead back in his constituency.

He ordered a car from the pool to take him home to Proutt and chatted to the driver for a while. But then, as the Mercedes left the M25 and joined the M13 towards South Herewardshire, he opened his briefcase and began reading through the pile of paperwork he'd been avoiding all week. It concerned the draining of Gertie's Plash and the surprising reasons why an otherwise unremarkable pond had become the focus of so much local attention, and a personal bugbear for him.

The story began in the 1740s when the notorious rake Sir Francis Dashwood had created a private gentlemen's club called the Knights of St Francis of Wycombe. Its membership, consisting of politicians, aristocrats and other bigwigs, would dress up as monks and hold gluttonous dinners with bawdy entertainments provided by young professional ladies known as 'nuns'. Their meeting place was a set of caves that had been specially dug into the side of a chalk hill on Dashwood's Buckinghamshire estate and the events held there were secretive, decadent and, some said, sinister – so much so that, in time, the Brotherhood would become known to outsiders by a new name: the Hell-Fire Club. It was known that Dashwood would often stage mock-religious ceremonies and that some club members took it all a bit too seriously. But not so an MP called John Wilkes, who, during one such event, released a baboon into the caves as a practical joke. However, as most of the revellers had never seen one before, they believed they had accidentally conjured up the very Devil himself and fled from

West Wycombe in terror. Among their number was a certain Sir Redvers Whorne, who returned home to Harpax Grange desperately in need of a clean pair of breeches but thankful to have avoided Satan's clutches.

It took a little while for the shock to pass but, once it had, Sir Redvers began to pine for the club's hedonistic delights, a longing made keener by the realisation that his Hell-Fire Club days were over. He had exhibited outright cowardice before his peers and betters, and even after the truth of Wilkes's prank was revealed, his shame was too great to consider ever returning to Wycombe. But South Herewardshire, though a prosperous county, was somewhat staid and pedestrian in the range of saucy diversions available to a man of his lusty tastes. He was therefore left with only one option: he would have to create his own Hell-Fire Club.

The Diabolical Club boasted a less distinguished roster than did the Knights of St Francis, but it was no less sybaritic in its pursuits. The Diabolicals would meet in Black Dog Wood on warm summer evenings to hold wild parties and faux-Satanic rituals, but rather than cultivating an air of mystery among local people, they found themselves subjected to ridicule, especially among envious men whose applications to join the club had been blackballed. Sir Redvers and his club members were called foppish weaklings and mocked for not being manly enough to hold their parties during the winter. But the final straw came with the publication in 1758 of a comic engraving by William Hogarth, himself a member of the Hell-Fire Club, entitled 'The Fair-Weather Fiends of Harpax'. The artwork depicted Sir Redvers and a crowd of his miserably cold followers warming their frozen hands on blazing emissions from Satan's backside. Embarrassed and enraged, Sir Redvers decided to commission a secret chamber in which his parties could be held all year round. But having no handy chalk hills nearby to tunnel into, he was forced to build it underground at the edge of the woods nearest to Harpax Grange. Excavation began during the summer of 1759, with Sir Redvers insisting on it being ready for use by All Hallows Eve, even if that meant cutting a few corners. However, the tight deadline was met and the Diabolicals were then invited to a grand opening ceremony, during which they were all killed outright when the hastily built and inadequately supported roof came crashing down, burying them all under tons of soil and stone.

The sudden collapse left a large depression in the landscape, which the Whorne family – who'd been told by Sir Redvers that he'd been digging for coal – initially assumed to be the result of natural subsidence. However, as the truth began to emerge, they quickly ordered the eyesore to be filled by diverting water from the River Gew in an attempt to avoid a scandal and awkward questions from relatives of the missing partygoers and their female guests. The resulting pond was named after the newly widowed Lady Gertrude and, with some suitable planting and landscaping, it soon became one of the prettier features of the Harpax estate. However, Sir Redvers had one last surprise up his sleeve. At the same time as the chamber was being constructed, he'd also ordered that a tunnel be dug to connect it to the cellars of the house. This meant that he would be able to make private visits, by way of a secret trap door, whenever he chose to. With the creation of Gertie's Plash, the undiscovered tunnel had flooded and now, after some 250 years of seepage through its poorly made walls, water had begun creeping up into the foundations of the school, threatening structural damage and eventual collapse.

It was traditionally the role of the local MP to sit as chair of the school's independent board of governors and Sir Giles thoroughly enjoyed nitpicking over the school accounts, interfering with the appointment of teachers, and taking any and every opportunity to oppose Miss Bultitude's plans for expansion or modification of the building. However, because he had a vested interest in the health of Harpax Grange, he'd had no choice in this instance but to support her various grant applications so that the Plash could be drained, the tunnel dried out and sealed, and then the pond returned to its former state. Annoyingly, it was incumbent upon him to help lead the fight to save the one building that he wanted most in the world but couldn't have.

The loudest opposition to the drainage plan had come from environmentalists and animal rights groups, who had pointed out that the Plash was home to a number of rare plant and animal species including Boffly's bladderwort and McAlister's snipe fly. It was also one of only two places in the UK where Europe's rarest duck, the critically endangered Nagle's red-headed merganser, was known to breed. But on the other hand, there was a small army of historians who had pushed for the plan to go ahead because the site of the Diabolical Club had never been subjected to archaeological study. To complicate matters even further, there were the descendants of the Diabolical Club members and their guests; some wanted the bodies exhumed so they could be given a proper burial, while others – particularly those who suspected that their ancestors might have been providing the entertainment – insisted that they be left to lie in peace. Sir Giles had been forced to broker negotiations between all of the parties concerned and, while it had not been easy to find a compromise, an agreement had eventually been reached. The plan would be unveiled at the public meeting in Nasely Village Hall the following evening.

The documentation made tedious reading and after ten minutes or so, Sir Giles stopped to give his eyes a break. And as he stared out of the window at the fields beyond the motorway, he daydreamed about what it must have been like to be the lord of the manor back in Sir Redvers' day, when a rigidly enforced class system had ensured that anyone lower than him on the social scale would have had no choice but to bow to his will. It was a time when all of the tiresome hands-on work of running an estate would have been gladly done by forelock-tugging flunkeys and illiterate farmhands. And, best of all, it was a time when every whim and pleasure would have been his to enjoy because he was aristocratic and wealthy. He wouldn't have had any problems with Joan Bultitude back then. Nor with Phoebe, or Cecily for that matter. They would all have been brought up to speak only when spoken to and would never have dreamed of questioning his authority on any matter. His word would have been law.

He considered taking a nap but too many worries were racing around in his mind. To distract himself, he took a lengthy surveyor's report out of his briefcase and began to read. The report's tedious prose and the car's soft leather seats acted as a soporific and he was asleep within minutes. He didn't wake until the car arrived at the gates of Proutt House.

Chapter 7

'I think we're all done here,' said Turvey. 'I have everything I need.'

What had begun as a few exploratory scrapes with a trowel had ended up as a rectangular pit from which he and his assistant had extracted the skeleton and several bags of soil. Jaine watched as the tarpaulin containing the skeleton was carefully folded.

'And you're sure that his hands were bound behind his back?' he asked.

'Looks that way,' said Turvey. 'Similar material to the stuff that was used for the blindfold. It's looking like a case of foul play to me.'

'I guess so.'

'We'll fill in the hole and leave some barriers up for a day or two while the ground settles. We don't want anyone tripping over it, though I doubt you get many people wandering around the woods at night.'

'Except doggers,' said Jaine.

'Doggers? Here?'

'It's a popular location, apparently. You didn't know?'

'They'll have to rename it Black Dogging Wood,' said Turvey.

Cecily sat in the library at Proutt, checking her diary and making notes on her calendar regarding upcoming social events and appointments. Giles was always so busy with company and parliamentary business that he had no time for the day-to-day business of running the estate. Therefore, anything considered 'domestic' was left to her. She finished her tasks and then sat back in her late father's comfortable old Chesterfield and absorbed the ambience of the space. The library was her favourite room in the house, as it had been his. He had filled the shelves with beautifully bound books as he'd wanted to appear well-read and learned, but it was an artifice easily dismantled by a closer look at the titles. Hidden among the Shakespeares, Brontës, Miltons and Defoes were titles such as Michael Southcott's *Death Has Windows*, D. Mandeville's *The Great Trunk Murders*, Sid Abernathy's *Lindy-Hop Lunatic* and any number of similar potboilers, which he would furtively enjoy here, in his private retreat. There were also Westerns and pulp thrillers and full sets of classic murder mysteries by the likes of Lady Abigail Austin, Ariadne Oliver and Gerald C. Potter. Having them rebound in rich leather with gold-embossed spines had provided the library with the literary 'wow factor' he'd been after – as long as no one looked too closely past the camouflage.

Cecily considered her own circumstances and was struck by the realisation that she truly was her father's daughter. She looked like him, to be sure – the same square jaw and firm chin, the same steely blue eyes and chestnut hair cropped short and parted on the side. But it was more than just a physical similarity that bonded them. He had presented to the world a fictitious version of himself, an educated and erudite man who could quote from Bertrand Russell and Thomas Mann. But as soon as he was out of the public eye, he had rushed home to spend his time with Bulldog Drummond, Richard Hannay and Shalako Carlin. Cecily too had created a mask of respectability to hide the reality of her true passions and it was, perhaps, no surprise that she excelled at theatrical performance. A capacity for imposture and role play was a family trait, it seemed.

The sound of car tyres on gravel broke her reverie and she looked out of the window. She hadn't expected Giles home so early but she didn't mind. It was an opportunity to push him, or one of his companies, to sponsor the next production by the Bowcester Theatre Group, of which she was patron, director and, more often than not, female lead. Not that he'd take much pushing. He certainly didn't dare to push back.

The door to the library opened and a pretty, gamine face, framed by shoulder-length brown hair, peered around the jamb.

'The master of the house is home,' said Jenny Highnote. 'Do you want me to start grinding up the glass for his kedgeree?'

'Oh, stop it,' said Cecily. 'And go and put some clothes on, for heaven's sake.'

Dressed in nothing but a chef's apron, Jenny turned on her heel and left the room, but not before presenting Cecily with a pair of shapely buttocks to admire.

As the bell rang for the end of the school day, Miss Bultitude gathered up her things, collected her dogs from the hunting lodge that had been her home for the past ten years, and set off down the drive in her boxy old Volvo estate. The yapping of the dogs was clearly audible until the car was nearly out of sight. Phoebe watched her go and then hastened to the headmistress's office, where she set about photographing everything in the room with her phone before recommencing her search. She hoped that if she was successful and found what she was looking for, it would provide the tipping point in her and Giles's relationship.

When the advertisement for secretary to the Head of Harpax Grange School had appeared in the *Times Educational Supplement*, Sir Giles had spotted a golden opportunity to place a spy in Joan Bultitude's inner sanctum and, as chair of the board of governors, he knew that he would have a significant say in the appointment. Phoebe Kingshaw's credentials were impeccable and, with a few choice amendments to her CV to hide any connection to him, she had easily got the job. Consequently, she had now been at the school for nearly a fortnight and the task she had been set by Giles was very simple.

'I want you to find some dirt on Joan Bultitude,' he'd said. 'It shouldn't be too difficult. I mean, a single woman running an all-girls' school with all women teachers? She must be copping off with someone. Maybe her deputy, that Dyke woman.'

'Deak,' corrected Phoebe.

'All I know is that neither of them is ever seen in male company. And Miss Bultitude is butcher than butch. I reckon she could wrestle a bear to the ground.'

'That doesn't mean she's unsuitable to run a school, any more than a straight teacher would be,' said the more progressive Phoebe.

'With all those pretty young girls around?'

'What decade are you living in?' snapped Phoebe. 'Even if she is gay, and that's a big if, it's ridiculous to suggest that she'd be interested in children. Plus, they have checks these days.'

'OK,' conceded Giles. 'But the parents might not like the idea of a gay head.'

'Then they are as old-fashioned and prejudiced as you seem to be. Would they prefer a man in charge? I mean, blokes can fancy schoolgirls too. In fact, the costumes you sometimes get me to wear strongly suggest that—'

'Yes, OK, forget what I said. Just dig up some dirt for me. All I need is just a hint of inappropriate behaviour, a whiff of scandal. Irregularities in the accounts. Girls being beaten. Topless photos on holiday. Anything that will give me an excuse to start an enquiry. Even if she's cleared, the mud will stick and, rightly or wrongly, the parents will demand her removal. I don't give a damn about her private life. I just want her out of my house!'

And so Phoebe had spent the past ten days unenthusiastically peering into drawers, rummaging in box files, flicking through photo albums and reading emails in the hope of finding the one elusive piece of evidence that would destroy her employer. It was not a task she relished; in the short time she'd known the woman, Joan Bultitude had never shown herself to be anything other than decent, kind and utterly passionate about the welfare and education of the girls in her care. Miss Deak had even said that the headmistress would die for her girls or, at least, do almost anything to protect them and to keep the school open. To be part of a plot to smear the reputation of such a woman felt seedy and shameful. But Phoebe also knew that if Sir Giles could get possession of Harpax Grange, he'd probably feel less duty-bound to Cecily and Proutt House. It was, she believed, the nudge he needed to overcome his reluctance to leave his wife, and this thought was what kept her focused on her unsavoury task.

She finished foraging in a cupboard and, having found nothing more surprising or incriminating than some fabric freshener, flea powder and an industrial staple gun, she turned her attentions to an old wooden chest that sat in a bay window

53

and which, with the addition of a long cushion, served as an extra seat. Miss Bultitude had told her that it had come with the building as part of the fixtures and fittings and that she didn't have a key for it, which Phoebe thought sounded plausible but a mite suspicious. Who wouldn't want to look inside a vintage chest? She removed the cushion and tried to lift the lid on the off-chance, but it was firmly locked. She looked around for something to use as a pick.

Chapter 8

'Delicious pheasant, isn't it?' said Cecily.

Sir Giles smiled a bilious half-smile.

'I can't remember finer,' said Cecily. 'From the estate?'

'Shot them myself,' said Jenny as she gathered up the dirty plates. 'Then hung them for three days to bring out the flavour.'

It seemed to Giles that she put unnecessary emphasis on the word 'hung'. On days when he was at home, she was obliged to fulfil the role for which she was officially employed, that of cook and housekeeper. However, subservience was not a role in which she excelled.

'Good show,' said Cecily. 'Is there a pudding?'

'Oh yes,' said Jenny, looking at Giles. 'A really thick and stodgy one.'

She collected the last of the plates and walked slowly across the dining room and out into the hall. Giles gulped his wine as he watched her go. Opposite him at the long dining room table, Cecily tried unsuccessfully to stifle a smile.

'You may well smirk but it's not bloody funny,' he hissed. 'I realise that she doesn't like me but does she have to make such an obvious show of it? I am her employer, after all. Whatever other… duties… she performs, she is still a member of staff and she should not be so… so…'

'Disrespectful? Unfriendly? Don't be so thin-skinned, Giles,' said Cecily. 'She's paid to cook your meals, not to like you. Do you think the gardener likes you any better? Or the window cleaner?'

'She just called me thick and stodgy.'

'Don't be paranoid. She did no such thing,' said Cecily. 'Although, to be fair, you have become a little stouter of late.'

'The woman hates me, just because I'm married to you and she isn't.'

'We can rectify that situation tomorrow if it bothers you,' said Cecily. 'Admittedly, there would be a certain amount of sanctimonious finger-pointing, but I have broad enough shoulders to bear it if you have.'

Giles had visibly paled.

'Of course, my less tolerant relatives won't be best pleased to find out that we've been living a lie, and my Great Uncle Jasper – you may recall that he's the Bishop of Coxeter – will probably have a heart attack when he finds out what I've been up to. The man has been phobic about vaginas his whole life and the thought of two of them ru—'

'Cecily, really.'

'But, relatives aside, a divorce would mean that Jenny and I would be free to get married and to rub whatever we like with impunity. Come to think of it, your secretary would be delighted too, wouldn't she? Smiles all round, I'd say.'

'That's not the point—'

'Listen. You know as well as I do that the only reason I ever agreed to play this absurd charade with you was that it was Mummy's dying wish. But now she's gone and Proutt is restored, I do find myself wondering why we carry on with it. It seems to be solely for the benefit of your career.'

'You don't mind the money.'

'That is true. And, I suppose, if my family's influence can make you even more rich and powerful, there will be even more to divide up when the inevitable divorce happens.'

'That's a very mercenary attitude.'

'But practical, dear. Jenny won't wait for me for ever and my ridiculous family will eventually realise that the prospect of us producing an heir is about as likely as finding a horse on the Moon. You're going to have to bite the bullet one day and you should start preparing yourself for it. Now, speaking of horses, I need to talk to you about sponsorship for the new play. We're doing a musical adaptation of *Animal Farm* this year and we'll need some good costumes…'

Phoebe worked at the lock of the ancient chest with a pair of bent paperclips and waited for the telltale click of pins falling into place. Years ago, her somewhat maladjusted older brother had shown her how to open simple locks with a makeshift pick and tension wrench. He'd since matured and gone to work for a short-term loans company and was consequently involved in an entirely different form of daylight robbery, but the skills he'd taught her in their youth had proven to be more useful than any of her degrees or diplomas. Knowing what was locked away in your employer's desk drawers and filing cabinets was an excellent way of ensuring that they didn't take advantage of you.

The chest was made of old, dark oak, beautifully patinated by centuries of time and by the many hands that must have stroked its tactile surface. The Whorne family crest with its skewered-boar motif dominated the engraved lid and it was generously decorated with carved hunting scenes of cruelly tusked pigs running among twisted, gnarled trees while men on horseback pursued them with huge dogs and long lances. But Phoebe barely noticed as she worked at the lock. Age had made the mechanism stiff and the paperclips she had employed were proving too flimsy for the task. She found a metal letter opener that was a little more substantial and used that as a tension wrench instead. Almost immediately she was rewarded by the lock turning. She carefully lifted the lid and winced as the old, dry hinges gave out a loud creak. For a long moment, she held her breath and waited silently for any sign that someone might have heard the noise. It was possible that Miss Deak was back from her trip to Bowcester and the woman had the hearing of a moth. A long, tense minute passed without incident and, feeling reassured, Phoebe exhaled and peered inside the chest. Disappointingly, it contained very little, just a large leather dog collar, a brown paper package bound with ribbon, and an impressive collection of dead spiders and cobwebs. She took a photo of the interior for reference and then turned her attention to the package, carefully lifting it out and grimacing at the desiccated invertebrates. She laid it on the parquet floor and opened it up. Inside was a sheaf of typewritten paper. She read the line at the top of the first page and her heart skipped a beat.

'Bloody hell,' she whispered.

'Roly-poly pudding,' said Jenny as she placed a bowl heavily in front of Sir Giles.

'Really? I'd expected spotted dick. Or a fat rascal at the very least.'

Jenny rolled her eyes. Giles's phone began vibrating in his pocket. He looked at the screen and saw that it was Phoebe calling. 'Strangely enough, I'm not really in the mood for pudding any more,' he announced, leaving the dining room in a huff. Outside in the hall, he accepted the call.

'Sorry I couldn't answer just then. I was having dinner with her indoors. You won't believe the gall of our cook. She jus—'

'You need to meet me ASAP,' said Phoebe urgently.

'I thought we said at the weekend? I haven't booked anywhere yet.'

'No, this is different. We have to meet tonight.'

'Tonight? Does this mean that you've found something?'

'You don't know the half of it,' said Phoebe. 'Meet me by the golden pig at nine o'clock.'

Sir Giles looked at his watch.

'But that's only half an hour away. I'm not sure that I— Hello? Hello?'

But Phoebe had either hung up or the mobile phone signal had been lost.

'I just have to pop out for a little while,' said Giles, returning to the dining room and pulling on his jacket. 'Constituency matters.'

'Send her my best regards, won't you?' said Cecily with a knowing smile.

Phoebe took photographs of the first and last of the typewritten pages before retying the bundle, placing it back inside the chest and locking it using the letter opener. She then went quietly downstairs, all the while checking around and ahead of her to make sure she wasn't being observed. She arrived at reception, intending to grab a torch before setting off into the woods, when suddenly her phone rang. She jumped and desperately grabbed it out of her pocket, stabbing at the call connect button.

'Jesus Christ, Giles! Are you trying to get me caught?'

'I was just calling to say that I'm on my way,' said Giles. 'What do you mean, caught? What are you up to?'

'Listen. I've found something that is absolute dynamite but I'm saying nothing over the phone, OK? Just get your arse to the golden pig as quick as you can. And don't phone me again.'

Phoebe left the building quietly and a brisk ten-minute walk brought her to the mausoleum and Monty's Folly. She caught her breath and checked her phone for messages. She half-expected to find a text from Giles with some excuse for not turning up; he let her down so often that she frequently felt like she was some kind of inconvenience to him. She certainly felt less important than his job or, for that matter, his wife, and she wondered what kept their marriage together. It wasn't love, or so he claimed. A sense of duty, perhaps? That was often the way with old families. Or maybe Cecily had some sort of hold over him? After all, Giles was her cash cow. It was surely in her best interests to find some way to keep him on a short leash and, presumably, whatever Cecily had on him was damaging enough to ensure that he always came home, credit cards at the ready. But not after tonight, she thought. Oh no. Everything would be different after tonight. She looked at her phone again and it read 8:51 p.m. She also noted that there was even less signal here than at the school, so even if Giles had sent a message she wouldn't have received it. A sudden noise among the bushes made her jump.

'Giles?'

Something heavy smashed into the back of her skull and made her fall to her hands and knees. Her consciousness began slipping away as she toppled sideways, her head connecting heavily with the cold flagstones.

She never felt the second blow, the one that killed her.

Sir Giles parked his Bentley in the public car park and switched off the engine. It had felt good to be totally in control of something for a change, even if it was just a car and only for twenty minutes. Most of the time he was chauffeured about and, in both his public and private life, other people had their hooks into him twenty-four hours a day. Whether it was the party whip, his PA, his shareholders, his board of directors, his constituents, his wife or his mistress, the demands and desires of others ensured that his life was never quite his own.

He stepped out of the vehicle and pulled his collar up against the chill of the evening. October had brought northern winds, bearing the promise of frosts and snow to come. He tested his torch and then took the path signposted towards the mausoleum.

The walk was lined with skeletal trees clothed in the last dying leaves of the year, but at least it was a clear right of way and he was glad not to be going into the woods themselves. The tall obelisk of Monty's Folly soon became visible ahead and, as he walked towards it, Sir Giles considered some of the Whornes who were interred beneath its shadow. There was his great-grandfather, Jolyon, who had been a lieutenant colonel in the First World War and whose disastrous decision-making had killed off more of his own soldiers than Germans. And then there was Jolyon's older brother, Sir Rufus, who in 1924 had been the only person ever to die by way of Harry Grindell Matthews' 'death ray'. Matthews had claimed that his ray could stop a car engine, shoot down aeroplanes and incapacitate soldiers from up to four miles away. At a private demonstration, Sir Rufus – then attached to the Chiefs of Staff Committee – had been standing beside a box of dynamite when it had unexpectedly gone up. Whether it was set off by the ray or, as many suspected, Matthews was a con artist and the explosion had been rigged but accidentally triggered too soon, was never decided. The family hadn't cared; they'd delighted in telling the world that one of their number had been killed in such an eccentric fashion. That had always been the way with the Whornes: in life or in death, they had always done extraordinary things. They had hunted dangerous wild boars, climbed the highest peaks, crashed and burned in scratch-built racing cars, ballooned over oceans and trudged through crocodile-infested rivers to bring civilisation, usually in the form of Christianity, tobacco and alcohol, to tribes that had never met white people before. And at the top of the list, there was Sir Redvers – dilettante and pleasure-seeker, eldest son of the tragic Sir Veryard Whorne and founder of the ill-starred Diabolical Club. His bones still lay crushed under Gertie's Plash but there was a suitably over-the-top memorial to him inside the walls of the mausoleum. Giles wondered whether he would ever do anything as noteworthy as his forebears had. Or was he destined to be simply a dull, if successful, meat producer and politician? Thanks to a special dispensation agreed during the sale of Harpax Grange, his ashes would one day be stored here among those of his ancestors. As things stood, he realised, his urn would be the one that visitors skipped quickly by because he was 'the boring one'.

He arrived at the building and almost tripped over the body. It took a second to register that it was Phoebe who lay at his feet, and the sudden shock of discovery made him let out a loud bestial cry that was part anguish, part revulsion. He'd never been this close to a dead body before, let alone the body of someone he cared for. He hadn't even been allowed to visit his mother during her final days at the hospice as he'd been a child and his father had wanted to spare him further upset. The thought occurred to him that perhaps Phoebe wasn't dead, just seriously injured? He knelt down and tried to rouse her but she was limp and lifeless. He felt clumsily for a pulse on her neck but found nothing. As he took his hand away from her still-warm flesh, he realised that it was slick with blood – rich, red and vital. It hadn't started to coagulate, which told him, even with his limited knowledge, that she must have died just minutes before. No, not died. Been killed. Even by the indirect light from his dropped torch, he could see the extent of her terrible injuries. And there was so much blood. Stifling the urge to be sick, Giles frantically grabbed up his torch and shone it all around for fear that the killer was still lurking somewhere nearby. An image of the Shaggy Beast, extravagantly fanged and talons unsheathed, flitted through his mind. Giles dismissed it as, with trembling hands, he took his phone out of his pocket and tried unsuccessfully to dial 999. There had been a weak signal back at his car, he remembered, but here there was nothing at all. He swore and, with a speed quite remarkable for a man of his bulk and sedentary habits, he raced back to the car park.

Somewhere deep in the woods, among an area of densely planted conifers some distance from where Sir Giles was frantically calling for the emergency services, a courting couple were doing their best to have fun despite the bitter cold.

'You do love me, don't you, Jamie?'

'Of course I do. This is our second packet this month.'

'It's just... you don't seem to be very enthusiastic.'

'I'm just cold, Keeley love. I'm not sure that I'm cut out for this kind of— Ooh! That felt good.'

'Someone walked over my grave.'

'Tell them to do it again,' said Jamie, and he began thrusting with renewed vigour.

'Wait... listen,' said Keeley.

'What?'

'I thought I heard something…'

From somewhere close by came a sound like heavy, laboured breathing. Jamie withdrew and quickly got dressed.

'Let's get out of here,' he whispered. 'I've heard funny stories about this place. We should have stayed on the path.'

'Don't be daft,' said Keeley, groping in the darkness for her knickers. 'It's probably just some other dogger copping an eyeful. Let them watch. That is sort of the idea.'

'If it is, he has chronic asthma and— Fuck!'

A shambling, hairy figure emerged suddenly from among the trees, sporting long white teeth, burning red eyes and a monstrously large erection. As the couple ran away in terror, it lifted its head and howled at the shrouded moon.

Chapter 9

'Something nasty in the woodshed?' said Mr Levinshulme, the profoundly deaf reporter for the *Bowcester Mercury*. 'I remember reading that...'

'Not woodshed! Woods!' yelled Barry Chetwynd. 'I said that there's something nasty in the woods!'

The murder of Phoebe Kingshaw was the talk of the village. And, thanks mostly to Chetwynd's enthusiasm for the subject, so too was the overnight Shaggy Beast sighting. An anonymous courting couple had described their terrifying encounter to the lad who worked the night shift at the petrol station in Larock. He'd told his sister who worked at the sausage factory, who had then told her colleagues, and the extraordinary bush telegraph that exists among small countryside communities had done the rest. Within hours, the story had spread by word of mouth across half of Bowcester Borough, the facts becoming more exaggerated and sensationalised with each retelling. Somewhere along the way it had also somehow become enmeshed with the other big story of the day and, in his butcher's shop, Barry Chetwynd was taking every opportunity to further cement the two events together in his customers' minds.

'I told you the Beast was real and now it's on the rampage! They say she was torn limb from limb, poor girl.'

'What rubbish,' snapped Miss Shelmerdine, in whose classroom Chetwynd had sat as a child. She upbraided the other people in the shop. 'Shaggy Beast indeed. Don't listen to his foolishness. You'll only encourage him.'

'Wonderful book, *Cold Comfort Farm*,' continued Mr Levinshulme, oblivious to the fact that the conversation had moved on. 'A splendid parody of those old "loam and love child" novels…'

'Don't you want there to be a monster in Black Dog Wood?' said Chetwynd, smiling. 'I'm quite excited by the idea.'

'I'm not the least bit surprised. You've always been a very childish boy,' said Miss Shelmerdine, leaving the shop.

'You can talk,' said Chetwynd under his breath. 'You're the one who has to wear nappies these days.'

'Did you just say something about a monster?' asked Mr Levinshulme.

Across the street in the mini-market, Sid Munsun was also discussing overnight events with the people queuing at his till.

'It's no wonder they call it the Shaggy Beast if what I hear about the size of its doodah is true. As big as the one on Gladys Brockhole's side wall; that's what young Jessie Tremblett told me the other day.'

'That's ridiculous,' said café owner Mrs Anne Moore.

'It would have made her eyes water and that's for sure.'

'Sidney Munsun!'

'No one has suggested that the Shaggy Beast humped the victim to death, have they?' said shoe-shop owner Percy Bingle. 'Though it would explain the name.'

'And you're just as bad, Bingo,' tutted Mrs Moore.

'It was probably just a big old dog fox gone rogue,' said RSPCA inspector Inderpal Verma. 'It can happen, you know. They break into a coop and kill all the chickens without eating a thing.'

'Yes, but dog foxes don't have willies the size of a baby's arm.'

'Sidney Munsun!' scolded Mrs Moore.

'And they don't roger school secretaries to death,' said Bingle.

'Bingo!'

'I suppose it could be one of those ABCs – an alien big cat – like the Beast of Bodmin,' mused Verma. 'Maybe an escapee from the Trembletts' menagerie over at Ordon? I should call and ask.'

'But surely then Jessie would have recognised it?' said Mrs Moore.

'All I know is that sightings have become more regular recently,' said Munsun. 'And now there's been a death, you can guarantee that Barry Chetwynd will be organising a monster hunt. You wait and see. He did one once before.'

'Surely that's a job for the police?' said Mrs Moore.

'That would mean them having to admit that the Beast is real,' said Munsun. 'And I can't see that happening, can you? Good morning, Len. The usual?'

Len Youlden had come to the till for his paper and daily pouch of tobacco.

'Arr,' he said. 'You'll never guess who's been arrested for killing that secretary. Only our local MP, that's who.'

'No!' said Mrs Moore. 'Sir Giles? Really?'

'That's what I was told by Rowan Fadly,' said Youlden. 'Her son works in Leverett's hardware shop in Bowcester and he's married to that Battock girl whose sister is courting that lad from Curse God Farm who works as a special constable on Friday nights and—'

'Did you say monster hunt?' asked Mr Levinshulme, who had come into the shop for some onions to go with his liver and bacon.

By midday, he had submitted a wildly inaccurate version of the story to his editor at Bowcester and by 1 p.m, news trawlers on the London tabloids had picked up on the words 'shaggy beast' and 'werewolf'. As a result, a handful of cub reporters were on their way to South Herewardshire by 3 p.m.

The senior reporters had been despatched several hours earlier, when the news had broken that a member of parliament had been arrested on suspicion of murder.

At Bowcester Police Station, Sir Giles sat hunched over an interview room table and sipped at a cup of miserably poor instant coffee. A distinguished-looking man of six feet, he usually cut a fairly imposing figure, but he now looked smaller, meeker and somehow older. His greying hair was unkempt, his chin was stubbled and his bespoke tailored clothes had been taken away for forensic examination and replaced by a shapeless grey jogging suit supplied from police stores. Having spent a fitful night trying to sleep on a hard mattress in a cell that reeked of stale sweat and disinfectant, he was also exhausted.

He attempted, once again, to make sense of the situation in which he found himself. He couldn't quite process the grim reality of it all. He had said as much to the police officers who had questioned him upon his arrest the night before. And there had been so many questions: Why was he at the mausoleum at that time of night? Had he arranged to meet the victim? What was his relationship to her? Despite being in a state of shock,

Giles had elected to keep his mouth shut until he could speak to a solicitor. The night duty custody officer had therefore postponed all further questioning until the morning and had let him sleep. Upon rising, he'd eaten a greasy breakfast off a paper plate and had then contacted a genuinely shocked Cecily to find him a legal representative among her relatives who would have the right amount of clout.

Cliff Jaine knocked twice on the open door of his DI's office and stepped inside. The room was spartan, with plain magnolia-coloured walls dotted here and there with small grey spots where the removal of posters and maps had taken off some of the paint. The previous occupant, DI Brian Blount, had left under a cloud following the terrible mistakes he'd made during the Shirley Pomerance murder investigation. And as the DI before him had been found dead in the office from autoerotic strangulation, the Detective Inspector post at Bowcester had now acquired a reputation for being cursed. Certainly, it had taken a long time to find a replacement for Blount as no one, it seemed, wanted to fill the vacancy left by his demotion and transfer. But Derek McNabb had had no such qualms or superstitious concerns. Since moving in two months ago, he had erased every trace of the room's former occupants but had then utterly failed to stamp his own identity on to it. There were no family photos or certificates of merit, no pot plants or executive toys, no personal touches at all; just bare walls and an uncluttered desk behind which he now sat, apparently deeply engrossed in some paperwork. He didn't look up.

'Morning, guv.'

'It's "sir", not "guv",' said McNabb, running his fingers through his short-cropped red hair. His fingers lingered on an emerging bald spot at the crown. 'This isn't an episode of *The Bill*.'

'Yes, gu— sir. Sorry. Force of habit. DI Blount was happy wi—'

'I am not DI Blount. What do you want?'

'Just letting you know, sir, that I'm driving over to the lab to talk to Topsy – SOCO Turvey, I mean – to see what else he's discovered about the skeleton. Things get done quicker if you stand over the boffins rather than waiting for them to email you. Is that—'

McNabb's phone rang. He held up his hand for silence and snatched the receiver to his ear.

'DI McNabb. He is? Good. I'll come down.' He stood up, smoothing his goatee to a crisp point and making eye contact with Jaine for the first time. 'Luscott-Whorne's solicitor is here.'

'Nasty business, that,' said Jaine. 'I met the victim yesterday, as it happens. When I was at the sch—'

'Keep me posted of any developments, Sergeant,' interrupted McNabb. 'And for God's sake tidy yourself up, before you get seen in public. You look like a bag lady.' He marched briskly out of his office.

'Tosser,' said Jaine, under his breath.

Derek McNabb hadn't risen to the rank of Detective Inspector by brilliant police work or by being particularly smart. He'd done it by taking necessary but unglamorous positions that no one else wanted, roles in which obstinacy, penny-pinching and quibbling were considered virtues and where a lack of personality was invaluable. He had spent the previous three years working in the complaints investigation department following up on allegations of police misconduct and he'd been very successful at his job. But while it had boosted his promotion chances, it had also sunk the possibility of him forming any genuine friendships within the constabulary.

It wasn't the fact that he had investigated fellow police officers that had made him unpopular; if there was one thing cops hated, it was a bent cop. Rather, it was the gusto and enthusiasm with which he had pursued his quarry. The majority of decent officers viewed him as a coward who picked on soft targets among his own sort rather than villains, and it hadn't been long before he was being referred to as 'Judas'. McNabb had been quick to stamp on that. But he'd then picked up the nickname of 'Kipper' and he'd initially naively assumed that it was because he'd grown up in Arbroath – his father had been with the Royal Marines, based just outside the town at RM Condor. However, upon learning that it actually meant 'dead-eyed, two-faced, yellow, no guts', he'd become even more isolated, intolerant and resentful of his fellow officers. He had subsequently sought promotion on the basis of 'if you can't join them, beat them', but he had stalled at the rank of inspector – a halfway house between street cop and senior management and uncomfortably sandwiched between two bodies of officers who disliked him equally. He very much wished to be a chief inspector. However, further promotion was unlikely.

McNabb had fallen victim to something known as 'The Peter Principle', and had been 'promoted to his level of incompetence'. As a sergeant, he'd been proficient at investigating complaints but the role of inspector demanded an entirely different skill set that included leadership, compassion, empathy, adaptability and a willingness to learn from others – all behaviours, abilities and people skills in which he was clearly lacking. It meant that he was passed over during selections for chief inspector on a regular basis. It also ensured that a whole extra layer of angry resentment had been added to his style of management.

As he walked downstairs to the interview rooms, he saw officers improperly dressed or lounging about chatting. Everywhere he looked there was sloppiness and unprofessional behaviour. His predecessor had, in his opinion, been far too soft on the men and women under his command and McNabb was doing his best to rectify that with regular inspections and the use of invasive micro-management. It had done nothing to improve his standing with his staff.

He arrived at the door of Interview Room 2 and went inside. A bored-looking uniformed constable who had been slouching against a wall abruptly straightened up. Sir Giles was sitting at a table staring vacantly into a now-empty polystyrene cup, while a furious-looking man in a blue pinstriped suit whispered into his ear. McNabb drew himself up to his full height, which was considerably shorter than either Sir Giles or his visitor, and introduced himself.

'I am DI Derek McNabb. I am the lead on this investigation.'

The man in the suit interposed himself between McNabb and his prisoner. He had ruddy cheeks and a tidy black moustache and his eyes sparked with intelligence and umbrage.

'About time too,' he said brusquely and without the offer of a handshake. 'Julian Luscott-Vent QC. I trust that this will not take very long, Inspector. My client has been through a very distressing experience and has spent the night in a police cell with the rudest of facilities. I'd like him taken home as soon as possible.'

'Home? With all due respect, your client is a murder suspect.'

'Nonsense.'

'Have you not seen the arrest report?' said McNabb.

'Of course I have. But I've seen no evidence to substantiate your frankly surprising allegations.'

'No evidence?' said McNabb incredulously. 'He was found at the crime scene.'

'A public place with unrestricted access. And he wasn't "found" there. He dialled 999 and asked you to come. But do go on.'

'Yes. But the victim was murdered at almost exact—'

'I think you mean killed, rather than murdered. Until proven otherwise.'

'All right. She was killed at almost exactly the same time that Sir Giles was there. And there was no one else around,' said McNabb.

'No one else that you have found. What about that couple who reported that they'd seen a werewolf or something?'

'We don't know who they were.'

'You don't? Why not?'

'We're tracking them down,' said McNabb, starting to feel much like he felt when under cross-examination at court. 'But look, Sir Giles had the victim's blood on his hands and clothing. That's pretty damning evidence.'

'Damning? In what way?' asked the barrister. 'Anyone could have found her lying there.'

'At nine o'clock at night?'

'Are you claiming that no one goes into Black Dog Wood at that time of night? You've already admitted that there were at least two other people in the vicinity.'

'No, but—'

'My client stumbled upon the body of that poor unfortunate woman while he was visiting his family's mausoleum. It's pure coincidence, nothing more. Unless you have witnesses that say otherwise. Perhaps your werewolf spotters? Not that they sound very credible.'

'But you must see how unlikely—'

'See? What I see is a member of parliament, a respected

businessman and a trusted friend in some distress,' said Luscott-Vent. 'If Sir Giles says that he came across the body of a woman, I see no reason to disbelieve him. He's had a dreadful shock. And all you have, Inspector, is a wicked allegation based upon the flimsiest of circumstantial evidence. You don't even have a murder weapon, do you?'

'We're searching the woods again now that it's light and—'

'No weapon. No witnesses. And no forensic evidence to link Sir Giles to that unfortunate woman's death other than the blood on his hands and clothes, which is commensurate with him attempting to render first aid, as any decent human being would do upon finding a person who has been injured or attacked. And, I might add, it was my client who called for the police and ambulance. It's not much of a case, is it, Inspector? In fact, it's not a case at all. For all you know, the victim was climbing the walls of the mausoleum and fell, landing on her head.'

'That doesn't seem very likely,' flustered McNabb. His face had become puce. It clashed with his hair and goatee.

'Nor does a knight of the realm randomly killing some stranger he meets while visiting his relatives' last resting place,' said Luscott-Vent. 'And yet, that seems to be the basis of your case.'

'That's not how I see it, and—'

'You have no evidence to show that he is a danger to anyone. In fact, you have barely any evidence at all other than Sir Giles being in the wrong place at the wrong time,' said Luscott-Vent, summing up. 'Had he chanced to arrive just a little sooner he might even have saved Miss Kingshaw's life and you would now be hailing him as a hero. All of which means that you have insufficient reason to keep my client in custody. I therefore insist that he be released and allowed to go home. I'm sure that if you require a recognisance to secure his bail, Lady

Luscott-Whorne will be more than happy to organise one. The family is not without funds, as you know.'

'But I need to interview him.'

'There will be no interviews. I've instructed him to say nothing,' snapped the barrister. 'The onus is upon you to find evidence of his guilt, not for him to protest his obvious innocence. There, I think we've covered everything. So, Inspector, as I'm sure you have other more important work to be getting on with, such as catching the real murderer for example, perhaps we can bring this sorry business to a close?'

'I'm not releasing him,' said McNabb, his voice sounding a little more strained than he would have liked.

'Quite right. That sort of decision needs to be made by someone far more senior,' said Luscott-Vent. 'I'll call your Chief Superintendent.'

He produced his phone and selected a number.

'Hello, Eddie? Julian here. How are you? Yes, absolutely. What? I know! Three under par! That's put the fear of God into old Roseblade and his nine-hole record! Ha ha! Now then, this isn't entirely a social call, I'm afraid, old chap...'

McNabb growled and stomped out of the interview room. Up until this moment, nothing in his life had been more important than showing the world that he was a man to be reckoned with. But that had now been superseded by the desire to see the look on the barrister's face when Sir Giles Bloody Luscott-Whorne got sent down at Crown Court for murder.

Clifford Jaine arrived at the police laboratory in Coxeter and drew himself a mug of coffee from the vending machine. It was almost impossible to get a decent cuppa anywhere within the South Herewardshire Constabulary, but even a desperately poor one went some way towards removing the bad taste that he always got in his mouth when dealing with McNabb. His previous DI had been a disagreeable man, but he hadn't been as obnoxious and deliberately self-serving. Jaine wondered whether he'd been bullied at school; the bright red hair would surely have made him a ripe target for taunts by the crueller of his childhood peers. And he was shorter than average, so perhaps he suffered from some kind of Napoleon complex? Whatever the reason, Derek McNabb seemed to thrive on being thoroughly unlikeable.

'Hi, Cliff, come on through,' said Turvey, emerging from a door marked with a radioactive symbol. He saw the concerned look on Jaine's face. 'Don't worry, that's just because we have X-ray equipment in here. I promise not to roast your love spuds.'

The two men walked down a short corridor and entered a room marked Path Lab C. The skeleton was laid out on a table, the bones arranged in their correct positions. The skull, refusing to stay upright, lay on its side and seemed to be watching them as they entered.

'I guess now that Kipper has a real-life murder to play with, you've been lumbered with the cold case, eh?' teased the SOCO.

'Something like that,' said Jaine. 'Talking of which, have you got anything new that I can take back to him on Phoebe Kingshaw?'

'Not yet. I've organised the autopsy for later this morning but I doubt that there'll be any surprises. It's obviously death due to massive head trauma. With any luck we might get some sort of idea of what the weapon was.'

'Then please let him know sooner rather than later. He's gunning for Luscott-Whorne and being even more of a pain in the arse than usual. If that's possible.'

'Will do. Now, about Billy Bones here. I've found a few

76

things of interest,' said Turvey. 'First off, everything points to him being buried sometime in the 1930s and I reckon he was between thirty-five and forty-five years old. So he would have been born around the turn of the century. He has numerous shrapnel injuries to his face, upper arms and shoulders. As we suspected, he'd seen some action, this lad.'

'First World War?'

'I reckon so. He was too young to have been a Boer War vet. And then there's the blindfold and the fabric used to tie his hands.' Turvey pointed to two long, threadbare pieces of green cloth lying on the table next to the body. 'Standard army issue puttees, both of them.'

'Puttees?'

'Those long strips of thick cloth that soldiers wound around their lower legs.'

'Weird choice.'

'Not really. Almost every able-bodied man signed up for the Great War and they would all have had at least one pair each. There must have been a lot of them about.'

Jaine picked up one of the pieces of cloth. 'What were they for? They couldn't have offered much protection, surely?'

'Not from bullets or shrapnel, no. But they kept out ticks and lice. Plus, they were cheap to produce, one size fits all, and they could be easily washed and used as bandages. Which, incidentally, is what *puttee* means in the original Hindi.'

'I never saw you as a military history buff.'

'I can read Wikipedia.'

'Ah. What about cause of death? The skull is a bit mangled.'

'As I said, those are shrapnel injuries,' said Turvey. 'But the bone had healed sometime before his death, so they probably happened during the war. He might have been facially disfigured. As for cause of death, I'm not sure yet. He'd definitely been roughed up before he died. There are a couple of cracked ribs and several broken fingers. Probably not enough to kill him, though. And I doubt that he blindfolded himself or tied his own hands together either. Someone did this to him and then buried the body. So, whichever way you look at it, the game's afoot.'

Chapter 10

The morning was cold but dry and bright and it seemed to Frank Shunter that it was the perfect day to rake up the leaves on the lawn and add them to his compost heap. He still had a hundred and one small jobs to do indoors on the new extension but the weather was too good to waste. An ancient radio stood on a wall, belting out a crackly version of the altogether appropriate 'Autumn Almanac' by the Kinks. There was a new DAB radio in the kitchen but Shunter persevered with his old paint-spattered and held-together-with-duct-tape device. He had once claimed that it was a metaphor for his life – that just because something was old and there were newer options available, there was no reason to throw it away if it still worked. But having made this declaration, he'd been hoisted with his own petard. He was now lumbered with terrible sound quality until the radio was truly beyond repair.

Mrs Shunter emerged from the kitchen with two steaming mugs of tea and he propped the rake up against the wall and stretched.

'Perfect timing,' he said, pecking her on the cheek. 'No biscuits?'

'And undo all the good work you've done?' she said, patting his stomach. 'I hope you're minding your back.'

'I'm not a masochist. I know when to stop and... Hang on...'

He turned the volume knob on the radio and was rewarded by a storm of crackles and pops through which he could just about make out the local news.

'*...where the body of a woman, identified as Phoebe Kingshaw, a secretary at Harpax Grange School, was discovered last night. A man is helping police with their enquiries. In Pawley today...*'

'I know that face,' said Mrs Shunter, folding her arms.

'What?'

'That's the same face you pulled two years ago when that author woman was murdered in the village.'

'It's just curiosity,' protested Shunter. 'Professional interest, you might say. Or, rather, retired professional interest. It's not like I'm getting involved.'

'You said that last time and look what happened. Explosions, police shoot-outs—'

'Hardly my fault. And I did help to catch the murderer.'

'You're too old for that kind of thing now.'

'I'm fifty-eight. I'm not Methuselah.'

'You stick to your composting. We don't want a repeat of things, do we?'

As his wife walked back indoors, Shunter turned the radio up further to make a point about obsolescence. And then turned it down again as it was making Ray Davies sing like a dalek.

Sir Giles arrived home at Proutt but couldn't remember any part of the journey. Lack of sleep and the succession of bizarre events that had marked the past twenty-four hours of his life had led him to a state of dazed confusion from which he was finding it hard to escape. He was woken from his funk by a series of sudden, fierce blasts of light. A mob of paparazzi had gathered at the gatehouse that marked the entrance to the estate and they crowded around the car, shouting unintelligible questions and pushing their cameras up against the thankfully tinted windows. Giles tried to shield his eyes from the glare of their flashes as the electric gates opened ponderously slowly. But then he was through and the gates swung shut behind the car and all was quiet and calm again. Proutt House loomed welcoming in the near distance.

Cecily was waiting to greet him on the doorstep. Seeing his pitiful state, she led him straight upstairs to his room and put him to bed.

'So what happens now?' asked Jenny.

'Cousin Julian says that he's been bailed until next Monday pending further enquiries. The police seem to be convinced that he killed her but I just can't see it. Can you?'

'If I'm honest, no. But if he didn't kill her, who did?'

'I hadn't really thought of that,' said Cecily. 'The real murderer will still be out there, won't they? And if the police aren't looking for anyone else, they can carry on murdering.'

'Starring Sid James as Jack the Ripper?'

'This is serious, Jenny.'

'We're safe enough here. This place is like a fortress. And I have my guns.'

'Yes, but we're not hermits. We do go out occasionally,' said Cecily. 'I have to go into Nasely this evening.'

'Why?'

'The public meeting. About the draining of Gertie's Plash.'

'What's that got to do with you?'

'I'm one of the school's trustees and I'm married to the chair of the board of governors,' said Cecily. 'Giles is obviously in no fit state to attend so I'll have to show my face in his stead. Civic duty and all that.'

'Want me to come with you?'

'I'm sure I'll be fine.'

'Oh yes, I forgot. There may be a psychopath on the loose but a couple of lesbians can't be seen together in public, can they?'

'That's not what I meant. I was talki—'

'I really thought that his fling with his secretary might give us some hope of ending this nonsense,' said Jenny. 'But now we're stuck with the idiot.'

'You can be quite heartless sometimes, Jenny. A young woman has been murdered.'

But Jenny had already walked off down the stairs.

In his room, Sir Giles stared up at the high ceiling with its pendant chandelier and decorative plaster mouldings and a tear escaped the corner of his eye. He rolled over in an attempt to get some much-needed sleep but as soon as his eyes closed, all he could see was the lifeless, bloodied face of Phoebe Kingshaw.

Chapter 11

Dr Owen Pantridge had once heard a university lecturer defined as 'a person who talks in other people's sleep' and he was happy to concede that his own style of delivery could be described as soporific. He was softly spoken and his topics were never controversial or likely to provoke strong feelings in his listeners, which suited him just fine as he was not a man who enjoyed conflict. However, the audience he faced this evening was very different from his usual student crowd. He knew for a fact that some of them were unconvinced by the plan he was about to outline and that one animal rights group in particular was very much opposed to it. He looked around the people gathered in the village hall with some trepidation and tried to imagine them all naked, a trick that he'd been taught on a training course many years before. But it didn't help; how the sight of seventy-five nude pensioners and red-faced pig farmers could possibly fill him with confidence he couldn't imagine.

People had drifted into the hall during the past half hour and had formed into small groups around the refreshments table to discuss the weather, their families, the murder of Phoebe Kingshaw, the recent Shaggy Beast sightings, the big cock on Gladys Brockhole's side wall and the quality of the tea and biscuits. Cecily sat stoically alone in the front row of chairs and used a rare instance of half-decent phone reception to check her emails. Somehow the identity of the man 'helping police with their enquiries' had leaked out, and while she found the whispers and sideways glances discomfiting, she was determined not to react or respond.

The clock of St Probyn's struck seven and Dr Pantridge felt a kaleidoscope of butterflies suddenly take flight inside his stomach. He cleared his throat.

'Ladies and gentlemen. If you would like to take your seats, please, we'll begin.'

He smiled, in what he hoped was a friendly and disarming way, in the direction of the small knot of angry-looking young adults that stood at the back of the hall. They didn't smile back. Nor did they move as people began to fill the rows of chairs.

'Thank you all very much for coming out this evening,' he said, nervously fiddling with a pair of spectacles that hung on a cord around his sweaty neck. 'My name is Dr Owen Pantridge and I am senior lecturer in history at Saltonstall University and the project leader for this… er… project. I hope you'll find this evening informative and also that my colleagues and I can put to rest any concerns or worries that you might have. I thought we'd start with a short presentation.'

He signalled for the lights to be lowered and nervously pressed a button on a remote control. A projector threw a fine image of the school onto the screen behind him, partially obscured, to the amusement of the audience, by a magnified silhouette of his own bald head. A small clump of lonely hairs stuck up from the crown, making it look like a cartoonist's desert island. He quickly shuffled out of the way.

'As I'm sure most of you know, Harpax Grange is a Grade II listed building dating from 1720 and designed by the celebrated architect Edmund Greasley at the behest of Sir

Veryard Whorne. Upon his death, it passed to his eldest son, this fine fellow, Sir Redvers Whorne.' A change of slide showed a portrait of the man wearing an extraordinary plumed hat, a beautifully embroidered silk gown with ermine trim and a particularly lascivious grin. Gentle laughter filled the hall. Pantridge pressed a button and a new slide showed an aerial view of Harpax Grange and Gertie's Plash with the location of the tunnel connecting them overlaid as a drawing.

'In the past eighteen months, the building has developed some very serious instances of rising damp and dangerous black mould. The cause is this previously undiscovered underground passage, shown here on the photo. It became flooded when the Plash was created and water has been permeating out through its walls for over two hundred years. The surrounding soil has now reached saturation point and, with nowhere else to go, the water has begun to creep upwards into the foundations and brickwork. There was never any damp-prevention work done because no written record was ever made of the tunnel's existence. Not even the Whorne family knew it was there.'

'First rule of Diabolical Club is you don't talk about Diabolical Club,' whispered Gerry Waxleigh. Len Youlden nodded but utterly failed to get the reference.

'Consequently, the problem has been quietly growing under everyone's feet for years and it's now become a serious health and safety issue. That is why the decision has been taken to drain the Plash – just for a few weeks – so that we can pump the tunnel dry and seal it off where it connects to the pond. It also allows us the first ever opportunity to recover bodies and artefacts that have lain buried under the pond since it was created.'

'What about the wildlife?' shouted a pretty Goth from the back of the hall. The group of young people around her loudly echoed the sentiment.

'We have taken a great deal of advisement on this and we are confident that we can complete the work without lasting detriment to the ecology of the area,' said Pantridge. 'When we've finished our dig, we will refill the pond using the River Gew to ensure that the water quality remains constant and appropriate for this area. We have already installed a pair of water tanks that can accommodate a goodly number of fish and amphibians, plants and invertebrates. We will use these to restock once the project concludes. Inevitably there will be some casualties but we aim to keep them to the absolute minimum.'

'The absolute minimum is zero,' said Oberon Tremblett, eliciting a chorus of agreement from the other members of FLAN.

'Fascists,' muttered Willy.

Pantridge waited for the murmurs to subside but didn't get a chance to speak.

'Changing the subject, if I may, but what do you intend to do with any remains that you find?' asked shopkeeper Sid Munsun. 'One of my ancestors was present at the Diabolical Club's opening night.'

'That poor, poor strumpet,' said Gerry Waxleigh.

'Actually, he was a mill owner,' said Munsun indignantly over the noise of the audience's laughter.

'I can probably answer that,' said the Reverend Tirbett, rising to his feet. 'I have discussed this issue at length with Dr Pantridge and the County Archaeological Board. St Probyn's will provide a full and proper burial service for those who don't have family or whose remains cannot be identified. Sir Redvers himself will be joining his descendants at the family mausoleum, of course.'

'Thank you, Reverend,' said Pantridge. 'Meanwhile, any finds of particular historical significance will go on display at the county museum.'

'What about the ducks?' shouted Onions.

'That question will be answered shortly,' said Pantridge.

'Why can't you just block off the tunnel without emptying the Plash?' asked Bron. 'Concrete sets underwater. Surely you could put some frogmen in to do the job? Then you could pump the tunnel dry from the school end.'

The members of FLAN, with the notable exception of Colin Cheeseman, cheered the suggestion.

'That is a good idea and we did consider something similar,' said Pantridge. 'But then we wouldn't have access to the dig site, would we? The pond needs to be drained if we're to get diggers in there to clear away the mud and rubble.'

'Ah. I did wonder why an engineering project was being headed up by an historian,' said Bron.

'You're just after the treasure!' shouted Onions.

'Historical artefacts,' corrected Pantridge.

'Greed is the inventor of injustice,' said Bron. 'And greedy people will always find justification for their actions.'

'It really isn't about money,' protested Pantridge.

'It's always about money!' shouted Onions. 'A school for posh kids based in a mansion? All that buried gold and silver? That's what this is about, really.'

'I can assure you that—'

'You wouldn't be going to all this trouble if the tunnel was under a council estate!'

'And the Plash is one of the few places in England where Nagle's red-headed merganser is known to nest,' added Cheeseman, deciding that he should make his voice heard too.

'And you can't rebuild a duck,' added Bron.

Cheeseman shot him a glance full of loathing.

'As I said, we are aware of the wildlife issues,' said Pantridge, concerned by the abrupt change of mood among the protesters. 'The mergansers are not due to nest for another six months and by then we will have everything back as it was. We are sure tha—'

A chant began of 'Save the Plash! Save the Plash!' and Pantridge found himself wishing that the village had a police officer who could intervene. Cecily wondered whether she should say something but, before she could act, Joan Bultitude was on her feet.

'That's quite enough!' she barked in her most stentorian voice. 'If you can't be civil, go and wait outside. You are quite entitled to air your views and concerns, many of which I share, by the way, but I will not tolerate this kind of hooliganism. Go outside and do your shouting. Go on! Outside! Out!'

The intimidated protesters were quickly shooed out of the door. The equally cowed audience applauded quietly as Miss Bultitude walked back and retook her seat.

The meeting then proceeded as planned with a second presentation by the project engineer, a down-to-earth Yorkshireman called Ken Arthur, and then a third by an expert on rare ducks, who explained the provisions that were being made to encourage the birds to continue to nest in the area. At the end of the meeting, the plan was accepted as being necessary by the vast majority of those in attendance.

Outside the hall, a small minority disagreed vehemently.

'Extraordinary meeting of FLAN. My house. Ten minutes,' said a florid-faced Colin Cheeseman.

Sir Giles awoke from a dream of madness and dark horror. He'd been walking across a desolate landscape made entirely of corpses, as if in the aftermath of some impossibly large battle. A sea of blanched and bloodless flesh had stretched to the horizon in all directions and there had been no break to the grisly monotony – no trees, no buildings, nothing. The dead were packed so tightly together that he'd found it difficult to find gaps between them in which to plant each footstep and he'd been forced several times to turn a body onto its side to make room. Each time he had done so, he'd found himself staring into the lifeless face of someone that he had once cared for and lost: his grandparents, his mother, beloved aunts and uncles, and Phoebe; there had been so many Phoebe Kingshaws. His horrifying walk had seemed to go on for an eternity but then he had been somehow transported to the inside of a prison that looked remarkably like a scaled-down version of his family's mausoleum. He'd stood at the iron-barred windows, protesting his innocence as a jeering crowd of men on horseback rode about outside the walls. They had hurled abuse at him, taunted him by saying that he was unworthy of the name Whorne, and they had stabbed at him with long pointed boar lances. Every thrust had opened a new wound in his flesh, bringing gouts of fresh blood and ever more pain. There had been no escape from their screaming accusations and their savage attacks. Waking had been a blessing.

He sat on the edge of the bed letting his feelings of fear and helplessness dissipate, but the nightmare of his reality remained. Phoebe was dead, murdered, and the police believed that he was responsible. And why shouldn't they? Everything pointed to him. His situation looked grim, but Sir Giles had never been the kind of man to give up just because the going got tough. He would be the first to admit that he wasn't the most ruthless or unscrupulous of people but neither was he a pushover. He hadn't let anything get in the way of growing his business empire. Nor had he ever let up on his crusade to acquire Harpax Grange. He was persistent and he had money and influence. And there was one sure way to extricate himself from his current predicament, he realised: he could find the real killer himself. However, he would have to do it without police assistance as the damnable McNabb seemed to be fixated on proving that he was the murderer.

He got off the bed and paced the room in thought. If this were America he could easily hire a private eye, but gumshoes were thin on the ground in rural South Herewardshire and even if they weren't, they certainly wouldn't have the resources or the powers granted to their licensed counterparts in the USA. But then, as he glanced at the bookcase in his room, filled by the late Lord Milverton with his favourite bedtime reading, he spotted a copy of Grant Peabody's thriller, *The Stranglers of Bolton*, and his thoughts turned to the murder of author Shirley Pomerance at the Agnes Crabbe Murder-Mystery Festival in Nasely two years previously. And an idea suddenly formed in his mind.

He walked across to his writing desk and powered up his laptop. He typed the words 'Shirley Pomerance murder' into a search engine and then clicked on a newspaper report of the case. He recalled reading at the time that the officer in charge of the investigation had pursued the wrong suspect with disastrous results. But someone else, a retired London police detective who happened to live in Nasely, had doggedly followed the clues, methodically and patiently gathering the evidence, and had helped to catch the real murderer. Sir Giles couldn't recall the man's name but he scanned through the report until he found him.

'Gotcha,' he said as Frank Shunter's name appeared on the screen.

Colin Cheeseman had founded Free Lab Animals Now! exactly one month before the only such laboratory in the county had moved its operation to Wales. He had therefore transferred his attentions to local dairy and pig farms and had established regular demonstrations outside the abattoir at Ordon. His proudest claim was that, over the course of two years, FLAN had 'liberated' more than twenty pigs – cows had proved too cumbersome – and released them onto land owned by the eccentric Tremblett family. Consequently, the family's modest estate now boasted an aggressive, inbred and feral population of Herewardshire Hogs that didn't take kindly to strangers, and Cheeseman had achieved some small degree of local notoriety. Now, as he looked around his sitting room at the faces of his would-be guerrillas, he felt as if a new chapter in FLAN's story was beginning.

'Well done everyone,' he said. 'Another solid victory.'

'Being thrown out of two venues in two days is a solid victory, is it?' asked Bron. 'We were made a laughing stock. And we lost our opportunity to vote against the drainage plan. Not that it would have made any difference to the result.'

'It's still a victory. They'll think that we're weak now.'

'True. We've shown them that we do as we're told,' said Bron.

'But they'll underestimate what we're really capable of. They won't expect us to go on the attack now, will they?'

'Attack?'

'Exactly.'

'There are eight of us.'

'Numbers aren't important,' said Cheeseman. 'One man can make a difference.'

'Or woman,' said June.

'Or woman. Mandela. Gandhi. That student in front of that tank in Tiamin... Tianmanin... that square in China. One ma— person can make a huge statement that resonates around the world. Imagine what we can do with eight!'

'Yeah,' said Terry, punching his left hand with his right.

'I hope you're not suggesting violence,' said June. 'I can't condone violence.'

'Nor me,' said Willy.

'Not towards people. Towards the pump machinery,' said Cheeseman. 'We won't give our enemies the satisfaction of claiming that we've made any kind of threat towards them. We must retain the moral high ground.'

'Fascists,' said Willy, the gleam of civil disobedience in his eyes.

'Do you even know what a fascist is, Willy?' asked Bron.

'All we need is dedication, passion and a willingness to act,' said Cheeseman. 'And—'

'And a couple of dozen more protesters,' interrupted Bron. 'Be realistic, Colin. How about we bring in some people from other groups?'

'No. This is our fight.'

'Which we will lose.'

'You're always so bloody critical, but I don't see you making any suggestions.'

'I just did. I said that we should bring in—'

'Look, it doesn't take many people to chop a power lead in half or smash a pump, does it?' said Cheeseman. 'The important thing is that we show the world that FLAN is a force to be reckoned with.'

'Surely the important thing is to stop the draining of the pond and save the wildlife? It doesn't matter who does it.'

'Yes, that too. And with one concerted effort tonight, we can do that.'

'Oh. Does it have to be tonight?' asked June. 'Only, we're both on early shift in the morning. We have to be in at seven and Mr Sandilands gets very tetchy if we're late.'

'I've never understood how two such passionate animal rights campaigners manage to square their beliefs with working in one of Luscott-Whorne's death camps,' said Cheeseman.

'That's a bit strong,' said Terry.

'We don't kill the animals,' said June defensively. 'They're already dead when they get to the factory. And, anyway, I work in admin and Terry works in sales. We're not involved with the physical side of things.'

'Nor me. I just chop the onions,' said Onions.

'We could stay up later on Friday,' suggested Terry.

'You must do as your conscience dictates,' said Cheeseman sourly.

'It's what our bills dictate,' said Terry. 'It's all right for you. Your parents left you this house and money. We need the work.'

'And jobs aren't exactly in huge supply around here,' said Onions.

'And I can't risk getting arrested,' added Bhavin, a bespectacled mobile phone salesman. 'I'd lose my job. And I'm up for a promotion.'

'No one will know it's us. We'll wear masks,' said Cheeseman in exasperation.

'So where do we meet?' asked Onions.

'The Knicker Tree at midnight. Bring something heavy that you can do some damage with. Right, meeting adjourned.'

Cheeseman stood at the window and watched as Bhavin, Onions and the unfortunately named Terry and June walked off down Hope Street. He sighed.

'Imagine how different things would have been during the French Revolution if no one had turned up because "Mr Sandilands might get a bit tetchy".'

Maisie smiled at him in a way that pleased him immensely.

'Mr Sandilands isn't French,' said Willy. 'He's from Quedgeley.'

Cheeseman sighed again.

At the village hall, the caretaker and a few volunteers were stacking chairs and sweeping up after the public meeting. Dr Pantridge was putting his projector away when Cecily approached him.

'I'm terribly sorry that my husband wasn't here for your talk this evening,' she said. 'He's had a trying day or two, as you might have heard.'

'Yes. Terrible business, your Ladyship,' said Pantridge awkwardly.

'He is quite innocent, of course. And rest assured that he is still very much behind what you're doing at the Plash.'

'Thank you. That's good to know.'

'And I feel that I must also apologise for the behaviour of those louts. It quite put my bristles up.'

'Hardly your fault,' said Pantridge, smiling.

'Admittedly, but it's something of a rarity in these parts and I'm sorry you had to endure it.'

'Ah, we shouldn't be too harsh on them,' said Pantridge. 'At least they care. I was the same at their age, full of righteous anger. It was all about saving the whales and banning the bomb back then, of course. And even though I doubt they'd believe me, their concerns are our concerns too.'

'Thankfully, our feisty Miss Bultitude brooks no nonsense. So, when will the pond be drained?'

'We switch on the pumps tomorrow,' said Pantridge. 'How long to empty the pond, Ken?'

Ken Arthur did some mental arithmetic. 'It's Tuesday today, isn't it? Barring any hiccups, by Saturday or Sunday, I reckon.'

'Then here's to a trouble-free operation,' said Cecily, lifting the dregs of her cup of tea in a toast.

'Hear hear,' said Pantridge.

Chapter 12

The Shaggy Beast liked to patrol the woods for a few hours every night and autumn was its favourite time of year to do so. The evenings came in early, visitors to the woods were few and it enjoyed the bite of the refreshingly cold air. Things were more difficult during the summer months when it stayed light until late and the warm weather made the woods popular with dog walkers and, in recent years, doggers. There were some nights when there seemed to be someone involved in a lewd act at every turn. By contrast, this time of year was very satisfactory.

An unexpected sound caught its ears and the Beast ducked behind an ancient oak. It peered out from its hiding place and saw a small group of people standing beneath the lacy and elasticated foliage of the Knicker Tree. They didn't seem to be dressed, or undressed, for any kind of exhibitionist sexual activity; if anything, they looked as if they were on their way to a fancy-dress party. One was definitely wearing a Spiderman mask and there was a Frankenstein's monster too. They were also carrying an assortment of heavy tools, such as hammers and crowbars. The Beast wondered what kind of fancy-dress party required guests to bring such things rather than the more traditional bottle of cheap booze.

As the clock of St Probyn's struck midnight in Nasely some two miles away, the sound was carried faintly on a chilly breeze to the ears of the would-be saboteurs. Colin was dressed in nondescript dark clothing and a black full-face balaclava that revealed only his eyes and mouth. Onions and Bhavin had brought rubber Halloween masks. Willy had made a real effort, or he hadn't understood the brief, because he had turned up in full Mickey Mouse costume, including white gloves, red shorts and a pair of outsize boots. Much to Cheeseman's annoyance, Maisie had brought the same mask as Bron: a *V for Vendetta*-inspired Guy Fawkes mask of the type often seen at political rallies. Terry and June were no-shows, which, though disappointing, had come as no great surprise. At the twelfth stroke of the distant bell, Colin and his team of protesters set off towards the Plash.

The Shaggy Beast watched them leave and then followed at a distance, exhibiting a great deal more stealth than they did. They soon arrived at the perimeter of the pumping site and ducked under the tape barrier. The Beast positioned itself behind another thick oak tree, where it could remain undetected while having an unobstructed view of whatever drama was about to ensue.

Colin brought his followers to a halt.

'They may have some sort of security guarding the site,' he whispered. 'Keep your masks on at all times and follow me as quietly as you can.'

With all of the assurance and swagger of a man who had secretly visited the site twice in the past hour to ensure that it was devoid of people before rendezvousing with his fellow activists, Colin crept forward in the dark and almost immediately stumbled over a twisting bramble, landing face down in the leaf litter. The noise was enough to send groups of startled ducks honking and splashing to the furthest edges of the pond. His heart hammering in his pigeon chest, Cheeseman stood up, brushed himself down and waited for the Plash to regain an air of calm tranquillity. He signalled for his sniggering troops to follow him.

Knotty branches cast fingery shadows over the surface of the pond and the water, rendered almost monochrome by the weak light from a sliver of moon, rippled gently in the fading wake of the panicking waterfowl. The two newly installed pumps sat silently by the pond's edge like a pair of small long-necked dinosaurs that had come down to drink, their trunk-like intakes resting in the water and their long outlet hoses trailing off to the nearby river. Between them stood a large and chunky diesel-powered generator. A small cabin and a Portaloo had been erected nearby, and at some distance from the machinery stood two large plastic water tanks, each at least five feet high and ten feet square and supported by a framework of steel scaffolding poles. A small battery-powered pump hummed between the two, oxygenating the water within. Occasional dark shadows appeared as fish swam close to the wildlife tanks' translucent walls.

'They're very trusting, leaving everything here unguarded like this,' said Onions, surveying the site suspiciously. 'I don't like it.'

'The machinery isn't likely to get stolen,' said Cheeseman. 'You'd need to bring in a tractor with all this mud.'

'I still don't like it,' said Onions. 'Perhaps they have CCTV?'

'I didn't se— can't see any cameras,' said Cheeseman.

'That doesn't mean there aren't any.'

'Does it matter?' said Cheeseman. 'We're in disguise.' He stalked purposefully towards the generator, nearly falling over again as his boots slipped in the thick, wet mud. He raised his lump hammer high in a pose that he hoped would make him look like some mighty Norse god about to smite a Frost Giant or two, and then brought it down with a resounding clang upon the generator's metal cowling. The shock jarred its way up his thin arm and rattled his teeth and, for a moment, his eyes went out of focus. The sound echoed its way into the dark and silent woods.

Bhavin looked around in a panic. 'Shit, man. That was loud. I didn't realise it would be so loud.'

'Nor me,' said Onions.

'I can't afford to get nicked.'

'Nor me,' said Onions again.

Colin shook the feeling back into his hand and examined his handiwork. The metal displayed the smallest and shallowest of dimples. He frowned and prepared to try again.

Bron appeared at his side. 'Are you trying to get us caught?' he hissed.

'We're here to stop these machines from being used,' said Cheeseman.

'Yes, but there are quieter ways to do that,' said Bron, holding up a bag of sand. 'We can pour this into the generator's fuel tank and disable it.'

'You do things your way, I'll do things mine,' said Colin. 'And—'

'Jesus Christ!' shouted Onions. 'Look!'

A tall dark figure had appeared at the perimeter of the pump site. It had burning red eyes and long white teeth. It raised its hairy arms and wicked talons flashed in the moonlight. As did its spectacularly large penis.

'Has… has that thing got an erection?' said Maisie.

'It's the Shaggy Beast!' shouted Onions as he and Bhavin ran off into the woods. Colin looked at Maisie and then at Bron in their identical masks and a sudden, irrational jealousy settled upon him. In an adrenaline-fuelled act of spontaneity, he grabbed hold of her hand and the two of them ran off together. Bron looked closely at the apparition at the edge of the clearing and dropped his unused bag of sand. Then he and Willy ran away as fast as Willy's huge yellow boots would let them.

The Shaggy Beast raised its head and uttered a blood-curling howl before melting away into the trees.

Chapter 13

'Call for you. Someone with a posh voice,' said Mrs Shunter, bringing the phone to her husband, who was reading the paper over breakfast.

Shunter took the phone. 'Hello? Frank Shunter.'

'Who is it?' mouthed Mrs Shunter silently.

'Our MP,' mouthed Shunter back at her, covering the receiver with his hand.

Mrs Shunter's face crumpled into a frown.

Dr Pantridge surveyed the overnight damage to the generator and shook his head in annoyance.

'I knew we should have laid on some security after that public meeting,' he sighed.

'It's only a dent, no real damage,' said Ken Arthur. 'I wouldn't even have noticed it if I hadn't seen the CCTV footage. We can start pumping today as planned.'

'That's all well and good,' said Pantridge. 'But what's to stop those hooligans coming back and doing more substantial damage?'

'Local police?'

'They're hardly going to supply a couple of bobbies to guard our equipment all night,' said Pantridge. 'And we can't afford private security on our budget. I suppose we could ask the school to stump up for it. It's in their interest, after all.'

'Or we could stay on site ourselves.'

'And risk being duffed up?' said Pantridge. 'And, don't forget, there may be a murderer on the loose.'

'We could ask some of the excavation team to come here a few days early to bolster our numbers, ' said Arthur.

'That's not a bad idea.'

'Meanwhile, I can rig up some floodlights, which should put the buggers off coming back.' He turned to his laptop and opened a folder. 'Talking of which, let's have another look at the CCTV footage from last night. I'm pretty sure we know who they are already but if we're lucky, we might have some video evidence we can use to get the little sods arrested.'

'I'd just be happy if they didn't come back,' said Pantridge, looking at the Portakabin upon which someone had written 'You can't rebuild a duck' in purple spray paint.

McNabb arrived at work and spent the first hour poring over his staff's duty sheets in the hope of finding evidence of someone fiddling their overtime claims, but his mind wasn't on the task. The fact that Sir Giles Luscott-Whorne was walking around, in every sense a free man, grated on him. Despite his protestations, he had been forced to release the MP on bail to reappear at the station in a week's time, pending the results of further enquiries. To add insult to injury, bail had been unconditional – no house arrest, no electronic tag, nothing. He hadn't even had to surrender his passport, even though he was known to own properties in Florida, the Cayman Islands and the south of France. To top it all, McNabb's own divisional commander was golf buddies with the man's barrister, which was as good as proof that his line manager was susceptible to influence. It just went to show what he had always believed: if you dug deep enough, everyone was dirty. Just like his father had been with his drinking and gambling. Just like his mother had been with her string of affairs.

That said, McNabb knew he hadn't had enough real evidence with which to hold the MP in custody, let alone charge him with the crime. Despite several intensive searches by his officers, no murder weapon had been found and Phoebe Kingshaw's autopsy had simply confirmed that she had been beaten to death by some kind of blunt object that had left behind minute traces of beech wood. As the woods were full of beech trees, looking for one particular branch that might have been the weapon was like looking for a needle in a haystack. No, it was like looking for a needle in a stack of needles. He was no closer to being able to prove that Sir Giles was the killer and the thought fluttered through his mind that maybe he was pursuing the wrong suspect. He dismissed the idea immediately. There were no other likely candidates. It had to be him.

Idly, he turned to his computer, popped Sir Giles's name into a search engine and flicked through the many photos that appeared. The man seemed to spend half of his life at parties and in every shot there was a glass of wine or champagne in his hand. McNabb sat back in his chair and recalled a phrase often used by his mother during his childhood, especially in the context of his father's bullish behaviour: 'What soberness conceals, drunkenness reveals.' Was Sir Giles, he wondered, the sort of man who let his guard down while under the influence? A slip of the tongue could go a long way towards helping to build a case against him. But how to get close enough to spy on him? He had the authority to set up an undercover operation but such things cost money and he would have to justify the expenditure. And, besides, he didn't trust any of his staff enough to do it properly. Jaine was competent but far too laid back for his liking and, besides, he now had his own murder investigation to be getting on with. McNabb therefore resigned himself to the fact that, for the moment at least, he would have to spy on Sir Giles himself.

Colin Cheeseman woke up and stretched. He ached all over and his arms and legs were bruised and criss-crossed with scratches sustained while stumbling through Black Dog Wood in the dark. But it had all been worth it. He had shown himself to be a capable leader, and FLAN had made its opposition to the drainage plan clear. And he had received a wonderful and wholly unexpected additional benefit. He looked at the pale, freckled shoulder of the semi-naked woman sleeping next to him in his bed and smiled. High on a cocktail of adrenaline and the several ciders they'd shared back at Colin's cottage, Maisie had ended up staying the night. Not that she and Colin had done anything more than kiss and cuddle; his clumsy and inexpert fumbling had ended with her explaining that it was the wrong time of the month and they'd fallen asleep together after the rush of their overnight adventure had worn off. But she had stayed and Colin was still reeling from his good fortune.

Maisie stirred in her sleep and rolled over, exposing a breast. Colin resisted the urge to touch it. It was over a year since he'd been this close to a semi-naked woman but he knew that touching things without consent was the best way to ensure that he wouldn't get close to one again for some time. Meanwhile, he found himself analysing her decision. Had she stayed because she genuinely liked him or because of the euphoria they'd experienced as fellow guerrillas? Or had it been out of fright, having witnessed what might have been the Shaggy Beast? Whatever the reason, would she feel the same about him when she woke? He hoped so. He talked a good fight but when it came down to it, he had neither the disposition nor the physical build for conflict, and while he had always claimed that he'd be willing to go to prison for his beliefs, it was an idle boast. The thought of it terrified him, which was why his bouts of civil disobedience tended to be low-key and as non-confrontational as he could make them. And, besides, he now dared to hope that he might have someone to stay out of prison for.

His thoughts then turned to the Shaggy Beast. Logically, Colin knew there had to be a rational explanation for the apparition he'd seen. It had to have been someone in a suit. But who? And why? Was it some kind of security for the pump site? And why had it been sporting that monstrous phallus? Perhaps the best thing to do would be to lie low for a day or two, he thought. He'd suggest it to Maisie; that way, he'd know for sure whether her interests lay in him or in the buzz she got from being part of FLAN. It would also mean that she'd be kept away from the annoyingly charismatic Oberon. Self-centred and socially inept, Colin had never had much success with women. Bron, on the other hand, always seemed to have a girlfriend. But not Maisie, decided Colin. Maisie was his.

By midday, Sir Giles was feeling much more like his old self. He had never been the most sentimental of men, perhaps as a consequence of growing up on farms where animals regularly went to slaughter, and he'd gone through life relatively free from hurt. However, Phoebe's senseless death had awoken feelings in him that he was wholly unused to processing. He had genuinely been fond of her; it hadn't been love – or, at least, he didn't think it had – but he had felt her loss keenly. That, and his subsequent arrest and detention, had left him feeling emotionally drained and physically exhausted. However, a night of sleep in his own bed had been very restorative. It had helped to put things into perspective and his upset had now turned to resolve. He was going to find Phoebe's killer, prove his own innocence and, furthermore, take that cocky police inspector down a peg or two into the bargain. He went downstairs for lunch in a much improved frame of mind.

Cecily was already at the table and, having asked after his well-being, she brought him up to speed with events at the public meeting.

'Hoodlums, eh?' said Giles through a mouthful of cheese and chutney. 'So what do we do about them?'

'Actually, I think the more pressing concern is that there's a murderer on the loose.'

'You don't mean me, surely?'

'Of course not. But if you didn't do it…'

'Ah. I see. I'm taking steps towards dealing with that,' said Giles.

'What sort of steps? Legal ones, I hope.'

'Of course. I'm not without resources, you know. I intend to identify the real culprit and prove my innocence.'

'Isn't that what we pay our police for?'

'You'd think so, wouldn't you?' said Giles. 'But the local CID chap seems to be fixated on prosecuting me, and I'm afraid that your cousin-in-law made matters considerably worse by treating him like some kind of idiot child. So, if the police are unwilling to look at any other possible scenarios, I rather think that it's down to me to push them in the right direction. And this morning I have set the ball rolling.'

'I hope you're successful then,' said Cecily. 'For all our sakes.'

'Don't worry. Whatever happens, you'll be looked after.'

'Actually, I meant the fact that there won't be a killer running amok,' said Cecily.

At the Happy Onion, the regulars were also discussing recent events over a lunchtime pint.

'An MP in the woods at that time of night with a woman who isn't his wife? Don't take much imagination to figure out what he was up to,' said Len Youlden. 'Bloody buggers are all at it. Never seems to matter how old or ugly they are neither. What do women see in them?'

'It's power,' said Charlie Barnfather. 'It's an aphrodisiac, apparently.'

'I didn't think Sir Giles was that powerful,' quipped Waxleigh.

'Or else they pay some prostitute,' said Youlden.

'The Diabolical Club then. A Soho dominatrix now,' said Waxleigh. 'It's always been the way. An MP can't change his spots.'

'I still can't see him as a murderer, though,' said Barnfather. 'Personally, I rather like the chap. Typical posh boy and a bit puffed up sometimes, but he always struck me as a decent sort.'

'But if he didn't kill her, who did?' asked Youlden. 'Someone from the village?'

'Some people are saying it was the Shaggy Beast,' said Chetwynd.

'Nope. Just you,' said Waxleigh.

'You don't really believe that there's some kind of monster running around, do you?' said Barnfather.

'No, not for a minute,' said Chetwynd. 'But every story has a basis in truth and there have been too many sightings for there to be nothing. There must be something in those woods. Maybe some kind of big cat?'

'But it walks upright like a man.'

'OK, a bear then. Or a gorilla. But still an animal that's escaped from a zoo.'

'But the nearest zoo is in Bristol and that's nearly a hundred miles away,' said Barnfather. 'I suppose it could come from a private collection though. What about that mad family, the Trembletts? They have lots of exotic pets.'

'No werewolves though,' said Waxleigh.

'Indy Verma was going to phone them and check,' said Chetwynd. 'But I've spoken to Jessie Tremblett and she says that they have nothing like that. And she saw the Shaggy Beast herself.'

'It's probably just some long-haired old hippy living rough,' said Barnfather.

'Whatever it is, sightings are becoming more frequent and I reckon we should be capitalising on it,' said Chetwynd.

'What do you mean?'

'You know how busy we get around Agnes Crabbe festival time, Charlie. From May to August we do a brisk trade but, come the autumn, visitor numbers drop to almost nothing. Imagine if we had an all-year-round attraction.'

'The Shaggy Beast?' said Barnfather. 'How would that work? It probably doesn't even exist.'

'Ask the Loch Ness tourist office. They get hundreds of thousands of visitors every year based on a few alleged sightings and a handful of blurry photos, most of which have been discredited. Then there's Roswell in America and the Bigfoot Discovery Museum and any number of supposedly haunted houses and castles. Tourists are queuing up to spend their money anywhere where there's even just a whiff of a monster. So why not us? We'd be quids in.'

'You mean by selling tea towels or something like that?'

'Think bigger, Charlie. A life-size model for tourists to pose with. Memorabilia. A museum...'

'How do we do all of that?'

'We start by getting some press coverage,' said Chetwynd. 'There are loads of reporters in the village at the moment. Let's use them. We drop hints that the Shaggy Beast may be responsible for the murder. And we could form a posse and spread the word that we're going to try to catch the thing. We could put Nasely on the map.'

'Assuming the Beast exists – and that's a big assumption – how would you catch it?' asked Barnfather. 'You had a go at it back in the nineties. What did you do then?'

'I had the net from an old set of goalposts,' said Chetwynd. 'And an air rifle. Both gone now though.'

'I can ask Mad Connie. She'd know,' suggested Youlden.

'She'll just go on about phases of the moon and silver bullets and rubbish like that,' said Chetwynd. 'We need something more concrete than old wives' tales, Len.'

'I meant that she knows a lot about handling wild animals. All of the Trembletts do.'

'We want one of those dog-catcher things,' said Chetwynd. 'Those long poles with a sort of noose on the end. Or a tranquiliser gun.'

'I bet Indy has that kind of stuff,' said Waxleigh. 'I'm playing bowls with him tomorrow. I'll ask.'

'Great! Can't do any harm to have an RSPCA inspector on board. Adds credibility. Shall we do this then? How about Friday night? That'll give us a chance to spread the word to all those reporters.'

McNabb left the police laboratories with a smile on his face. He had spoken to Phoebe Kingshaw's family to arrange a suitable time for them to collect her property and had been surprised to learn from them that she was employed as Sir Giles's secretary at Westminster. They had been equally surprised to discover that she had been working at Harpax Grange School. It naturally begged the questions of why she was there and why she hadn't told her nearest and dearest.

More importantly, however, the tech guys had cracked the security on Phoebe's phone and the contents had been very revealing indeed. At the back of McNabb's mind was a niggling doubt as to the legality of his actions but, he reasoned, this was a murder investigation and surely anything that helped to identify the perpetrator outweighed any notions of invasion of privacy. And the gamble had been worth it. To his delight, he'd found records of numerous calls between Phoebe and Sir Giles; in fact, the very last call she had ever received was from him and was timed at just quarter of an hour before her death. There were also hundreds of texts ranging from mundane parliamentary business to nauseatingly frank sex talk, and quite a few photographs of Phoebe and Giles together that McNabb wished he'd never seen. He couldn't wait to reveal what he'd found to the MP and his snooty barrister.

He called Proutt House but was told by an abrupt-sounding female member of staff that Sir Giles was in Nasely, visiting his constituents. He therefore decided to drive over to the village himself. With it being such a small place, his chances of 'accidentally' bumping into Sir Giles were pretty high. He was looking forward to the encounter.

'Six of them,' said Ken Arthur, peering closely at his laptop screen and counting off the pale and ghostly green figures caught by the CCTV's night-vision lens. 'One lass and five lads, but they're all in disguise.'

'It's that lot who were at the public meeting. I'd put money on it,' said Pantridge.

'Hard to prove though.'

'Whizz to the end. We might just catch someone removing their mask,' said Pantridge.

Arthur clicked on a control and ran the footage at four times normal speed and, all of a sudden, the masked protestors scattered.

'Whoa! Stop. Go back,' said Pantridge.

Arthur put the recording into reverse and the group ran backwards to where they had been originally standing.

'Stop!' said Pantridge. 'There. What's that?'

Beyond the group of figures stood a strange, hair-covered apparition with arms raised. Its eyes burned white in night vision.

'What the hell is that?' asked Pantridge. 'Bigfoot?'

'That's not a foot,' said Arthur.

The Moore Tea, Vicar? café sat between Bingle's Shoe Shop and Witton's Florists and was something of a community hub. The place had a regular clientele of retired folk who popped in for lunch or afternoon tea and it was popular with people who worked in the shops on the High Street because of its generously filled sandwiches and delicious home-made cakes.

Mr and Mrs Moore's divorce – necessitated by Mr Moore being caught providing rather more than just fondant fancies to some of his female clients – had been acrimonious but fair. Everything had been divided fifty-fifty; he'd kept the catering side of the business and she'd kept the café. And she'd since made a great success of it, especially after taking on a talented full-time pastry chef called Ginger Keogh.

Mrs Moore was a boisterous, friendly woman in her fifties who had taken a particular shine to the similarly aged and recently slimmed-down Frank Shunter. On normal days, she enjoyed flirting with him and sharing the local gossip, whether he wanted to hear it or not. But this afternoon she was avoiding his table and was being uncharacteristically quiet, almost offish in fact. Her customers – and there were fewer than usual – were also unusually subdued. Shunter picked up on their mood but was not surprised, considering with whom he was drinking coffee.

'Can I get you anything else?' asked Ginger.

'We're fine, thank you,' said Shunter.

'And can you thank Mrs Moore for keeping the paparazzi outside,' said Sir Giles. 'They're relentless.'

'She won't have that kind of thing in here,' said Ginger. 'Not for anyone.'

He glanced once at Sir Giles, arched an eyebrow and walked back to the counter, where Mrs Moore was eyeing the MP balefully over a plate of cream horns.

'Well, this feels damned awkward,' said the MP. 'No one has said a word to me today. Except the reporters, of course. They've been following me around like a pack of hounds. Normally I have to fight the locals off if I show my face in the village. Probably afraid that I'll murder them if they complain about the bus service.'

A man at the next table choked on his tea and then moved to a table further away on the pretext of finding a newspaper.

'So let me get this straight,' said Shunter quietly. 'You want me to investigate a murder in which you are the prime suspect but without involving the police?'

'That's the gist of it, yes. I'm desperate. There's a truly awful little man called McNabb and he seems determined to pin this on me. But I swear to you, Mr Shunter, that I didn't do it.'

'Frank.'

'I swear to you, Frank, that she was already dead when I found her. And I called the police! Would a guilty man do that?'

'It's not unheard of. A couple has a row, one hits the other a little harder than they meant to, the assaulted person falls down and smacks their head on something hard. Perpetrator panics and calls the police. Accidental manslaughter. It happens.'

'But that isn't what happened. The last words we spoke to each other were on the phone to arrange the meet.'

'Look, tell me to mind my own business if you want to, but it's pretty obvious to me that you knew the victim pretty well, didn't you?'

'Well, I…'

'Consider this a test of good faith for both of us,' said Shunter. 'I promise that nothing you say goes beyond this table. I have absolutely no interest in your personal life and I'm not going to moralise about extramarital activity. But you need to understand that if I take the job, and I haven't said yet that I will, the truth will emerge. I'll need complete honesty from you.'

'Yes, I realise that.'

'OK. So, what was your relationship to Miss Kingshaw?'

'She is… was… my secretary.'

'But I'm guessing there was a bit more to it than that.'

'We were… involved.'

'Does anyone else know about this?'

'Only Cecily and—' Sir Giles suddenly realised what he'd said.

'Your wife?' said Shunter with some surprise. 'How does she feel about your relationship?'

'Do you mean, could she be a murder suspect? No. Definitely not. For reasons I won't go into here, she has no

112

desire for my relationship with Phoebe to be made public knowledge either. The thing is, we... that is to say, we have a... look, it's... complicated. Just believe me when I say that she is definitely not a suspect.'

'OK. So, who else knows?'

'I suspect my PA has a shrewd idea. But I've told no one else, and— Oh God! He can't be serious. Not here. Not in public.'

Shunter looked up to see what had suddenly horrified Sir Giles. A compact little man with a red goatee beard and short-cropped hair was making his way towards their table and looking unbearably smug.

'Good afternoon, Sir Giles,' said McNabb. 'Do you mind if I join you?'

'I don't have to speak to you. My barrister told me so,' said Sir Giles, as McNabb sat unbidden on a free chair at the table.

'Quite rightly so. And you're not under caution either, so anything you say right now would be inadmissible in court anyway.' With a flourish, McNabb produced a clear plastic bag containing a mobile phone and placed it on the table. 'I just wanted you to know that this was among Miss Kingshaw's personal property.'

Sir Giles's mouth opened and shut, guppy-like, but nothing came out.

'No need to say anything, Sir Giles. In fact, I'd rather you didn't. However, I will just point out that, as part of an ongoing murder investigation, it was necessary to examine the contents. Which, as I'm sure you can imagine, means that we'll have lots to discuss at our next meeting. I have, of course, downloaded copies of everything, just in case any of the content gets accidentally lost or deleted between now and next Monday. Here's a copy for you.' He pocketed the phone and produced a USB memory stick from inside his jacket. 'I have, of course, also sent a copy to your barrister as per the rules of disclosure. Well, I must be going. See you soon. Very soon.'

McNabb stood up and left the café with a big smile on his face and in the sure knowledge that he had scored a palpable hit against his foe. Sir Giles stared at the memory stick and groaned.

'That was McNabb, I take it?' said Shunter.

'Yes. And a nastier piece of work you could never hope to meet.'

'His predecessor wasn't exactly a charmer.'

'This one is the absolute pits. Even other police officers hate him,' said Sir Giles. 'Please tell me you'll take my case? That's why I tracked you down. You're my last hope.'

'Look, I can't just "take a case". This isn't like America. They have properly licensed private detectives over there. I'm just a retired London bobby.'

'But you can ask questions, surely? You can try to find out what really happened?'

'Yes, but so could anyone else.'

'But they wouldn't know the right questions to ask. You have knowledge and experience,' said Sir Giles. 'Look, Mr Shunter, Frank, I'm not a murderer but I am a wealthy man and I'm desperate. I'll pay you two thousand pounds up front to take my case and five hundred pounds per day, no questions asked, for as long as it takes you to complete your investigations. Find the evidence I need to prove my innocence and I'll throw in a ten-thousand-pound bonus. Identify the real killer and I'll double it.'

'That's very generous, but—'

'Worth every single penny if you succeed. Oh, and if we call them gifts and don't document them they'll be tax-free too.'

'It's not just about the money. I have no access to police records or anything like that. I would be starting from scratch.'

'Good. Then you'll be free from influence and bias. So do we have a deal?'

'I might need to ask some questions you won't like,' said Shunter. 'For example, I'd need to go through the contents of Miss Kingshaw's phone. Otherwise, I'm on the back foot when trying to second-guess McNabb.'

'Yes, of course, if you think it will help. But at least let me delete any... indelicate images or texts first? I'd like to preserve some of my dignity. And Phoebe's.'

'Of course. Delete what you want. As long as you keep in mind that there may be something on that memory stick that could help to prove your innocence.'

'There's nothing innocent about the stuff I need to delete,' said Sir Giles.

'So why were you meeting her on the night she died?' asked Shunter.

'She'd called me to say that she'd discovered something at the school.'

'And what was she doing at the school?'

Sir Giles quickly brought Shunter up to speed on Phoebe Kingshaw's mission. 'The thing is, she apparently did find something. The word she used was "dynamite".'

'Really? What sort of thing?'

'I don't know, frustratingly. But those were her words. Something dynamite, she said. Whatever it was, it was important enough for her to insist on meeting me to tell me face-to-face.'

'Important enough for someone to kill her to keep it a secret?'

'I can't imagine what that might be. All I'd asked her to do was dig up a little bit of dirt on the headmistress. You know... inconsistencies in the accounts or unsuitable behaviour. Stuff like that.'

'So, she obviously found something. And now she's dead. That sort of puts Joan Bultitude in the frame, doesn't it?' said Shunter.

'So you'll investigate her first?'

'I haven't said yes yet.'

Sir Giles placed a brown envelope on the table. 'Here's the two thousand,' he said. 'All I'm asking you to do is spend a week looking into the case. Not even that. Five days. I'm due to report back to McNabb on Monday. If, by then, you've found nothing or you've decided it's not worth pursuing, keep the money and I'll find someone else. Though God knows who.'

Shunter looked at the envelope.

'I can't make any promises.'

'I understand.'

'What if I find things that actually strengthen the police case against you?'

'That's a risk I'm prepared to take. I know that I'm innocent. I put my faith in the truth.'

'OK, I'll have a look,' said Shunter. 'I hope, for your sake, that you've been upfront with me.'

'Thank you,' said Sir Giles. 'You don't know what this means to me.'

Across the road in a nondescript car, McNabb knew exactly what it meant to him. He peered through the telephoto lens of his camera and pressed the shutter as he watched the brown envelope pass from Sir Giles to his lunch companion. He wondered who the tough-looking older man with the grey moustache was. All he knew for sure was that people who accepted brown envelopes from alleged murderers during clandestine meetings in cafés were generally up to no good. Which meant that he now had two suspects to keep tabs on.

Chapter 14

'What did he say? Are we going back tonight?' asked Willy excitedly. He was still buzzing from the events of the night before and had managed three bowls of sugar-frosted flakes for breakfast and two more for his lunch. He was now finishing off the box as a mid-afternoon snack.

'No, we're not,' said Bron, hanging up the phone. 'Colin has unilaterally decided that FLAN has done enough for the time being.'

'What?' said Willy.

'What?' echoed the African grey parrot sitting on his shoulder. He fed it a flake and then a second to the chubby hamster that sat next to his bowl on the kitchen table.

'He's saying that we should lie low for a while,' explained Bron.

'Why? Because of the Shaggy Beast?'

'No. Because I strongly suspect that he's letting the little man in the pink polo neck do his thinking for him.'

'Who?'

'His willy, Willy,' said Bron. 'Colin has copped off with Maisie and is bailing on us because he'd rather be screwing her instead of the drainage plan.'

'He can't do that.'

'Of course he can,' said Bron. 'Let's face it, Colin has always been more interested in his own welfare than any animal's. And now that he's had his moment of glory and things could start to get a bit hairy, he's backed off.'

'But he can't do that!'

'And yet, he has. Which means that we have to step up, Willy. The pumping will have started by now.'

'So what do we do?'

'There's nothing we can do on our own. There simply aren't enough of us and the authorities will be on their guard now,' said Bron. 'If we want to stop the Plash being drained, we have to bring in outside help.'

'Colin says that if we work with other groups they'll steal our thunder.'

'It's not our thunder to steal,' said Bron, picking up one of the many semi-feral cats that lived on the Tremblett family farm. The old tabby eyed the fat hamster hungrily and purred as Bron stroked its arched back. 'This isn't about FLAN. This isn't about glory or notoriety. This is about the animals and what's best for them. So what if the Morbridge branch of the Animal Liberation Front gets some publicity? If it prevents the decimation of the wildlife in Gertie's Plash, I say let them have it.'

'I suppose,' said Willy.

'Think about some of the most powerful protests in recent history, like Greenham Common. The women's peace camp lasted for nearly two decades. At one point seventy thousand protesters were there, enough to encircle the entire air base. They came from all over the country, all over the world even, representing a thousand different pressure groups. But do any of us remember who those groups were? No. Because it's what they were doing that mattered, not who they were. It's hard to ignore that number of people, Willy. It's all very well Colin talking about "one person can make a difference", but seventy thousand people can make a shitload more difference.'

'I suppose,' said Willy again.

'So, are we agreed?' asked Bron. 'And don't say "I suppose" again.'

'I suppose,' said the parrot.

'I guess,' said Willy.

'Then let's make some calls.'

Shunter placed his hand on the brown envelope sitting on the table in front of him and wondered if he was doing the right thing. He certainly wasn't breaking any laws that he could see. He was being paid to do some research, nothing more. And he was reasonably convinced that Sir Giles was genuine. Thirty years of interviewing suspects for everything from petty theft to murder had made him very familiar with the signs of guilt. They were always there, written in the micro-expressions on a person's face – a flicker of the eyelids, a sudden glance away, a tremble at the corner of the mouth, a quickening of the breath. The MP hadn't exhibited any of those signs and the thought had crossed Shunter's mind that maybe Sir Giles was a psychopath. But then the conversation had turned to his marriage and there had been a very definite reaction. It hadn't been guilt, but something more akin to embarrassment. Or shame, perhaps? Whatever it was, it ruled out psychopathy, and Shunter's natural curiosity made him wonder just what was going on behind closed doors at Proutt House.

He finished his coffee and one of Ginger's delicious chocolate brownies, which he would conveniently forget to tell his wife about later, and thought about where to start his investigations. He needed to think of a plausible reason to visit

Miss Bultitude. In the meantime, there was the crime scene in Black Dog Wood to examine. He left the café, carefully avoiding Mrs Moore and all the latest village gossip, and walked home to collect his car.

The Empire Hotel stood diagonally opposite the Happy Onion at the far eastern end of Nasely High Street. It had been completely rebuilt following a disastrous oil tank explosion two years ago, but no one had shed tears for the old building. It had been a monstrous Modernist eyesore, quite out of keeping with the village, and it was something of a mystery how it had been built in the first place. Local feeling was that money had changed hands between the architect and the county planning office but nothing had ever been proven. By comparison, the new hotel was much more aesthetically pleasing, a mix of mock Tudor and Revivalist styles that didn't jar with the pretty stone-built shops and cottages around it. The foyer too was delightfully faux-vintage with exposed, if fibreglass, beams and lots of dark wood and plush leather furniture. At this time of year there were very few guests – a sprinkling of retired people on walking tours, commercial travellers who fancied somewhere a little less homogenous than the chain hotels in Bowcester or Sherrinford, or amorous couples enjoying illicit assignations. But mostly they were Agnes Crabbe fans. Even out of festival season they were drawn to Nasely, as if on a pilgrimage to see the village in which the great author had lived her entire life and upon which she had based her fictional hamlet of Little Hogley.

In a seating area off the main reception, a man with luxuriant greying shoulder-length hair and a moustache that was waxed at the tips indulged himself in a game of people-watching. It was something he did without malice and there was no judgement or criticism in his gaze. It was purely a mental exercise in which he challenged his own cultural and behavioural biases. He liked to observe strangers and guess what sort of people they were, the jobs they did, their likes and dislikes, and then question himself as to how he'd arrived at those assumptions. For instance, the woman sitting opposite him was in her mid-forties and was dressed in a skirt and jacket over a white blouse that was just a little too tight for her. She looked vaguely familiar but he couldn't think where he might have seen her before. Her make-up was subtle and her hair was tidily cropped at the shoulder. There was no wedding ring but there was a faint impression in the skin that suggested she had once worn one, and for some time. Her dress and demeanour suggested to him that she was a career professional – a businesswoman or a sales rep, perhaps. He idly wondered what she might imagine him to be with his tweed jacket, red corduroys and Panama hat. She was tapping something into her phone, but then stopped and looked up. His eyes met hers and he felt compelled to say something, in case she thought that he'd been staring.

'I see you have a copy of *A White Stone* there,' he said, smiling and pointing to a book resting on the coffee table in front of her. 'Are you a Milly? That's what Agnes Crabbe fans call themselves, isn't it? After her detective heroine, Millicent Cutter?'

'It's not mine. It belongs to the hotel,' said the woman. 'Are you a Manly, then? I believe it's what male Millies have started to call themselves.'

'Ha ha! No, not at all,' laughed the man. 'I'm a parapsychologist.'

The woman raised a quizzical eyebrow.

'What the popular press likes to call a ghost hunter,' he said. 'Professor Noel Gravestock.'

'Pleased to meet you,' said the woman, smiling as they shook hands. 'Pamela Dallimore, journalist.'

Frank Shunter looked at his watch and wished for summer and longer days. It was only four o'clock but already the sun had dipped below the tree line and the temperature had dropped sharply. He pulled his scarf tighter around his neck as he walked along the woodland path from the car park towards the Whorne mausoleum, his eyes scanning the ground for any small clue that McNabb's people might have missed. But he saw nothing of any note, bar the occasional scrap of litter and a condom packet lying among the fallen leaves.

The mausoleum was a charmless hexagonal building made of Portland stone and punctuated with a Corinthian column at each of its six corners. Each wall was inset with pairs of carved marble tableaux featuring the labours of Hercules and, on the wall immediately in front of him, Shunter could see scenes of the demigod wrestling the Nemean lion and victoriously holding aloft the girdle of Hippolyta, Queen of the Amazons. It was notable that each depiction of Hercules looked remarkably like the portraits he'd seen of Sir Montgomery, who had commissioned the building; Whorne men were nothing if not cocksure and self-promoting. It was said that the face of the golden pig that stood atop the high obelisk also bore more than a passing resemblance to the man and that it had been hoisted up high before he'd had the opportunity to spot it and remonstrate with the underpaid sculptor.

The building was effectively a walled graveyard with restricted access via a set of iron gates. It had no roof and the high walls were pierced by small square windows, into which were set bars in place of glass. A crown of savage iron spikes topped the walls thanks to Charles Whorne, who had added them in the 1820s when his fear of the Resurrection Men had begun to border on paranoia. Shunter peered in through one of the windows and raised an eyebrow upon seeing the monument to Sir Redvers, creator of the Diabolical Club. Entirely in keeping with the man's character, the central figure was an unflattering depiction of him as Bacchus surrounded by semi-naked nymphs and frolicking satyrs. Beyond the monument, the great stone obelisk rose from the centre of the structure, and all around the interior walls he could see specially constructed alcoves, each one sporting a funerary urn in which the ashes of some dead Whorne resided. There were also burial vaults, some ornate, some plain, depending upon the mores and tastes of the times in which their occupants had lived and died. The mausoleum was an extravagant memorial to an extravagant family.

Shunter stepped away from the window and walked around the structure until he came to the locked and iron-barred gate. A path composed of large flagstones circled the mausoleum and Phoebe Kingshaw's body had been found sprawled across several of them, directly outside the gate. Shunter bent down and his experienced eye spotted a telltale stain on one of the stones; even though the blood had been washed away, the porous surface had retained an echo of it. He stepped back and began looking at each of the stones in turn. After four or five stones, a small flash of white suddenly caught his peripheral vision – something nestling in the un-mortared gap between two flags. He drew a Swiss Army knife from his pocket and used one of the blades to dig it out. It was a small, round, handwritten price sticker, easily missed or ignored by less experienced eyes. The edges were still sharp and the reverse side still had some tackiness left in the adhesive, so it could only have found its way there in the past day or so, he surmised. It was from a store called Crute's and from an item that had cost £18.66.

'Odd sort of price,' he muttered to himself.

'Still can't turn it off, eh?' said a voice.

Shunter dropped the sticker into his jacket pocket and turned to see the unshaven, jovial face of Cliff Jaine.

'Professor Gravestock? I'm Ken Arthur.'

The engineer had appeared at the hotel just as the professor was in the process of explaining to Mrs Dallimore what he did for a living.

'Pleased to meet you,' said Gravestock. 'This is Pamela Dallimore.'

'The journalist who was kidnapped by that murderer a couple of years back?' said Arthur, shaking her hand.

'For my sins,' said Mrs Dallimore.

'Ah! That's where I know your face from,' said Gravestock.

'One brave lass,' said Arthur.

'You're very kind,' said Mrs Dallimore.

'Did you bring it?' asked Gravestock.

'I did,' said Arthur, producing a laptop from his satchel. 'It was quite a coincidence contacting you and finding out that you were already in Nasely.'

'There were some newspaper reports yesterday about your recent Shaggy Beast sightings,' said Gravestock. 'And as I live less than an hour's drive away in Pawley, I thought I'd check the information at source. Some newspapers have a penchant for exaggeration and their research is shallow at best. No slight intended, Pamela.'

'None taken,' said Mrs Dallimore. 'I don't work for the tabloids.'

'Well, here you go,' said Arthur, swivelling the laptop around to face the other man.

'Excuse us,' said Gravestock. Mrs Dallimore nodded and returned to checking her phone. The parapsychologist stared at the screen for a few seconds and then sat back in his chair.

'What do you reckon?' asked Arthur. 'You're the expert.'

'I'm not sure I can be an expert on something whose existence, after twenty years of research, I haven't found any proof of,' said Gravestock. 'But, as paranormal videos go, it's pretty much the kind of poor quality that one expects from cheap night-vision cameras.'

'Bugger,' said Arthur. 'I was hoping it might be worth a few quid.'

'Twenty years ago, maybe,' said Gravestock. 'But everything's shared on the internet these days. There are thousands of videos like this. But, that said, there aren't many videos of British werewolves, let alone priapic ones, and that gives it some rarity value.'

'That's more encouraging,' said Arthur.

'I'm sorry, but I couldn't help overhearing,' said Mrs Dallimore. 'Did you really say priapic British werewolves?'

'Do you mind if Mrs Dallimore sees the video?' asked Gravestock.

'I can't see any reason why not, especially if it's worthless,' said Arthur, setting up the laptop for the journalist to watch.

'Oh, I wouldn't say worthless,' said Gravestock. 'You see, the reason I came to Nasely is the consistency of recent sightings. They are all remarkably similar and have been made by people unconnected to each other. That suggests there might actually be something interesting in the woods. If it turns out that there is, your video will be the first recorded sighting. Then it will have real value.'

'That's more encouraging,' said Arthur. 'Can I get you a drink, Professor?'

'Call me Noel. A decent local ale would be nice, thank you.'

'I'll get you a pint of the Cockering IPA. Mrs Dallimore?'

'A gin and tonic, if you don't mind.'

As Arthur headed for the bar, Mrs Dallimore smiled. She had caught the whiff of a fresh breaking story. And if there was one thing she loved, it was a scoop.

'So, old Luscott-Whorne has got you fighting his corner, has he?' said Jaine. 'That's actually the best thing I've heard all day.'

'Really?' said a surprised Shunter. 'You're not going to tell me to back off?'

'Not unless you want me to. You're a pretty useful guy to have around, as I discovered during the Pomerance investigation.'

'Hmm,' said Shunter. 'It just feels a bit... mutinous, like I'm working against the police. I'm not terribly comfortable with that. I'm still not sure I should be getting involved.'

'Old habits die hard. You did the job for half a lifetime.'

'I guess so. My wife reckons I'll never retire. Are you working on this case?'

'No. I've got my own murder to solve.'

Jaine brought Shunter up to speed with the skeleton found by Miss Bultitude. 'Weird, isn't it? Nothing happens at the school for decades, other than the odd unwanted schoolgirl pregnancy, and then two dead bodies turn up at once. Like buses.'

'Don't buses come in threes?'

'Don't even joke about that,' said Jaine. 'I had to pop into the school to get the headmistress to sign her statement and I thought, while I'm literally in this neck of the woods I may as well take a quick gander at where Kingshaw was murdered, just in case I spot something that might have been missed.'

'So why is the fact that I'm doing some snooping for Sir Giles the best thing you've heard all day?'

'Because my DI is an arsehole,' said Jaine. 'And the possibility that you might make him look like an even bigger arsehole makes me smile.'

Sir Giles left the M13 and joined the M25 with the intention of picking up the M4 towards London. Once again he was enjoying the feeling of being in complete control and he had decided that if he managed to escape the nightmare in which he found himself, he was going to have a much more active say in how his life was run from now on.

His first positive act had been to drop off the edited memory stick at Frank Shunter's cottage before heading to London where, perhaps, a return to work would provide some distraction from his worries. Cecily had taken over his duties regarding the draining of Gertie's Plash and there was nothing else to keep him in South Herewardshire for the moment. And besides, it put welcome distance between him and McNabb. He would spend the night at his rooms at the Albany and then attempt to pick up some of the strands of his life in the morning.

'So you have no idea who your mysterious blindfolded man was?' asked Shunter, looking at the freshly turned soil.

'None at all, other than he was most likely a soldier during the First World War,' said Jaine. Having found nothing of further interest at the mausoleum, the two men had decided to visit the site where the skeleton had been unearthed.

'The grave was pretty shallow so it's surprising that it didn't get unearthed before now,' explained Jaine. 'But I guess it's quite a way off the beaten track. And local people tend to stay on the paths.'

'I wonder if he was one of the Lucky Six?' said Shunter, twirling one end of his moustache, as he so often did when thinking.

'Lucky Six?'

'Nearly all of the able-bodied men in this borough fought in the Great War but only a handful of them came home. They called them the Lucky Six. If your soldier was a local man, there's a good chance that he was one of them. I have some contacts I could ask if you like.'

'Great,' said Jaine. 'And if you have any more insights to share, I'm more than happy to listen. At the moment I have nothing. And in return, if I hear anything that might help you in your investigations, I'll pass it on.'

'To help me or to piss off McNabb?' said Shunter, smiling. 'That's a nice offer, Cliff, but don't break any rules or confidences for me. The truth will worm its way to the surface. It almost always does.'

'He's quite... excited, isn't he?' observed Pamela Dallimore. After several drinks in the hotel bar, she'd persuaded Ken Arthur to show her the video footage again. 'So what do you think that thing is, Professor?'

'If you don't know by now...' sniggered Arthur.

'Some kind of prank or fraud, as these things invariably are,' said Gravestock. 'But I try to keep an open mind. After all, new species are being discovered all the time.'

'But how could something that big stay hidden?' asked Mrs Dallimore.

'That's not what I'd call hidden,' said Arthur.

'I meant the werewolf,' said Mrs Dallimore, with a smile.

'You'd be surprised,' said Gravestock. 'Larger animals like badgers and deer are incredibly good at hiding from human eyes. We unknowingly walk within feet of them all the time.'

'But that's not an animal. That's… whatever it is.'

'A man in a suit, I expect,' said Gravestock. 'It's certainly not a traditional werewolf, anyway. For a start, its appearances are not tied to the full moon. But this is all speculation. What we need is evidence – better video footage, decent photographs, some suggestion of a population rather than just an individual, spoor…'

'Spores?'

'Spoor. The traces an animal leaves behind it as it moves about. Tracks, scent markings or droppings.'

'Do werewolves shit in the woods?' said Arthur, with a grin.

McNabb booked off duty and stopped off at a chip shop in Dunksbury on his way home – cooking for one was a chore he could do without – and, as he waited in the queue to be served, he quietly fumed. Sir Giles had snuck away to London, a predictable move on his part and one of the reasons McNabb had been opposed to unconditional bail. It meant that the man was beyond the reach of his surveillance and there was no way he could justify a trip to the capital to follow him around. But it had just occurred to him that his sister lived in London and might be willing to do a little MP-watching on his behalf. All she'd have to do was keep an eye on where he went and who he met. There was no danger involved. And besides, she owed him – he'd loaned her the money she'd needed to set up her business – so perhaps he'd call her in the morning. In the meantime, there was Sir Giles's coffee companion to learn more about, and there was Lady Luscott-Whorne too; her husband had clearly been having an affair with his secretary for quite some time, but did she know, he wondered? Bitterness and revenge were good motivators for dishing the dirt and she might prove to be a useful ally. Of course, they were also good motivators for murder, but McNabb put such thoughts to one side. He was sure that Sir Giles was his man. But, either way, it was worth paying her Ladyship a visit, just to be sure.

He collected his cod and chips and headed home.

Giles had planned to spend the night at his apartment in Piccadilly but the rabble of reporters and photographers crowded around the forecourt of the Albany put paid to that plan. He therefore drove to Pimlico and his flat in Dolphin Square. He'd bought it because of its proximity to Westminster and it had been his and Phoebe's love nest, which was why it hadn't been his first choice for an overnight stay. He knew that her make-up still sat on the bathroom shelf and her clothes still hung in his closet. However, beggars couldn't be choosers and he was too tired to become maudlin. He settled down in front of the television with a very large single malt and was asleep before the six o'clock news had ended.

Frank Shunter ate his supper in silence, knowing full well that a domestic storm was brewing. His wife had barely said a word to him since he had got home, which didn't bode well.

'So...?' she said eventually over the apple crumble and custard.

'If you're asking whether I met Sir Giles, yes I did.'

'I knew it. I knew you wouldn't be able to say no. You just can't resist getting involved, can you?'

'It depends what you mean by getting involved,' said

Shunter. 'He wanted to ask me for a favour, that's all. And, for what it's worth, I don't think he's a murderer.'

'Oh, good. Because he turned up on the doorstep earlier.'

'He did?'

'Gave me the fright of my life.'

'I'm sure you were perfectly safe. I genuinely don't think he killed that girl.'

'The police seem pretty sure that he did.'

'That doesn't make it true,' said Shunter. 'I worked on plenty of cases where the obvious suspect turned out not to be the guilty party.'

'That's as may be, but I don't want suspected murderers turning up at my house and—'

Shunter retrieved a brown envelope from a drawer and dropped it on the kitchen table. Mrs Shunter opened it and her eyes grew wide.

'There's two grand there,' said Shunter. 'All he wants me to do is a little investigating on his behalf to see if I can turn up anything that might prove his innocence. Nothing dodgy. Nothing illegal. And I keep the money whether I find anything or not.'

'But isn't that…'

'What?'

'Unethical?'

'I don't see how,' said Shunter. 'He's innocent until proven otherwise and I'm not a copper any more so there's no issue of bribery or being offered a backhander. I'm not doing anything that a private investigator wouldn't do. I might even find evidence that works against him.'

'But won't you upset the police?' said Mrs Shunter. 'Again.'

'I hope they'd be professional enough to accept the evidence when it's presented to them.'

'Hmf. Well, anyway, he asked me to give this to you.' She

put the memory stick on the table and pushed it across to him. 'I can't say that I'm happy about this, Frank. You're too old for this sort of thing.'

'So you keep saying,' said Shunter. 'But you're only as old as you feel and I don't feel decrepit yet. There are people in their eighties running marathons. Nicholas Parsons is still presenting radio shows and he was around when dinosaurs ruled the Earth. All I'm being paid to do is ask a few questions, that's all. I'm not bungee jumping off the Forth Bridge. And it is two grand.'

Mrs Shunter pursed her lips in thought.

'That pays for a nice holiday,' said Shunter.

'Just don't do anything stupid,' said Mrs Shunter.

'I won't.'

'And promise me you'll call the police if there's any hint of danger.'

'Of course.'

'I don't suppose you'll ever properly retire, will you?' she said, shaking her head.

'I will, when I'm actually too old,' said Shunter with a wink. 'The Grim Reaper retires everyone eventually.'

Chapter 15

Sir Giles awoke and found himself still sitting in front of the television, which was showing a breakfast interview with Helen Greeley, the actor who played Miss Cutter in the television adaptations of Agnes Crabbe's books. He groaned and turned it off. Wasn't it possible to have one day without hearing any references to South Herewardshire and murder? He stood up and stretched. The armchair, comfortable though it was, had not been the best place to spend the night and his neck ached where his head had lolled to one side. He threw open the curtains and gazed out onto the monolithic buildings of Dolphin Square. It was still quite dark but there were already people busily moving about, despite his watch telling him that it wasn't long after seven and the fact that many of the residents were retired. He showered and ordered a cab to take him into Westminster.

With a gust of black diesel smoke, the generator chugged into life and the powerful pumps began to hum. Two long, fat hoses, each the diameter of a grapefruit, began to throb as water was slurped out of Gertie's Plash. In the near distance could be heard the sound of it gushing with some force out of the outlet pipes and into the River Gew. Ken Arthur smiled. Dr Pantridge yawned. Despite their reservations, the two men had elected to spend the night in the Portakabin in the hope that their presence would scare away potential vandals. The installation of powerful floodlights had been an additional preventative measure and the plan appeared to have worked. However, Pantridge had barely slept a wink.

'The lights were so bright, and I kept expecting at any minute to be threatened by some protester with a hammer,' he explained to Arthur who, annoyingly, seemed to have slept like a log. 'Then, when I finally did drop off, I had a dream where I got attacked by a werewolf with a placard saying "You can't rebuild a duck".'

'Ah well, it's just the one night,' said Arthur. 'Some of the dig team will be here later today. Both pumps are up and running and if they run twenty-four hours a day, the pond will be empty sometime over the weekend.'

'That's reassuring,' said Pantridge. 'Good morning!'

He directed this greeting towards Miss Bultitude, who was walking her poodles, as was her morning routine, and who had just appeared at the safety barrier. The dogs, upon spotting the two men, began barking loudly and straining at their leashes.

'Good morning!' she shouted above the hullabaloo. 'How are things progressing?'

'Fine,' yelled Pantridge. 'Thanks again for sorting out those troublemakers at the meeting the other evening.'

'Much appreciated,' added Arthur.

'I'm not sure that I did much good,' said Miss Bultitude, pulling her slavering pets back to her side and pointing to the graffiti-covered Portakabin with the hockey stick she was carrying. 'The same ruffians, I assume?'

'Possibly. A minor inconvenience,' said Pantridge. 'The show will go on.'

'I'm pleased to hear it.'

'You expecting trouble?' asked Arthur.

'You mean this?' said Miss Bultitude, holding up the stick. 'Just a precaution. In the light of recent events, it seemed wise. Well, I must be off. Enjoy the day. We're going to have some autumn sunshine by the looks of it.'

Miss Bultitude made a brisk circuit of the woods and returned home to drop her dogs off before heading into the school. She found Miss Deak in the school secretary's office, sorting through a pile of correspondence.

'It's a perfectly lovely morning out there, Tiggy.'

'I'm sure it is,' replied Miss Deak. 'I'm just catching up with Miss Kingshaw's work.'

'Awful business. You've heard, I assume, that she was apparently Sir Giles's secretary all along?'

'Yes, on the local news. I always knew there was something fishy about her and her appointment. Right from Day One, I knew. She was his spy in the camp.'

'Do you think so?'

'What other reason could there be?' said Miss Deak. 'My guess is that he was hoping to find something to use as leverage against you. Some reason to get us thrown out on our ears. He'd do anything to get his hands on Harpax. The man needs strangling.'

'Oh dear. How upsetting.'

'I imagine you'll be advertising for a new secretary now?'

'It seems so callous. But I have to think about it, I suppose. Have you the capacity to deal with some of her work for a while? I'm happy to share the load, of course.'

'Yes, I think so. She's left everything in good order.

Whatever else she might have been, she was a very competent secretary.'

'Well, that's good news,' said Miss Bultitude. 'And goodness knows we could do with some of that. Talking of which, I checked the Millerick Society message board this morning and the members are asking when the next fundraiser is likely to be. We didn't fix a date at the last one, did we?'

'A fundraiser?' said Miss Deak. 'With everything that's going on?'

'I don't see why not,' said Miss Bultitude. 'Society evenings are always such fun and I think we could do with something to take our minds off the awfulness of recent events.'

'I can check for possible dates,' said Miss Deak.

Sir Giles hadn't anticipated the reactions that his appearance at the Palace of Westminster would provoke among his colleagues. He'd expected sympathy and kind words, but instead he'd found himself to be persona non grata. Everywhere he went, people peered at him from the shadows or whispered in doorways or took circuitous routes between venues – anything to avoid passing by him too closely and necessitating conversation. He ate a solitary breakfast in the members' café and then went to his office, where his PA was looking just as tetchy as when he'd last seen him. Clyst was a man for whom subterfuge, obfuscation and political manoeuvring were meat and drink and he deeply begrudged being left out of the loop. Any loop.

'This is ridiculous,' complained Sir Giles. 'Everyone is giving me the cold shoulder, Raif. Surely no one actually thinks that I killed Phoebe, do they?'

'I'm sure I don't know.'

'What does that mean?'

'It means that I have tried to avoid conversation on the subject altogether. I don't want people asking me awkward questions that I can't answer.'

'Yes, but you can assure people that I'm innocent, can't you?'

'I could,' said Clyst. 'But then they'd ask me why Miss Kingshaw was working at the school, especially as she's on the civil service payroll here. And as you'd kept me in the dark regarding her absence, and in what capacity you were employing her, I didn't have an adequate explanation to give to people. I still don't. Consequently, all I had was fabrication or admitting that I have no idea what my employer is up to, both of which would make me look either incompetent or untrustworthy, and I am neither.'

'Yes, but...'

'Nor could I explain why you might have been with her when she was killed.'

'There is a perfectly logical explanation for that.'

'Which, again, I have not been made privy to. So what was I supposed to say to people? The chief whip certainly wasn't very happy. He has asked me to extend to you his best wishes and he suggests that a spot of "gardening leave" might benefit both your health and that of the party.'

'But I didn't do it, Raif!'

'I'm quite sure that you didn't. However, with the election coming up, the prime minister is concern—'

'Ah, now I see why everyone is avoiding me,' said Sir Giles. 'They're afraid they'll be tainted if they associate with me, aren't they? I'm toxic.'

'Not my words,' said Clyst.

'Whatever happened to presumption of innocence?' said Sir Giles, pulling on his overcoat. 'Well, if there's nothing for me to do here I may as well go. In the unlikely event you need me for any reason, and it doesn't sound to me like you will, I'll be at Titters.'

'Actually, you probably shouldn't…'

'What?'

'The membership secretary politely asks that you don't visit the premises until such time as you are cleared of all charges, which he believes you undoubtedly will be, of course. He says that his first priority is to shield the club and the other members from any scandal.'

'Any scandal? The place was built on scandal! Their past membership includes Crippen, Lord Lucan and Oswald fucking Mosley!'

'That's as may be, but they didn't have gutter tabloids, Twitter and paparazzi back then,' said Clyst. 'You can't keep these things quiet like they used to in the good old days.'

'The good old days? Jesus Christ…'

'I also have requests here from Boodle's, the Carlton, Whites…'

'Save your breath. I'm going.'

'Home to Proutt? Shall I organise a car for you?'

'To hell with your car.'

Sir Giles stormed out of his office and out of the building.

Tents had begun to sprout on the banks of Gertie's Plash. Five archaeology, engineering and history undergrads from the university at Uttercombe had come at Dr Pantridge's request and the remaining ten would be arriving on Sunday when the dig commenced. Their spokesperson was a ruddy-faced postdoctoral research fellow called Dougie Fancey.

'There's a wee bit of concern about these protesters,' he said. 'How many did you reckon there were?'

'No more than six,' said Arthur. 'There are more of us than

them and they're pretty poor specimens, to be honest. We'll be fine.'

'The facilities are a bit basic at the moment,' added Pantridge. 'We only have the one toilet but we have two more being delivered on Sunday when you were originally scheduled to arrive. There's a sink in the cabin for washing. Or there's the river, I suppose.'

'Aye, well, it's better than we get at most festivals,' said Fancey.

'It's a very odd price. I doubt we stock anything that retails for £18.66. Are you sure it came from us?'

Shunter produced the price label that he'd found near the spot where Phoebe Kingshaw had been killed. 'It's written on one of your stickers and it looks reasonably new.'

The manager of Crute's department store concurred.

'And handwritten too, which is unusual as we normally use a pricing gun. I wonder if it was a sale item? Shop-soiled or something like that?'

'Is there any way to find out?'

'Not without going back through the accounts,' said the manager. 'Which, with all due respect, would take a great deal of time and effort. I couldn't authorise that unless it was for something like a police investigation. It's not, is it?'

'I'm not a police officer,' said Shunter.

'No, but I do read the papers, Mr Shunter,' said the manager, tapping the side of his nose and winking. 'And I'm well aware of your reputation. Miss Pomerance was a regular customer here. Such a tragedy.'

'Indeed, but I assure you that I'm just doing some research. Perhaps I could leave you my number on the off-chance you think of something?'

'Yes, of course,' said the manager.

Shunter left the shop and stepped outside into Fisher Street, one of Bowcester's two main shopping thoroughfares. It was surprisingly busy for a Thursday lunchtime, he thought to himself. But, then again, anywhere looked bustling when compared to sleepy Nasely, and Bowcester was the largest town in this part of South Herewardshire. Along with Uttercombe, Morbridge and Coxeter in the north and Pawley in the south, Bowcester had been one of the county's primary market towns, where local farmers had come to sell their stock. The market was long gone and the modern age had seen the arrival of ubiquitous high street franchises, supermarkets and fast-food joints. But there were still echoes of the past to be found in the names of local businesses that had defied regeneration and still clung to life, such as Leverett's hardware shop, Libman and Marr's Whisky Shop, and Crute's, a delightfully old-fashioned family-owned department store that had been trading since the 1930s.

There was also Holland and Pendlebury's antiquarian bookshop, which had first opened its doors to Victorian readers. Shunter always enjoyed rummaging among the shelves on his occasional visits to the town but invariably went home empty-handed, as most of the books he'd love to have bought were beyond his means. But not today. Sir Giles had offered him £500 a day and hadn't specified on what it should be spent. And there was an envelope containing £2,000 sitting in a drawer at home. With some small degree of nervous excitement, he walked towards the shop in Lackery Lane, where he dithered over first editions of George Summersbee's *The Wheels of Justice* and Rex West's *Mystery of the Pink Crayfish* before settling on a signed first edition of Douglas Adams's *Dirk Gently's Holistic Detective Agency* for £120. And then, because it was on expenses, he had his lunch in a swanky brasserie. Over the best fish and chips he'd eaten in years, he fondled his new acquisition and tried to suppress the pangs of guilt he felt in buying it. It wasn't useful. It wasn't essential or even necessary. And the money he'd used to pay for it came from a man who, despite his instincts telling him otherwise, might possibly have brutally beaten a young woman to death. But the book had called to him. Shunter traced the blue biro squiggle that was Adams's illegible signature. Writing was a form of immortality, he mused, and thanks to his books the author would never be forgotten. But a signed book was something more: it created a physical connection between writer and reader. Shunter suddenly realised that what had made him buy the book was the knowledge that his favourite author had once held that very same volume in his hands. It was even possible that the pages still contained microscopic traces of his DNA. His phone rang, abruptly breaking his train of thought.

'Hello, Mr Shunter?' said the voice at the other end. 'It's Mr Jeal, the manager of Crute's department store. I may have found something.'

Sir Giles sat on a public bench near to Cleopatra's Needle and looked out onto the River Thames, as he so often did when deep in contemplation. His political career was dead; he knew that now. The general election was very close and no one in their right mind would select a person for their new cabinet who was suspected of committing a murder. He'd be lucky to even retain his seat. Of more concern, however, was the very real possibility of being convicted of a crime that he hadn't committed. Prison was a terrifying prospect. And so too was the divorce that would inevitably follow. The Luscotts would take him to the cleaners and even though he'd be left with a reduced, though still substantial, personal fortune, the family name would be sullied for ever. Unless new evidence emerged, he'd achieve notoriety as 'Giles the Murderer'. But at least he wouldn't be quite so invisible among his deceased ancestors, he thought wryly.

The future looked bleak. He wondered whether to call Shunter to ask for an update.

Mr Jeal was at the back of the store tidying up a display of men's jackets when Shunter appeared.

'Thank you for popping back, Mr Shunter. I had a light-bulb moment. After you left I was thinking about your enquiry and it suddenly occurred to me that the unusual price tag might be due to a bulk discount. If someone ordered several similar items at once, for example. So I had a quick look and I think I've solved your mystery. Our sporting goods department sold thirty hockey sticks in a bulk buy about a month ago. The customer was eligible for a fifteen per cent discount, which brought the item price down to... exactly £18.66.'

'Very nicely done,' said Shunter. 'Ah, but customer information is of course confidential, I suppose?'

'Naturally.'

'Although, with that many items... do you, perhaps, offer a fifteen per cent discount to educational establishments?'

'We do,' said Mr Jeal.

'So, hypothetically, that sort of discount might apply to somewhere like a girls' school?'

'It might indeed,' said Mr Jeal, smiling. 'Hypothetically, of course.'

'Just one more thing, Mr Jeal. You said that the labels were usually done with a pricing gun. So why would items be individually labelled with handwritten stickers?'

'It's common practice these days for schools to insist on their pupils paying for their own sports equipment,' said Mr Jeal. 'We supply them with blank labels so that they can be sold in the school shop. It's free advertising for us. In this instance, it looks like the school has priced the sticks at the same price they bought them for. One might assume, therefore, that the school is probably fairly well off and wasn't concerned about making a profit.'

'Thank you,' said Shunter. 'I'll leave you in peace now and with your integrity intact.'

'I hope I've been able to help,' said Mr Jeal.

'If I can find the owner of one particular item, you may have helped to catch a murderer,' said Shunter.

'How thrilling,' said Mr Jeal.

As Shunter left the shop, Sir Giles called. The temptation had proved too much for him.

'It's early days,' explained Shunter. 'Although I may have a line of enquiry regarding a possible murder weapon. I'll keep digging until I know for sure. This is only Day One.'

'And you've already uncovered more than the police have,' said Sir Giles. 'Good work, Frank. I have every faith in you.'

Chapter 16

The weather had been kind to the lawn bowls players of Nasely. The season normally ended in late September but as it had been mostly dry and the turf was still usable, the chairing committee had allowed the green to stay open for a few extra weeks.

'A Shaggy Beast hunt?' said Inderpal Verma. 'Count me in.'

'Excellent,' said Gerry Waxleigh. 'We're looking at tomorrow night if you're free.'

'I am. Is it my turn to throw out the jack?'

At a nod from Waxleigh, Verma threw the white ball out onto the rink.

'If there really is some kind of wild animal in Black Dog Wood, it would be good to be there and see it,' said Verma. He bowled his first wood, which sailed past the jack and fell into the ditch beyond.

'Oh dear,' he said, repositioning his heavy spectacles on his nose. 'Dead bowl.'

'On the subject of wild animals, did you call the Trembletts to see whether they'd had any escapees?' asked Waxleigh as he bowled his first wood.

'I spoke to Constance, the elder Miss Tremblett. She said that the only animals ever to escape from her farm were peacocks. And, once, a llama. But no bears or wolves or big cats or anything like that.'

'Ah well, it was worth asking,' said Waxleigh. 'So, do you have any specialist equipment that you'd be allowed to bring? A dog catcher? Or a tranquilliser gun, perhaps?'

'I have both but I would only ever use the gun as a last resort,' said Verma. He played his second wood, which also clunked into the ditch.

'Perhaps just bring the dog catcher, eh?' said Waxleigh.

It had been said of Pamela Dallimore that she had 'the gift of turning base allegations into gold', a reputation that rested mostly on the back of her book, *The Secret Queen of Crime*. Written to mark the tenth anniversary of the discovery of Agnes Crabbe's cache of novels, it had caused a sensation on publication. Mrs Dallimore had obtained most of the book's more lurid content by talking to local people. Everyone, it seemed, had a theory about what had gone on behind the closed doors of Crabbe Cottage after the great author had withdrawn from village life. All Dallimore had needed to do was collect those stories and string them together into a narrative. To the dismay of Crabbe fans, the book had been a bestseller, despite being built entirely upon unfounded rumour. To their further annoyance, it had also cemented Dallimore's reputation worldwide as the media's go-to person on the author, despite the fact that she wasn't a fan herself and hadn't even read most of Crabbe's work.

Central to the book had been the contentious idea that the author might have been romantically involved with her best friend, Iris Gobbelin. There was no actual evidence that this was true but that hadn't bothered Pamela Dallimore. Nor had she been concerned by the anger of the Millies who had denounced her work. She hadn't written the book for them. She'd written it for the gossip-hungry, tabloid-loving masses who wanted to read prurient stories about famous people. That was what made them happy and made her money.

But now the time was ripe for a sequel. Dallimore had enjoyed a degree of fame after her kidnap by Shirley Pomerance's murderer, and had exploited it brilliantly. She had been a favourite of chat shows and a regular magazine interviewee for months. Her recovery from her injuries had been slow and mostly sedentary, which had resulted in her having a considerably more buxom figure than she'd had before, but she wore the extra pounds in all the right places and rather enjoyed the increased attention she now got. With her public profile never stronger, she knew that the conditions were perfect for publishing a follow-up volume. All she needed was a hook. Therefore, she had adopted the working title of *The Secret Queen of Crime's Biggest Secret*, and had decided to pursue an entirely specious angle involving the paternity of Crabbe's unwanted child. Circumnavigating the fact that Agnes's tragic young husband, Daniel, was undoubtedly the father, she had concocted an illicit romance involving an unnamed aristocrat that would make the book as sensational and lucrative as the previous one had been. Although she wouldn't go so far as to name her 'suspect', she had in mind to plant enough hints to suggest that Jolyon Whorne, Sir Giles's great-grandfather, was the guilty party. He had been well known as a ladies' man in his day and, more importantly, he was a soft target; she could allege whatever she liked because, as the law currently stood, you couldn't libel someone who was dead. And besides, his alleged incompetence during the First World War had already made him a figure of loathing for many people. Few would step forward to defend him.

She had come to Nasely out of festival season to see if there were any last little bits of scandalous Jolyon-related tittle-tattle to be mopped up and, by sheer good fortune, she'd arrived at exactly the right time to capitalise upon the arrest of his great-grandson on suspicion of murder. As a bonus, there was also the discovery of the mysterious blindfolded body buried in the grounds of the Whorne family's former seat. But the icing on the cake had been another story that appeared to be on the cusp of breaking. Some people might be claiming that the Shaggy Beast was some kind of werewolf but Mrs Dallimore had no such illusions. What she had seen on Ken Arthur's laptop was quite clearly a man in a dildo-augmented wolf costume, and if the respectable people of Nasely and its environs were dressing up as animals and meeting for sexy woodland fun, she wanted the exclusive. Something distinctly kinky seemed to be going on in Black Dog Wood and where there was muck, as the saying went, there was brass.

The Moore Tea, Vicar? café was, by far, the best source of titbits in the village and Mrs Dallimore had spent much of her day listening in on other people's conversations. To her delight, the topics under discussion had included several alleged affairs among the locals and a recent trip to Amsterdam by a newly divorced plumber called Mr Hemerton. As she suspected, if you picked at any village's scab of respectability, there was always hot-blooded naughty business to be found underneath. She had made copious notes, and after hearing rumours of Black Dog Wood being used as a dogging site, her potential story was becoming more interesting by the minute. But one snippet of conversation had been of particular interest – a man with a scar across his lower lip and chin had come in to buy sandwiches for his lunch and had mentioned to Mrs Moore that it would be a busy night in the woods on Friday because there was going to be 'another hunt'. When the café owner next arrived at her table, Mrs Dallimore gently broached the subject.

'Anne, you're a lady in the know. I've been hearing rumours of some kind of a hunt on Friday night. Is it pheasant? I know it's open season.'

'Not at night it isn't,' said Mrs Moore. She regarded Pamela Dallimore as one of her 'celebrity' customers and was keen to please. 'It's just some silly old duffers going off in search of the Shaggy Beast.'

'Shaggy Beast?' asked Mrs Dallimore, feigning ignorance.

'Our local monster. It's supposedly some kind of half-man, half-dog thing that's been prowling around Black Dog Wood for centuries. I'm not joking. It's how the woods got their name. Load of old tosh if you ask me, but plenty of people believe in it. Barry Chetwynd is the man to speak to.'

'Chetwynd... as in the butcher's shop?'

'Obsessed with it, he is. He says there wouldn't be any Shaggy Beast sightings without there being something that people think is the Shaggy Beast. Though if you want an entirely different kind of shaggy beast, you should speak to Mr Hemerton. Did you know that he's recently been on a...'

By the time Mrs Dallimore had finished hearing all about Mr Hemerton's alleged European brothel tour, it was starting to get dark outside. She left the café and walked down the High Street towards the Empire Hotel, deep in thought. In recent years there had been several successful 'reality' shows that purported to follow the activities of monster-hunters in search of Bigfoot, Nessie and their ilk. If she could somehow get herself invited to the following evening's hunt, it would provide some great copy for her potential story and maybe even enough material with which to pitch a TV show to production companies. She could rope Professor Gravestock into the project to add some credibility as well. Her visit to

Nasely was getting better by the hour, she decided. First thing in the morning, she would have words with Chetwynd the butcher.

Shunter arrived home and after carefully secreting his expensive purchase in the bookcase of his office in the new extension, he joined his wife for supper. Coincidentally, she'd chosen to cook fish and chips. He decided not to mention the champagne-battered turbot and triple-cooked chips that he'd eaten for his lunch.

'So, how did it go?' she asked him.

'I may have found a lead on the murder weapon,' said Shunter. 'But you know how slow these things can be. It can take a while for an investigation to pick up any steam.'

'I still don't like it,' she said. 'But I can't argue with the money. And if you are genuinely preventing an innocent man going to prison then it's a good thing, I suppose.'

'Or confirming that he's guilty,' said Shunter. 'We can't dismiss that possibility.'

'Did you find anything useful on that USB stick thing?'

'I haven't looked yet.'

'Why not?'

'It's the contents of the dead girl's phone. It just seems like a terrible invasion of privacy.'

'Don't be so old-fashioned. What if there's something on there that points to the killer? Threats or something?'

'The police have been through it already. And so has Sir Giles. I'm sure they'd have spotted something like that.'

'Hmm. What do you want for pudding? There's leftover crumble or yoghurt.'

'Do we have any custard?'

'I think so.'

'Crumble. No contest,' said Shunter.

As his wife took the dinner plates to the sink, Shunter fetched his laptop from his little office and powered it up. He slotted the memory stick into place and waited for the drive folder to appear. Inside it were four subfolders labelled as emails, texts, photos and misc. He went first to her text messages but there were hundreds to read and he didn't much fancy starting on them so late in the day. It was the same with her emails; searching through them would need a full day of work. His pointer hovered over the photo gallery icon. This was the content that he felt most uncomfortable viewing. Sir Giles had told him that he'd deleted anything particularly personal or intimate, but wasn't any part of a person's life intimate? Did he have the right to invade her privacy, to see where she had travelled to, what she had chosen to wear or, worse still, images of her and her loved ones? It felt to him like furtively looking through someone's photo albums without their permission. He then reminded himself that information of that kind was probably already in the public domain. If Phoebe was like most women her age, her life was an open book and many of her photos would already be online and visible via social media. Privacy, it seemed to Shunter, was a concept unfamiliar to the modern age. As a police officer investigating serious crimes committed by serious villains, he'd spent thirty years doing all he could to keep himself and his family anonymous and hidden away from the threat of possible repercussions. His phone was ex-directory and his online profile, such as it was, was minimal and never mentioned his wife or daughter by name. But people lived their lives differently now. It was almost as if Generation Y believed that they were living in some kind of reality TV show where every opinion they had, every drink they drank, every gig they attended, had to be shared with a worldwide audience. They also seemed to be oblivious to the consequences: how many would fail job interviews or be passed over for promotion at work because their social media profile suggested that they were drunk every night? How many had lost friends over ill-considered comments or off-colour jokes posted online? How many girlfriends and wives had seen intimate photos of themselves circulated in revenge by their ex-partners? And how many had been the subject of identity theft after giving away almost every detail about themselves? Their world was very different to the one in which Shunter had grown up and he found it alien and uncomfortable to visit.

He took a deep breath and double-clicked on the first photo in the folder. Phoebe Kingshaw appeared on his screen, sitting on a beach somewhere with palm trees in the background. She was dressed in a black one-piece swimsuit and was holding up a brightly coloured cocktail. She had a dazzling smile, he thought to himself, and she'd been a very attractive young woman. *Young.* Maybe his wife had a point; you were definitely getting old if you'd started to refer to women in their mid-thirties as young. He closed the photo and looked at the list of images. They were arranged in date order, so he clicked on the most recent – presumably the last picture that Phoebe Kingshaw had ever taken.

The full-size image appeared on the screen and caused his heart to skip a beat.

Chapter 17

Sir Giles was feeling rudderless. He had spent a second night in London and, upon waking, had realised that he had no idea what to do with himself. His political colleagues had shunned him, the press had surrounded his other apartment at the Albany, his clubs were off limits, and going home to Proutt would put him once more under the scrutiny of the terrible McNabb. Even the flat in Dolphin Square was too redolent of Phoebe to be entirely comfortable. He needed to get out and go somewhere. But where? He had nothing to do, no one to see and nowhere to go. Ironically, he was, for the first time in years, completely free to do whatever he wanted, and yet he couldn't. He was a public figure and his arrest for suspected murder had made the national news. He was just as trapped as ever.

He wandered into the bathroom and looked at himself in the mirror. A very different face to the one he was used to seeing stared back at him. He was unshaven and he'd definitely lost a bit of weight. He hardly recognised himself. And it made him wonder – would anyone else?

McNabb's arrival at Proutt caught Cecily by surprise. She and

Jenny had gone for a morning stroll around the estate and were walking near the main gates when the unmarked black Ford arrived. She had immediately dropped Jenny's hand, a movement that had elicited a growl of annoyance.

'For God's sake! I'm not leprous!'

'No, but—'

'Two women holding hands is not a crime. I can't believe we're still living this lie.'

'It won't be for much longer,' assured Cecily.

'You said that last year,' growled Jenny. 'And the year before that. I swear you love his money more than you love me.'

'Jenny, it's not as simp—'

'The sooner your stupid husband gets banged up the better. I won't wait for ever.'

Jenny stormed off back to the house, leaving Cecily to receive the visitor.

'Good morning,' she said, wondering whether the man in the car had seen the altercation. 'If you're here for Giles, I'm afraid he's in London.'

'Actually, it's you I wanted to speak to, your Ladyship. Detective Inspector Derek McNabb. Bowcester CID.'

He showed his warrant card.

'I see. I suppose you'd better come up to the house then,' she said.

If an unimaginative cartoonist had been asked to illustrate a pack of cards for a game of Happy Families, Barry Chetwynd would have been the perfect model for Mr Bones. He looked and acted, thought Mrs Dallimore, exactly like she imagined a butcher should. He was brawny and bawdy and every sentence he spoke came with a side order of meaty innuendo.

'What can I get you, miss?' he asked, with a broad toothy

grin. 'I can offer you the best pork you'll get this side of the Ridgeway.'

'I'm after something a little more exotic.'

'Exotic, eh? How about a bit of tongue?'

'Not quite what I'm after.'

'Venison? Wild boar? Ostrich, maybe?'

'I was thinking more of Shaggy Beast,' said Mrs Dallimore.

Chetwynd eyed her suspiciously. 'What do you mean by that?' he asked.

'I understand you're the local expert on whatever it is that's terrorising people in Black Dog Wood,' said Mrs Dallimore. 'And I've been told that you're going to try to hunt it down. How would you feel about press coverage?'

'Press coverage?'

'National press coverage is what I'm aiming for.'

'Perhaps you'd better come upstairs for a minute.'

Leaving his assistant to run the shop, Chetwynd washed his hands and led Mrs Dallimore up two flights of ancient rickety stairs to his office. The room occupied the gable and had low sloping ceilings papered with images of werewolves and monster dogs. A Lon Chaney Jr-style wolf-man figure stood on a desk, its outsize sprung head bobbing. Chetwynd squinted at his visitor and his face lit up in recognition.

'You're that reporter who got kidnapped by that—'

'Pamela Dallimore,' she said, sitting herself down on a dusty old chair. 'So, tell me about your monster.'

Chetwynd lifted a bulging lever arch file from out of a drawer in his desk. 'There you go,' he said. 'It's all in there. Every reported sighting.'

'My word. A lot of work has gone into this,' said Mrs Dallimore, leafing through the pages.

'I've been adding to it since I was a lad. I have pretty much every press cutting, right back to the glut of sightings between

1933 and 1934 that really kicked things off, legend-wise. But there are older reports too. Some go all the way back to the 1700s.'

'Very impressive. Not many photographs, though.'

'Photos are a rarity. The Shaggy Beast, whatever it is, only seems to come out at night when the woods are dark.'

'Yes, but modern cameras with automatic flash would catch it, surely? Even phone cameras are great in low light these days.'

'People are too busy running away to stop and find the camera app.'

'Then getting some good-quality photos is a priority,' said Mrs Dallimore. She finished paging through the file and sat back in her chair. 'So tell me, Barry, why the interest?'

'I don't know really,' said Chetwynd. 'What makes someone a stamp collector, or a trainspotter? We were told about the Shaggy Beast when we were kids and it was sort of a rite of passage for us to go into the woods at night and to step off the path, just to show how tough we were. I guess the thrill never left me. How about you? Most of the reporters I've spoken to this past day or so couldn't give a damn about it. What's got you interested?'

'I saw a video of it yesterday.'

Chetwynd's eyes lit up. 'A video? You're kidding me.'

'I'm sure I can arrange for you to see it if you're happy to work with me on this story.'

'Yes, of course. Be glad to,' said Chetwynd. 'I want all the publicity I can get. Not for me, you understand. For the village.'

'Great,' said Mrs Dallimore. 'Now, is it true that you're going hunting tonight?'

'We are.'

'Do I need to bring any kind of weapon with me? Just in case?'

'We've got that covered. We're meeting at the pub at nine o'clock.'

'Then I'll see you there,' said Mrs Dallimore. 'I hope we get lucky.'

'Me too,' said Chetwynd. He leaned in and grinned, the embers of mania glowing in his eyes. 'If I can prove this thing really exists, it could change my life.'

'Both of our lives,' said Mrs Dallimore. 'Partner.'

Cecily poured the tea and passed the police officer a jug of milk to add his own. It took McNabb a short while to register her action, having been distracted by the odd assortment of animal costumes that were piled up on a kitchen sideboard like so many trappers' pelts. Happy pigs lay atop a sandwich of gleeful goats, goofy donkeys, snarling wolves and, curiously, a buck-toothed smiling pink unicorn. All of them seemed to be staring blankly at him.

'Costumes for the Bowcester Theatre Group's musical production of *Animal Farm*,' explained Cecily. 'We all but cleaned out the fancy-dress shop.'

'I don't remember there being a unicorn,' said McNabb.

'A touch of fabric dye and a horn-ectomy and it will pass muster as Boxer,' said Cecily. 'So, what can I do for you, Inspector?'

'I wanted to ask you a few questions,' said McNabb. 'For clarity purposes.'

'What sort of questions?'

'Questions like… do you know where your husband was on the night that Phoebe Kingshaw was murdered?'

Cecily's eyebrows rose high on her forehead. 'So you still believe that Giles is guilty, then?'

'I'm afraid I do.'

'I see. He left here after supper but he didn't say where he was going.'

'And I do have to ask you if you were aware of any kind of personal relationship between Sir Giles and the deceased?'

'She was his secretary and had been so for a couple of years,' said Cecily. 'If their relationship was anything more than that, he's been very circumspect.'

'Do you know why she was working at Harpax Grange School?'

'I had no idea that she was until I heard it on the local news,' said Cecily. 'It did strike me as odd. But I'm sure that Giles can explain it.'

'And you're not aware of any reason why he would have met her at the mausoleum on the night she was murdered?'

'No, I'm afraid not. I must say that I was expecting you to treat me as a suspect.'

'You were?'

'Yes. Surely when a married man meets a younger woman at a remote location at night, it's not uncommon for the wife to be a suspect if that woman is subsequently killed.'

Somewhere in the near distance, a shotgun fired twice.

'My housekeeper. Out shopping for dinner, I expect,' said Cecily. 'So I'm not a suspect?'

'Everyone is a potential suspect, your Ladyship.'

'Hmm, should I perhaps have legal representation before answering any more of your questions then?'

'This isn't a formal interview,' explained McNabb. 'If it was, you'd be under caution. These are just routine questions. Investigation is a process of elimination. One way of building a case against your suspect is to prove that no one else could have done the crime.'

'Yes, I can see how that might be the case,' said Cecily. 'Well, just for clarity, I can assure you that I was here at Proutt at the time of the murder.'

'Can anyone verify that?' asked McNabb.

'Yes, my housekeeper can. Any more routine questions?'

'No, I think I have all I need at this time,' said McNabb.

'Well, do feel free to call me again if you want anything else eliminated,' said Cecily. 'But for now, Inspector, I must get on. The estate does not run itself, I'm afraid.'

'No indeed. Thank you for your time. And the tea.'

As he drove back down the long drive to the main gate, McNabb spotted Jenny Highnote walking along, a broken shotgun over the crook of her right arm and a brace of rabbits hanging from her left hand. He stopped alongside her and wound down the window.

'I take it you have a licence for that?' he said with a humourless smile.

'Of course,' said Jenny.

'Can I ask you if you know where Lady Luscott-Whorne was on the night of the murder?'

'She was here,' said Jenny. 'Don't you go suspecting her.'

'I have to keep an open mind,' said McNabb, taken slightly aback by the vehemence of her answer.

'Did she tell you that he got a phone call from the Kingshaw woman during supper? He dashed off to meet her like some lovesick puppy. Next thing, she's dead. It's pretty obvious to me that he's guilty.'

'I agree, but I need more than just circumstantial evidence

to ensure a conviction,' said McNabb. 'You say "lovesick". Are you saying that Sir Giles and the victim were—'

'At it like knives,' said Jenny.

'But Lady Luscott-Whorne said—'

'Her family doesn't like scandal and she has a reputation to maintain,' said Jenny. 'I, however, do not. And it's my job to protect her. As far as I can see, the best way to do that is to ensure that the murderer is behind bars.'

'Meaning Sir Giles?'

'If the cap fits…'

'Perhaps then, if you think of anything that might help my investigation, you'll let me know?'

Jenny nodded as she accepted his business card.

McNabb wound the window up and drove on. Her Ladyship might have sidestepped his questions but Jenny Highnote was clearly convinced of her employer's guilt. Besides, there was something distinctly peculiar about the relationships between the inhabitants of Proutt House. He had spotted the two women holding hands, and Cecily's rather blasé reaction to the suggestion that her husband was having an affair was a puzzle. He'd expected to meet a scorned woman but she seemed to be anything but.

'They're probably all swingers and sex fiends,' he said to himself. There was certainly precedent for it. He didn't know too much about the Luscotts but the Whorne family tree was peppered with Lotharios, from Sir Giles in the present right back to Sir Redvers and the infamous Diabolical Club. Another thing he was sure of was that people like the Luscott-Whornes looked after their own; he'd seen an example of that in the appointment of one of Cecily's relatives as Sir Giles's barrister. If he was going to build a watertight case, he would have to make sure that every possible alibi the man might try to employ could be disproved. He also needed a confession or, at the very least, some slip of the tongue that would suggest guilt.

He reached the gatehouse and turned on to the Bowcester Road. Half an hour later he arrived back at his office and phoned his sister.

Sir Giles returned to his flat in a buoyant mood. Having bought himself the kind of clothes that normally he wouldn't be seen dead in, he'd spent a couple of hours walking around the shops in Victoria, anonymous in his jeans, leather jacket and baseball cap and enjoying every minute of it. He'd done things he had never done before, like travelling on the Underground, eating in a burger restaurant, shopping in a department store – things that people did every day but, for whatever reason, he never had. It had been cathartic and eye-opening, and his disguise had worked well; the change of clothes, the careworn face and the five o'clock shadow had all come together nicely. He doubted that he'd fool someone who knew him well but he could certainly fool the general public. It had given him a new-found confidence and he wondered whether he should push it a little further. For some reason, he had the urge to go to a pub. Not some private members' club but a down-to-earth boozer. A location suggested itself to him and he phoned the porter to book him a cab.

McNabb had spent the early part of his evening at home, sitting in front of the TV and letting himself get worked up over old episodes of *Diagnosis Murder*. He couldn't decide what was worse, the absurdity of the plots or the stupidity of the villains who always left a welter of clues behind; so many, in fact, that even an elderly surgeon could figure out whodunit. But the most annoying feature of these shows was the fact that, when cornered and presented with the evidence against them, the suspects always launched into lengthy exposition, admitting their crimes and explaining why they'd committed them. It was utterly ridiculous and only marginally more believable than an episode of *Scooby Doo* after those 'meddling kids' had unmasked the obvious bad guy. Real life didn't work like that. Real bad guys denied everything and said nothing unless advised to do so by some la-di-da barrister.

He found himself wondering what Sir Giles was up to in London. Hopefully, he'd find out soon. He called his sister again.

'Are we in business?' he asked.

'We are,' said Ettie McNabb. 'I've been trailing him around the shops and he's now back home. Call me back in a couple of hours and I might have some news for you.'

'Nutty, hoppy. Nice aftertaste,' said Professor Gravestock. 'You keep a good ale, Mr Sallow.'

'Clean pipes mean happy customers,' said Vic. 'And the Cockering Brewery has been making this stuff for over a century. They know what they're doing. So, what brings you to Nasely? You don't look like the usual sort of Agnes Crabbe fan we get in here.'

'Oh, I see. The book,' said Gravestock, patting the copy of *A White Stone* that he'd borrowed from the hotel. 'I'm afraid her murder-mystery stuff leaves me cold but this one is a cracking ghost story. I did visit the Crabbe Cottage Museum this afternoon though, as I'm in Nasely. It was very interesting.'

'I'd take some of what you saw with a pinch of salt,' said Vic, smiling. 'She was a recluse for the majority of her life so the reconstruction of the interior is largely from people's imaginations.'

'Actually, the best bit for me was seeing some of her original manuscripts,' said the professor. 'To see the actual typewriter she worked on and the pages she'd hand-corrected. It's quite something to think that she held those actual pieces of paper.'

'You were saying something similar earlier, weren't you, Frank?' said Vic, throwing the question towards Shunter, who was nursing a beer further along the bar. 'About that signed book you bought yesterday.'

'You mean the Douglas Adams?'

'You have a signed Douglas Adams?' said Gravestock.

'The first Dirk Gently book. First edition hardback,' said Shunter.

'I'm envious,' said Gravestock.

A sudden burst of boisterous laughter erupted from near the fireplace. Len Youlden, Gerry Waxleigh, Charlie Barnfather, Sid Munsun, Indy Verma and a farmer called Janus Gugge had convened at the Happy Onion for a few pints of Dutch courage before they joined Barry Chetwynd on his Shaggy Beast hunt. Professor Gravestock saw that they were carrying a selection of golf clubs, tennis rackets, baseball bats and cricket bats. He looked concerned.

'My regulars,' said Vic. 'Nothing to worry about.'

'Are you sure?' said Professor Gravestock. He found himself particularly fascinated by Gugge, who looked as if he belonged on a lower branch of the human family tree. A resurgent Neanderthal gene or two perhaps, he wondered?

'Harmless loons,' said Shunter.

'They look like a lynch mob,' said Gravestock.

'No one is going to believe that we're playing sports in the woods after dark,' slurred Sid Munsun.

'It doesn't matter whether they believe it or not,' said Gerry

Waxleigh, waggling his ancient cricket bat. 'It's what they can prove that matters. They'd need evidence of my intent to cause someone harm before this could be considered an offensive weapon.'

'Well, don't say I didn't warn us all,' said Munsun. 'Let's hope it doesn't all end in tears.'

'Except for the Shaggy Beast,' said Charlie Barnfather, playing a fierce backhand stroke with his racket. 'Your round, Len?'

'And getting rounder by the day,' said Waxleigh, patting his friend's beer belly.

'Cheeky bugger. You're no beanpole yourself,' said Len Youlden.

The door opened and the Shaggy Beast hunters looked expectantly for their leader but, to their disappointment, it was Clifford Jaine who walked into the pub. He spotted Shunter at the bar.

'Cliff. Glad you came,' said Shunter. 'Drink?'

'Just a Coke. I'm late CID cover till 2 a.m. So, what's so important that you needed to drag me over to Nasely?'

'I have something to show you,' said Shunter.

Sir Giles climbed into his taxi and as it drove up Lupus Street towards Vauxhall Bridge Road, a second black cab emerged from a parking space and headed in the same direction. In the back seat, a glamorous-looking woman had delighted her driver by saying, 'Follow that cab.'

Chapter 18

The Coal Hole on the Strand was everything that Sir Giles had been looking for in a pub: high ceilings, dark polished wood, leaded windows and a gloriously ornate fireplace. The choice of ales was good, too, and the steak and kidney pie was excellent. He knew of the place because it was one of a handful of real pubs mentioned by P. G. Wodehouse in his books but, although he had been driven past it many times, he'd never popped in for a drink before. He was glad that he had now.

So far, no one had recognised him. The fact that his greying hair was under a cap helped, as did the pair of spectacles he'd perched on his nose. The pub boasted a mezzanine seating area where he could hide in a dark corner and peer inconspicuously over the banister at the drinkers in the main bar below. He imagined that they worked in the shops and offices around Charing Cross and Covent Garden and were now enjoying a stress-relieving drink with their workmates before enduring the daily hell of the commute home. London house prices, even rentals, had become so expensive of late that people now travelled in from places as far away as Cambridge, Brighton, Oxford and Gravesend to work. At this time of year, a commuter's day began in darkness and ended in darkness and he presumed that many of them would get to enjoy no more than an hour or two with loved ones before setting their alarms for 5 a.m. and heading for bed. And yet, for all that, Giles envied them. They might not have his money or his influence but their friendships were probably genuine, not just cultivated for advantage, and they were not bound by conventions of class or family history. There was no baggage that came with being a Reynolds, no stigma to being a Chowdhury or a Wójcik. They would never have to worry about being seen at the right events, talking to the right people, wearing the right tie. They lived outside the prison of expectation and duty, free to pursue whatever path they chose, free to decide who they could love and marry. Giles's obsession with restoring the family name to the upper classes had slowly but surely built the cage, albeit a gilded one, into which he had been locked. But things had changed now: the door was open and he had his life back. It was a life, he now realised, that he hadn't properly lived.

'Is anyone sitting there?'

Giles looked up into the smiling face of a woman dressed in a winter coat over a white blouse and black trousers. She was pretty, buxom and Titian-haired. He whipped off his cap.

'No. No, there isn't,' he said.

'Do you mind if I do then? Only there's nowhere else to sit. It's rammed downstairs.'

'Please do,' said Giles gallantly. 'It felt wrong to have this table all to myself anyway. I'm... Gi... Gerry.'

'Lorraine,' said the woman, extending a hand to shake. 'Can I get you a drink, Gerry?'

'No, let me,' said Giles.

'I knew you were a gentleman as soon as I saw you,' said Lorraine, smiling. 'Vodka and tonic, please.'

'Bloody hell. Is this for real?' said Jaine.

'I think it might be, yes,' said Shunter.

The two men had moved into a corner of the saloon bar and Shunter was showing the detective an image on his smartphone.

'Phoebe Kingshaw saw this somewhere and took a photo of it. In fact, it was the last photograph she ever took.'

'Taken at the school?'

'Undoubtedly. The question is, where? And why isn't its existence public knowledge?'

'Perhaps someone is trying to suppress it and Kingshaw was killed because she threatened to expose the secret?'

'That's plausible,' said Shunter, tapping the screen. It showed a neatly typed page of manuscript. 'After all, if this really is the lost manuscript of *Wallowing in the Mire*, this is huge news. It must be worth millions. And you're saying that McNabb doesn't know about this?'

'He hasn't mentioned it. I guess he's not an Agnes Crabbe fan and didn't recognise what he was looking at. He's so obsessed with nailing Sir Giles that he's pretty blind to anything else at the moment.'

'We need to get it verified,' said Shunter. 'I can talk to Andrew Tremens.'

'The solicitor who handles the Crabbe estate?'

'He's the expert,' said Shunter. 'I'll try to get hold of him, though it is the start of the weekend and he tends to go partying in London or Bristol. Not much of a gay scene in sleepy Bowcester. We might not get hold of him until Monday.'

'I'm not sure I can wait that long before telling McNabb about this.'

'Then don't. I'll text the photos to Tremens now.'

There was a sudden resounding cheer from the public bar as Barry Chetwynd arrived to lead the Shaggy Beast hunt. With him was someone that Shunter and Jaine both recognised.

'Bloody hell. Is that Pamela Dallimore?' asked Jaine.

'It is,' said Shunter, noting with interest the hockey stick that Chetwynd handed to her. 'Now what, I wonder, is she doing hanging about with that lot?'

Sir Giles and the woman he now knew to be Lorraine Butler – actor, single, no children, currently 'resting' between jobs – had enjoyed a lovely evening. For Giles, it had been a genuine pleasure to relax and to discuss subjects far removed from business and politics. He'd initially been wary, suspecting that she might be an undercover reporter, or even a call girl, which was why he'd plumped for giving her a false name. But as the hours had passed by and drinks had come and gone, he'd let his guard down a little. She didn't appear to have recognised him and she hadn't asked him anything that might have revealed any kind of hidden agenda.

The bar downstairs was starting to empty and Lorraine did the same to her glass. She glanced at her phone.

'Blimey, look at the time,' she said. 'I should be getting off home now. Last trains and all that.'

'I can pop you in a taxi if you'd like,' said Giles.

'No, it's fine,' said Lorraine. 'I've got my ticket already. Shame to waste it.'

'Of course. Well, it's been lovely to meet you, Lorraine.'

'Lovely to meet you too, Gerry. It's no fun drinking alone, is it? I went for an audition but no one else fancied a drink afterwards. You made my evening much nicer than I thought it would be.'

'I'm delighted.'

'Perhaps we could meet up again sometime. For coffee, maybe?'

'That would be nice. But I'm only here for a few days.'

'Is tomorrow good? Or is that too short notice?'

'No, not at all,' said Giles. 'Can I call you?'

Lorraine smiled and gave him her number. Then she leaned over the table to peck him on the cheek and was gone.

At ten o'clock, the Shaggy Beast hunters, many of whom had been drinking steadily for two hours, boarded the minibus they'd booked to take them to Black Dog Wood. Across the street in an unmarked car, McNabb watched them leave. He'd driven into Nasely out of boredom and in the hope that he might spot Frank Shunter, the man to whom Sir Giles had given the brown envelope. He'd quickly put a name to the face; there were plenty of interviews and press photos of Shunter online, and the man even seemed to be some kind of folk hero to his subordinates. The ex-detective had been instrumental in catching the murderer of Shirley Pomerance but, at the same time, he had helped to destroy the career of the previous DI, Brian Blount. McNabb wondered what Shunter's involvement was now, and at the back of his mind a tiny voice was already implying that Sir Giles had hired him to do the same kind of hatchet job on his career. He shook off his paranoia and concentrated on the task in hand.

The Happy Onion had been the obvious building to watch as it was the only place open at this time of night and, sure enough, he'd quickly sighted his quarry at the bar. He'd stopped short of going inside because the inhabitants of small villages like Nasely tended not to trust outsiders, especially ones who asked questions about one of the locals. Instead, he'd parked up nearby and waited. The subsequent meeting between Shunter and Cliff Jaine had momentarily made him extremely angry. But it had proven to him that his instincts were right – no one could be trusted.

As the Shaggy Beast hunters drove away in the minibus, he called his sister.

'Any news?'

'Lorraine has made contact,' said Ettie.

'Who?' said McNabb. 'No, never mind. I just need to know where he goes, who he sees, what he says.'

'You must want this bloke really badly to be going to all this trouble.'

'You have no idea,' said McNabb.

Chapter 19

The hunting party arrived at the mausoleum car park and discovered, to their surprise, that they were not the only visitors to Black Dog Wood on this particular night. As their minibus's headlights swept across a sea of steamed-up cars, panicky faces appeared at misty windscreens. A pair of white buttocks, pressed up against the glass of a Toyota's passenger door, gleamed brightly and, beyond the cars, groups of naked or semi-naked people suddenly found themselves bathed in the unflattering light. With all thoughts of sex forgotten, the doggers starburst in every direction. Some made a dash for their own cars and sped off, not taking the time to get dressed or to wait for their passengers. Still more plunged into the dark woods on bare feet, fearing that the white minibus that had suddenly appeared was full of police officers. The last person to disappear was seen desperately running as fast as any middle-aged man can run with his trousers around his ankles.

'Was that Tony Hemerton hobbling away with his pants down?' asked Charlie Barnfather.

'Must be on the last leg of his European sex tour,' said Gerry Waxleigh, laughing. 'Or last leg-over.'

'That'll teach the bloody bugger to go dogging in our woods,' snorted Len Youlden.

Everyone in the minibus was laughing, except the driver.

'I'm not waiting for you,' he said, a note of worry in his voice. 'If the police come along they'll think I'm with that lot. I'm not getting arrested for sex I haven't even had.'

'Then come back and pick us up in an hour,' said Barry Chetwynd. 'Unless we call you first.'

As the minibus drove off, several nervous-looking people dared to come out of the woods under cover of darkness and were creeping nakedly towards their cars when they saw the torches of the hunting party approaching. They also spotted the baseball bats, golf clubs and, bizarrely, a dog catcher. The beleaguered sex enthusiasts took once more to the trees.

The Shaggy Beast stopped to tackle an irritating itch. It was in a very awkward and intimate place and it required a degree of bodily contortion to reach it, a situation that wasn't helped by its formidable erection. As it scratched, its ears picked up distant shouts and cries of alarm and it turned its head to the left and right to get a better sense of where these new sounds were coming from. They weren't coming from Gertie's Plash; it had got quite used to the regular chug and hum of the generator and pumps. This was something else.

'Doggers,' grumbled the Beast, just as three naked women came crashing out of the undergrowth and onto the path. Upon seeing the monster, they stopped in their tracks. Two of the women immediately turned and ran back the way they'd come, screaming. The third stood her ground, her face aghast and her mouth opening and closing soundlessly as she pointed a shaky finger at the Beast's face and then at its engorged genitals. Her eyes rolled up into her head and she crumpled to the ground. The Beast cursed and moved to check that she was all right but then it caught sight of torches flashing among the trees in the direction from which the women had come.

'Blast it!' said the Shaggy Beast, and ran away in the opposite direction.

'Bloody hell, look at that!' said Barnfather, and the hunters' torches all shone in the direction that he was indicating with his finger. Two naked women could be seen dashing between the trees. Janus Gugge gurned lecherously.

'I swear that's the blonde waitress who works at the Gondolier restaurant,' said Munsun.

'Not a natural blonde, apparently,' said Waxleigh. 'I can understand the appeal of these hunts of yours now, Barry.'

The hunters emerged on to a path and found themselves staring at a large, unconscious and wholly naked woman lying on her back. Janus Gugge's lickerish grin melted away and he let forth a wretched primaeval howl of anguish as he recognised his mother.

Jamie Cordery's Friday night was also turning into a nightmare. In recent months, he and his partner, Keeley, had spiced up their sex life by adding a little jeopardy, but what had started out as sneaky knee-tremblers down alleyways and behind buildings had quickly progressed to ever more risky liaisons in public places such as changing rooms, cinemas and late night train carriages. They'd even joined the Mile High Club in the cramped toilet of a flight from Bristol to Zante. Keeley had been delighted but had soon wanted even bigger thrills. And having recently discovered the existence of a local dogging group, she had suggested that she and Jamie give it a go. Jamie had been less enthusiastic about the idea; while he wasn't averse to a woodland romp now and again, he wasn't so keen on the idea of being watched while on the job. Nor did he particularly like the thought of other men leering – and worse – over his naked girlfriend, especially as she seemed to enjoy the attention. And, to top it all, he wasn't going to quickly forget their recent encounter with the Shaggy Beast. But he'd agreed to give it a try and now, as he ran stark naked through the woods with a mob of what might be police officers chasing after him, he cursed the whole concept of dogging and promised himself that this would be his and Keeley's last time. There was always a chance of being caught – that was part of the rush – but this was infinitely more terrifying than the risk of being rumbled *in flagrante delicto* in a cubicle at Matalan.

A cruel bramble raked across his shin but Cordery didn't care. He was just thankful it hadn't been two feet higher where his genitals, despite doing their level best in the cold night air to look inconspicuous, would have borne the brunt of their attack. Running at such speed, and with so many tripping hazards around, it was a minor miracle that he hadn't already ended up face down in the dirt. The sound of voices behind him appeared to have receded so he decided to risk slowing to a gentle jog and then to a full stop so that he could catch his breath. The last time he'd run this kind of a distance was around fifteen years and three stones ago and he hungrily gulped the cool night air and wished that he was fitter. After a minute there were still no signs of pursuit, but a vague shape had appeared out of the gloom in front of him. It was impossible to identify the figure at this distance but, he reasoned, if it was coming from the opposite direction from which he had run, it was unlikely to be the police. It was probably one of his dogging companions, he thought, maybe even Keeley. Cupping his shrivelled scrotum in a gesture that was part modesty, part shame, but mostly an attempt to warm things up down there, he began to feel a slight sense of relief. But as the figure got closer, it began to morph into something strange and deformed and definitely not a fellow naked human.

'Fuck! Not again!' shouted Cordery as red eyes, snarling jaws and a massive penis came swimming into view. He turned on his heel and ran, but then his foot caught under a gnarled root and he slammed face-first into a silver birch. He dropped heavily to the ground, as senseless as a bag of cement.

'Not another one,' sighed the Shaggy Beast.

It looked down at the unconscious naked man at its feet and then up towards the sound of distant voices and torches flashing among the trees. In an instant, the Beast had made a decision. It unzipped its skin and quickly stepped out of it. It took several anxious minutes of hard physical work to push Cordery inside the costume and to zip it back up again but, with what seemed like seconds to spare, its former occupant ducked down silently among the browning fronds of a thick stand of bracken and waited.

The hunters came out of the dark, waving their sports equipment in a vaguely threatening manner and shining their torches around them. Mrs Gugge had regained her senses and was sheepishly walking along in front of her humiliated son, wearing his coat as best she could. Unfortunately, while Janus was a big man, his mother was a great deal bigger and the best she'd been able to manage was to drape the coat over her prodigious bosom. Meanwhile, her heavily applied make-up had been smeared across her cheeks and lent her face a tragic quality, like a clown that had been left out in the rain.

'Bloody hell!' yelled Barry Chetwynd excitedly. 'Look! We've caught it!' He pointed at the insensible hairy figure lying face down in the deep carpet of dead leaves. Mrs Gugge saw the Beast and stepped backwards, tripping over a log. Janus made a conspicuous show of failing to catch her as she fell. The hunters ran excitedly across the open ground to surround the recumbent figure. Inspector Verma pushed his way through the small crowd and went to place the loop of his dog catcher around the Shaggy Beast's neck in case it woke up.

'It's just a bloke in a wolf costume,' he said disappointedly, spotting the zipper that ran the length of the creature's back.

'Bollocks,' said Chetwynd.

The area was suddenly illuminated by a series of blinding flashes as Pamela Dallimore danced around the unconscious figure, taking photos from every angle. The Shaggy Beast stirred and rolled over, its mighty erection springing into view. Mrs Dallimore's camera went into overdrive. Cordery opened his eyes and, seeing the hunters standing over him, screamed once before Janus Gugge, in no mood for any more surprises, rapped him sharply on his costumed head with an antique baffing spoon and rendered him once again out for the count.

'Get that mask off,' said Len Youlden. 'Let's see who the bugger is.'

'And if he's still alive,' said Gerry Waxleigh. He held on to the Shaggy Beast's ears and slowly pulled the costume's head off.

'Who on earth is that?' said Chetwynd as Cordery's pink face appeared.

'Probably one of them doggers,' said Youlden. 'Serve him bloody right too for using our woods. Let's call for the minibus.'

'No signal,' said Waxleigh, checking his phone.

'Back to the car park then.'

'We can't just leave him here,' said Inspector Verma.

'Why not?' asked Youlden. 'He was like this when we found him.'

'What if something happens to him?' said Verma. 'I'm not

having that on my conscience. We should at least carry him back to the car park where he can be found by his friends.'

'Bloody bugger,' grumbled Youlden.

Keeley Flosser crouched among the bushes and sobbed. She wasn't someone who was given to crying and she had been known to mock others for being overly sensitive. But now that she was naked, alone and lost in a cold dark wood, she didn't feel quite so cocky. During their panicky flight, she and Jamie had become separated. Their pursuers, whoever they were, hadn't come her way but she hoped that Jamie hadn't been caught and that he'd made it back to the car and was even now sitting in the driver's seat with the heating cranked up, impatiently waiting for her to return. The problem was that she had no idea which way the car park was. She knew that it was close to a tall monument with a golden pig at the top, but her hiding place was deep inside the most densely planted part of the woods. Sir Redvers Whorne had indulged his family by creating a pinetum – it was rumoured to be the original meeting place of the Diabolical Club – and nothing was visible through the evergreen canopy. She had to venture out of the trees and find a path where she might be better able to spot Monty's Folly – a risky move, for sure, because if the police really were out in force in the woods tonight, there was a good chance that she'd be spotted. But would it be so bad to get arrested, she thought? It wasn't as if she'd been involved in a serious crime or anything, and at least then she'd be warm and safe. And besides, there was something else in these woods, something monstrous and frightening. She shivered as she thought about the creature that she and Jamie had seen just a few nights before, and she recalled childhood warnings to 'stay on the path'. She took a couple of deep breaths, slowly stood up and looked about her. There didn't appear to be anyone in sight so she broke off a couple of large fern fronds behind which she could preserve her modesty and then, looking something like a tatty Moulin Rouge fan dancer, she crept through the pinetum in search of the nearest footpath. After five minutes, to her dismay, there was still no sign of a path but her ears had started to detect a rhythmic throbbing sound. It was deep and regular and mechanical and where there was machinery, thought Keeley, there was probably some kind of building or vehicle to shelter inside.

The Shaggy Beast costume's original wearer shivered and watched from behind a screen of ferns as the hunters staggered off into the dark, four of them unenthusiastically half-carrying and half-dragging the Shaggy Beast between them.

Once the coast was clear, the former Beast made off nimbly through the woods with a familiarity that was quite lacking in any of the doggers.

As Keeley got nearer to the Plash she could see a small encampment of tents and four or five people sitting around a modest fire, swigging from cans of beer and chatting. Keeley stared longingly at the fire and the nearby Portakabin with its welcoming walls and likely heater within, and agonised over whether she dared to make a run for it.

'Are you thinking of trying to get to that hut?' said a whispered voice at her shoulder.

Keeley jumped. She turned and found herself unexpectedly facing a pretty young girl with brightly dyed red hair. She too was completely naked and Keeley felt immediately dowdy by comparison. She envied the girl's body confidence and wondered how she had failed to spot her among the doggers at the car park earlier.

'Jessie,' said the girl, extending a hand.

'Keeley.'

'So are we doing this?' asked Jessie. 'We can't stay out here all night stark bollock naked. I'm freezing my arse off.'

'Doing what?' asked Keeley.

'Come on,' said Jessie.

Jessie Tremblett strode boldly into the campsite and put her hands on her hips.

'OK, which one of you lot has some spare clothes they could lend us?' she said to her goggle-eyed audience. 'And a drink would be good too.'

The Shaggy Beast hunters arrived back at the car park and called for the minibus to collect them. There were fewer parked cars now than there had been before; most of the doggers had found their way back and made their escape. One unfortunate couple emerged from the trees while the hunters were waiting for their ride but, upon seeing the weapons and, more shockingly, the wolf-man-like figure lying unconscious or dead at their feet, they took to the woods once again.

The minibus arrived and the driver urged them to get on board as quickly as possible.

'Hey, Pamela! We need to go!' shouted Chetwynd from the passenger seat.

Mrs Dallimore signalled with her hand and took a final few photographs of the Beast with its mask now firmly back in place before climbing on board the bus. As she did so, she looked out of the window at Mrs Gugge, who had elected to remain behind to wait for her husband, who – to Janus's further cringing embarrassment – had apparently also been among the doggers. The family car was in the car park, which meant that he was still at large, and Janus had offered to remain behind with his mother out of a sense of duty.

'What a splendid evening,' said Gerry Waxleigh, grinning. 'Why don't we do this more often?'

At Gertie's Plash, the fire was out and the students had zippered shut their tent flaps. Jessie Tremblett had decided that she would spend the night with a big, good-looking Scot called Dougie and was now feeling warm and cosy in his arms. Keeley, meanwhile, had elected to sleep in the Portakabin on a makeshift bed made of donated coats. She wondered where her boyfriend was and what he was doing right now.

Elsewhere in the woods, the last few doggers had found each other and, after some initial huddling together for warmth, they had felt safe enough to continue doing what they'd come to the woods to do in the first place. Some had enjoyed themselves so heartily that they were already planning their next visit.

Chapter 20

The minibus deposited its cargo in Nasely High Street and the members of the hunting party made their way to their homes. Barry Chetwynd trudged despondently up the stairs to the office above his shop and poured himself a brandy. On his desk lay the Shaggy Beast scrapbook that he had meticulously curated since he was a boy. He flicked idly through the pages. He had always dreamed of being the first person to catch the elusive monster but now, at the age of forty-four, his dreams lay in ruins, shattered by some chubby bloke in a wolf costume. It hadn't even been a particularly convincing costume and, to make matters worse, Pamela Dallimore had taken hundreds of photographs. She would undoubtedly use them to accompany whatever feature she chose to write, and how the world would laugh at the country bumpkins and their ridiculous quest to catch a man in a panto costume. He felt sick. He downed his brandy and was about to pour another when he reminded himself that he had to open the shop at 8:30 a.m. He stoppered the bottle, locked up and walked home wearing a scowl that would curdle milk.

Jamie Cordery sat on a chair in front of the custody officer at Bowcester Police Station and protested his innocence. He'd been found and roused by a police constable called Dudfoot who'd responded to an anonymous tip-off, presumably from one of the doggers. He'd also found a shamefaced farmer's boy and his large and powerful mother who'd been trying to hide her nakedness under an ill-fitting coat. The lady had initially resisted attempts to get her into the police car but had eventually capitulated, and all three had been taken to Bowcester. The police doctor had been called to check Cordery over and had pronounced that he was fit to be interviewed, despite the egg-shaped lump on his head. Janus Gugge and his mother, meanwhile, were awaiting the arrival of Mr Gugge senior, who hadn't been best pleased to get a call on his phone to come and collect his family from the station. Mrs Gugge had barely said a word since getting into the car. She was saving up all of her anger and feelings of humiliation for the man who had abandoned her to save his own skin. Janus simply looked mortified, as any adult would upon discovering that his fifty-something aged parents engaged in public sex with strangers.

The custody officer recorded Cordery's personal details on her computer and then asked him to give his version of events.

'I swear I have no idea how I came to be in this suit,' he explained. 'I ran into a tree and knocked myself out. After that, it's all a bit hazy.'

'And you say that you were naked until that point?'

'Admittedly, yes.'

'So someone just randomly stuffed you inside it. Is that what you're saying?' asked the custody officer.

'Yes,' said Cordery, standing up. 'I've never seen this suit before tonight. Well, no, that's not true. I saw it a few nights ago but someone else was wearing it then. My girlfriend will tell you it's true, if you can find her.'

The custody officer looked with some small degree of disgust at the anatomically correct and monstrously oversized rubber penis that was stapled to the crotch of the costume. 'For pity's sake, please sit down, Mr Cordery,' she said. 'It's staring right at me.'

'You think I'm happy with this horrible thing hanging off the front of me?' said Cordery. He grasped the organ with both hands and began pulling hard on it. Janus Gugge attempted to shield his mother's eyes with a spade-like hand. There was the sound of tearing fabric and the dildo came away in Cordery's hands, taking just enough material with it to give the custody officer a brief glimpse of the rather less impressive set of genitals nestling beneath. Cordery sat down quickly and placed the offending sex toy on the desk. The custody officer seemed quite nonplussed by his act of self-emasculation and merely raised an eyebrow.

'All done?' she asked. 'Good. So tell me again, why were you running around naked in the woods?'

'I was... you know... dogging. In the car park by the mausoleum,' said Cordery. 'We weren't doing any harm. But then we got chased into the woods by a gang of nutters with torches and clubs and— Bugger!' Cordery thrust his hand through the hole in his crotch and scratched furiously at something. Janus Gugge went to cover his mother's eyes again but she slapped his hand away.

'Ah yes. You described them as pensioners earlier,' said Custody, referring to her notes. 'Terrifying.'

'There's no need to be sarcastic. It was dark,' protested Cordery, still scratching. 'We had no idea who they were when we first saw the van arrive. We thought they were coppers so we just ran. Then I saw this werewolf thing and I got scared and ran into a tree and knocked myself out. When I woke up, I was wearing the werewolf costume instead and there were these old blokes standing around me carrying cricket bats and tennis rackets and someone was taking photographs. Then something hit me on the head and when I woke up again I was in the car park. Shit!' He scratched angrily at his stomach. 'Have you got anything else I could wear? I swear this thing is infested. And it smells funny too.'

'We'll sort you out a tracksuit,' said the custody officer. 'Put him in Cell 2 and get him a jogging suit from stores, will you, Hillsy?'

'Righto,' said the gaoler. As the thoroughly miserable Cordery was led away, hands covering the window in his crotch, the custody officer scratched her chin.

'What do you reckon, Cliff?' she asked.

'What he says has a ring of truth to it,' said Jaine. Out of idle curiosity, he'd come into the custody suite during Cordery's questioning. There wasn't much going on that required a CID officer and anything that happened in Black Dog Wood was potentially of interest to him. 'And I'm pretty sure I know who those pensioners are that he was talking about and I wouldn't put it past them. It all looks like a prank gone wrong to me. No real crime being committed.'

'That's what I figured. In that case, all we really have is breach of the peace. We'll keep him in overnight and then let the magistrate have him in the morning,' said Custody.

There was a sudden commotion as Mrs Gugge leapt from the bench upon which she'd been quietly sitting and launched herself towards the small red-faced man who had just entered the custody suite with PC Dudfoot.

'I'll fucking kill you!' she screamed.

'Listen dear, I can— Oof!' pleaded her cringing spouse before being silenced by a big right fist landing on the side of his head.

Chapter 21

Constance Tremblett stood in the middle of a chilly, foggy field, her pack of assorted mongrels pronking and stotting around her ankles, and braced herself. Then, as she had done every morning for the past six decades of her eighty-two years on the planet, she spread her feet, raised her fists to the sky and shouted 'Bastard!' as loud as she could. Her morning ritual completed, she emitted a thunderously loud fart and then ambled back towards the farmhouse to oversee breakfast for her extended family.

Gertie's Plash was looking very sorry for itself. The steep sides of the bowl-shaped pond were covered in a green mat of drying algae and the water was now half its usual depth. Ken Arthur had made an early start and was checking over the equipment when Dr Pantridge arrived on site.

'I hear there was a bit of excitement here last night,' he said.

'No real problems on site,' said Arthur. 'But apparently the woods were full of doggers and Shaggy Beast hunters.'

'Looks to me like the pond will be drained by tomorrow so we'll need to get the students in there today to grab a few more plants,' said Pantridge. 'We don't have any specimens of marsh haseltine or Hodge's water iris yet. I have no idea what they are but they're on the list we were given by Natural England.'

'Best we go and wake them up then.'

As the two men roused their grumbling students, two pairs of eyes assessed them from a vantage point behind a dense screen of holly.

'Those pumps are bloody powerful,' said Bron. 'And there are people permanently on site now. I count six or seven, maybe?'

'So what do we do?' asked Willy.

'We go home and get some breakfast inside us. And then we need to talk to Colin.'

In Nasely, Shunter and Jaine had met for breakfast and, as usual, the proprietor of the village café was proving her worth as the fount of all knowledge.

'Colin Tossel from the Historical Society, he's your man,' said Mrs Moore. 'What he doesn't know about the Herewardshire Rifles isn't worth knowing. Or Mad Connie, maybe? Her father was one of the Lucky Six.'

'I've heard this woman mentioned before,' said Shunter. 'I'm not reassured by the word "mad".'

'Oh, she's not really mad, not in a medical sense,' said Mrs Moore. 'Eccentric, more like. She's what they used to call one of the "cunning folk". You know – wise women, fortune tellers, all that crowd. She knows all about local folklore and healing plants and I've heard stories of her curing people that medical science had given up on. I'm not joking. Some people say she's a witch but she doesn't do spells or anything. At least, I don't think she does.'

'So no dancing around naked under a full moon then?' said Jaine, with a smile.

'Connie Tremblett is in her eighties. I don't think she dances around anything these days, naked or otherwise,' said Mrs Moore. 'But talking of naked, did you hear about the shenanigans in Black Dog Wood last night? Apparently, there was some kind of orgy going on and...'

Professor Gravestock was reading a newspaper in the hotel's breakfast room when Mrs Dallimore appeared. She was looking tired, he thought, and he mentioned it as he invited her to join him at his table.

'It was a late night,' she explained. 'But I got some good photos and half an hour of decent video.'

'Of the monster?'

'Of some joker in a wolf suit,' said Mrs Dallimore. 'No surprises there. I hadn't expected there to be a real Shaggy Beast.'

'Try to keep an open mind. Just because last night turned out to be a bust, it doesn't mean that every sighting has been a hoax for the past two hundred and fifty years,' said Gravestock. 'And there are craftier ways to catch a Shaggy Beast than blundering about in the dark with a cricket bat. In my room I have motion-triggered trail cameras, tree cams, boulder cams, all sorts of covert devices that I plan to set up in various places around the woods. If there's anything there, I'll find it.'

'Perhaps I'll hang around for a day or two more then,' said Mrs Dallimore.

Constance Tremblett was still sprightly for a woman of eighty-two but her right hip was giving her gyp and it had caused her to adopt a clumsy, limping gait in which most of her weight was put onto her left side. It had also meant her relying on a walking stick, which was next to useless when traipsing across muddy fields. She had been offered a hip replacement but had refused the operation on the grounds that she would be taking up a bed needed by someone with more than a decade of life left to them. And besides, she had nothing but bad memories when it came to hospitals. She rubbed at her eyepatch. Her left eye had been missing for seventy years but it still itched regularly.

She shooed away a brace of feral pigs that were blocking her path and an alpaca that was begging for treats; the estate boasted over three hundred and fifty animals of various kinds and they all needed feeding. Keeping them alive and healthy was a daily chore that took the efforts of everyone who lived at Paradise Farm: Constance's three children, Finbarr, Eunice and Winifred, their partners, and the grandchildren and great-grandchildren.

In the large stone-flagged kitchen, she found Winifred and daughter-in-law Beatrice frying bacon. The pig it had come from, a fine fat Herewardshire Hog, had been freed onto Tremblett land by animal rights activists who had assumed that an estate with so many different kinds of animals must belong to an animal lover. Sure enough, Connie did love animals but not in any sentimental way. She ensured that every animal on the farm had a good, healthy, free-range life, but she didn't give names to any of her more edible menagerie and she discouraged the grandchildren and great-grandchildren from doing that too. She believed it was a fox-eat-chicken, cat-eat-mouse, human-eat-pig world, and she lived by the maxim that humans were part of the food chain, not something above or beyond it. It wasn't a view shared by her son, Finbarr, and his twin sons, Bron and Willy. They had been vegetarians their whole lives. But almost everyone else enjoyed a slice of bacon with some freshly laid eggs at breakfast time and the family nearly always ate together at the start of the day.

'Not a scrap of grass left in the lower fields,' said Connie. 'We'll have to move the cows onto the meadow.'

'Horses are in there,' said Winifred. 'And the zebra.'

'And the emu,' chipped in Beatrice.

'They won't mind sharing,' said Connie. 'Get the boys to put out some extra hay bales and water. When's breakfast ready?'

'Ten minutes,' said Winifred. 'The grandchildren are out collecting the eggs.'

'And did Jessie come home last night?'

'Early hours of this morning, but she came home,' said Winifred.

'Wonders will never cease,' said Connie. She walked out of the kitchen and as she ascended the staircase in the hall, Winifred and Beatrice were treated to a series of small farts, one for every step.

'I don't think she even realises she's doing it any more,' said Beatrice.

'We need to get her a stairlift,' said Winifred. 'For the sake of her hip and our noses.'

Jack Stillaway smiled grimly as he aimed his service revolver at a spot between Sir Charles's pleading eyes. He unwound a green puttee from around his lower leg and threw it at his kneeling prisoner.

'Tie it around your eyes like a blindfold,' he said. 'I want you to know how it feels to be blind and helpless like we were. Do it!'

Alyface, his hands still bound together at the wrists, began sobbing as he wound the cloth around his head.

'Please... don't do this,' he pleaded. 'I know that you don't want to do this... er...'

'You don't even know my name, do you?' said Stillaway, with a sneer on his disfigured face. 'I was just a number to you. Just one of the millions. Cheap and disposable, like that puttee.'

'I didn't know!' said Sir Charles. 'I'd never heard of chlorine gas before! I had no idea how dangerous it was. If I had, I'd never have ordered you to march forward. Please... don't hurt me!'

'I can still hear the screams as my friends' tears turned to fire,' said Stillaway. 'We tried to keep the gas out of our eyes with our puttees. But it didn't work. We escaped by desperately grasping on to each other, the blind leading the blind. The dark made the terror so much worse. I had to crawl over still-warm bodies, through the freshly spilled blood of men I'd grown up with, men I'd trained with, eaten and laughed with. And all the time with my eyes tightly closed and never knowing where or when the next shell would land and whether my name was on it. And now you're as helpless as your men were back there on the battlefield. How does it feel, your Lordship, not knowing when death will take you?'

Sir Charles stuttered and his face took on a ghastly pallid hue. His tears began to soak the puttee.

'Please... have mercy... plea—'

He clutched suddenly at his chest and, with a groan, collapsed and fell into the shallow grave that he'd been forced to dig.

Stillaway saluted the dead man at his feet. Justice had been done and he hadn't had to pull the trigger himself, for which he was thankful. He wasn't sure that he would have had the will to do so.

He finished shovelling earth on to the lifeless body and then dressed the freshly turned ground with leaves and branches.

The rain began to fall as he walked off into the darkening woods.

'Bloody hell,' said Jaine. He was reading an A4 printout of one of the two pages of manuscript that had been found among the photographs on Phoebe Kingshaw's phone. 'That is pretty much an exact description of my crime scene. That can't be a coincidence.'

'I agree,' said Shunter. 'And Agnes Crabbe wrote it around the time that your soldier was buried. It's like she was there. Or, at the very least, had it described to her.'

'But by who?'

'It's frustrating that all we have is two pages,' said Shunter. 'But we know where the rest of it probably is.' He tapped the screen of his phone. 'Check out the time stamps of the photos that immediately precede those of the manuscript.'

Jaine swiped through a series of images. 'That's Miss Bultitude's office. I recognise it. I took her written statement in there.'

'I thought it might be. The time stamps show that these were taken three minutes before she photographed the pages. So the manuscript is in Miss Bultitude's office and probably in that chest that sits under the window.'

'Unless Kingshaw took it with her for her rendezvous with Sir Giles,' said Jaine. 'Wait... do you suppose that's why he put her in place at the school? To look for the manuscript?'

'It's possible. Although that would mean that he had prior knowledge of its existence. The alternative is that Kingshaw found it by accident. Either way, I reckon she was taking the manuscript to Sir Giles, or maybe proof of its existence on her phone, when she was killed.'

'But why would he then kill her?'

'No idea. But I don't think he killed her anyway.'

'Who did then? Miss Bultitude? To keep the manuscript a secret, perhaps?'

'Whoever has possession is sitting on a gold mine,' said Shunter.

'Which points suspicion away from Sir Giles. He's a multi-millionaire already.'

'Not necessarily. It's been my experience that the richer some people get, the greedier they become,' said Shunter. 'Or maybe he simply didn't want Miss Bultitude to have it. It's no secret that he wants Harpax Grange, and if she's sitting on a valuable nest egg, she won't feel under any financial pressure to sell it to him.'

'But neither of them could profit from selling the manuscript, could they? Wouldn't it belong to the Crabbe estate, to her descendants?'

'That doesn't mean they can't publish the contents,' said Shunter. 'Copyright expires seventy years after the death of an author. Agnes Crabbe died in 1944.'

Jaine did some quick mental arithmetic.

'It's public domain now,' he said.

'Exactly,' said Shunter. 'Whoever publishes the book first reaps the benefits. I reckon the deal could be worth millions.'

'And that's a pretty good motive for murder,' said Jaine.

'So you're an actress,' said Giles. 'Would I have seen any of your work?'

'Depends on the sort of films you watch,' said Lorraine. 'They don't get a cinema release.'

'They're not porn films, are they?'

'No they are not, you cheeky sod!' said Lorraine, slapping him playfully. 'They're independent films.'

'Sorry, couldn't resist,' said Giles with a smile. He and Lorraine had met for coffee at a little café in the Newburgh Quarter of Soho. He was dressed in a nondescript pair of corduroys, flat cap and polo shirt. Lorraine was wearing figure-hugging jeans, a jumper and raincoat but, he noted, she looked just as glamorous as she had the night before.

'Anyway, enough about me,' said Lorraine. 'You never did tell me what you do.'

'I'm a meat producer,' said Giles. 'Is that all right?'

'Why shouldn't it be?'

'I'm always a little nervous about admitting it because some people have such strong objections. I had red paint thrown over me by a militant vegan once.'

'No, not me. I love my meat,' said Lorraine. 'It's funny, though... I thought last night that I recognised you. Like you'd been on the telly or something.'

'Er... maybe,' said Giles. 'In an old episode of *Countryfile* or something, I expect.'

'Maybe,' said Lorraine. 'So what brings you to London?'

'I have a... oh, hang on, I'd better answer this.' He took his mobile out of his pocket and walked away from Lorraine to take the call. 'Hello?'

'Hello. I hope I'm not calling at an inconvenient time.'

'No, you're fine,' said Giles. 'What can I do for you, Mr Shunter?'

'I need to ask you a quick question,' said Shunter. 'And I need you to be completely honest with me.'

'Very well.'

'Was Miss Kingshaw's appointment in any way connected to Agnes Crabbe?'

'Agnes Crabbe? No. Why?'

'Just one of several ideas I'm kicking about.'

'I'm intrigued.'

'It's probably nothing,' said Shunter. 'I'm just eliminating possibilities and following a few leads.'

'Well, if you could follow them a bit more quickly I'd be obliged. I'm due to report back to the police station on Monday and if there's nothing new to support my defence, I'm sunk. I'm relying on you, Mr Shunter.'

'I don't think he knows about the manuscript,' said Shunter.

'Do you believe that?' asked Jaine.

'He sounded genuinely surprised by the question.'

'So bang goes his motive for murder? That means we're back to square one and possibly Miss Bultitude as the killer.'

'Or it could just have been some totally random nutter who found her alone in the woods. Let's face it, it happens.'

'A case of wrong place, wrong time and a big dose of bad luck?'

'Maybe. And speaking of luck, I think we need to speak to someone about the Lucky Six. I suspect that the identity of your blindfolded soldier may be important.'

'Really?'

'I have a hunch that both murders are connected via the manuscript,' said Shunter. He counted off the points on his fingers. 'One: the manuscript is hidden somewhere in Harpax Grange. Two: your crime scene matches the finale of the manuscript. Three: the house and grounds belonged to Sir Giles's family at the time of your soldier's death. And four: Kingshaw was his mistress and she may have been killed because she found the manuscript. There are too many crossovers for me to ignore them, and nor should you. I reckon that if we assume both murders are connected in some way, we'll double our chances of success.'

'So who will you speak to? That Tossel bloke? The local historian?'

'Not if I can help it,' said Shunter. 'His writing is OK but he's the dullest man on earth. His voice is like white noise.'

'That bad, eh?'

'I think I might pay a call on Constance Tremblett instead. She sounds like a much more entertaining prospect.'

The two men parted company and returned to their cars. Jaine drove off towards Bowcester while Shunter headed out on the Coxeter Road towards the remote farming hamlet of Ordon. Some distance behind him, DI McNabb followed in his own car like a cat stalking a fledgling.

Chapter 22

'A man phoned asking to speak to you while you was out feeding the capybaras,' said Beatrice.

'What man?' asked Connie. She sat down heavily on a settle by the kitchen door and tugged off her Wellington boots.

'Said his name was Hunter. Or Thumper. Something like that. Asked if he could come and see you.'

'And can he?'

'I said you was out in the fields but if he pops by after twelve you'd probably be free.'

'Hmf,' said Connie. 'Not selling nothing, is he?'

'Said he just wants to ask you some questions about your dad and about when you was a girl.'

'Hmf,' said Connie again. 'Barely remember which way to put my knickers on most mornings.'

'Luscott-Whorne. Hyphenated,' said Lorraine. 'Very posh.'

'Maybe once upon a time,' said Sir Giles. 'But everyone's at it these days. Isn't there some footballer's wife who has about three hyphens now?'

'But you make it sound posh with your accent,' said Lorraine. 'And you're a Sir!'

'I must say I'm surprised by how well you've taken the news of my circumstances. I expected you to run a mile when I told you.'

'Oh, I don't think you did the murder,' said Lorraine.

'That's good to hear. Because I didn't.'

'I wouldn't be sitting here if I thought you had. Oh, hang on, it's my phone ringing now. Excuse me.'

As Lorraine walked off to take the call, Sir Giles found himself questioning what he was doing. Just a few days after the cold-blooded murder of his mistress, here he was, sitting in a Soho café laughing and joking with another attractive woman. And she was very attractive, he thought. In many ways, she reminded him of Phoebe – the curves, the dress sense, even the hairstyle, although it was the wrong colour. She didn't have Phoebe's quick wit and fierce intelligence but she more than made up for it with her bubbly personality and sense of humour. Giles had warmed to her from the start. Which was why he'd decided to drop the whole 'Gerry' business and come clean to her about his real identity. The fact that she had accepted things the way they were had endeared her to him even more.

McNabb sat in his car and ruminated like one of the large brown cows that regarded him balefully from the nearest field. He'd got up early in order to follow Shunter and had seen him meet with Cliff Jaine at the café. He was therefore no longer in any doubt that his detective sergeant had been compromised. He'd then tailed Shunter all the way to Ordon but had stopped short of following him up the drive to the Trembletts' farmhouse. Instead, he'd parked up in a lay-by and waited. He noted that the sign on the gatepost that had once said PARADISE FARMHOUSE now said AR...SE AR...SE. The ghosts of the letters that had fallen off, or more likely had been picked off, were still visible like dark shadows on the bleached wood. McNabb half-smiled, but his amusement was short-lived and he soon found himself, once again, fretting over the facts of his case. Sir Giles was due to surrender to bail in just a couple of days, by which time the Crown Prosecution Service would have decided whether or not to charge him with murder. McNabb knew that, based on the evidence he had gathered, it was far from a foregone conclusion. He reached for his phone and called his sister to gee her up.

'I don't know what kind of miracles you're expecting me to pull off in just a couple of days,' she replied. 'But it's in hand. Have some bloody patience.'

McNabb cursed and took out his frustration on a cold Cornish pasty.

Shunter's progress up the long drive to the farmhouse had been troublesome thanks to the surprising appearance of a dromedary that had blocked the road and glowered at him while languidly chewing the cud. At the same time, he'd found himself being studied by several horses and a furious-looking emu in an adjacent field. And now his car had been surrounded by some two dozen tough-looking pigs. He was debating whether he should sound his horn when a large, red-faced and mud-spattered woman emerged from the farmhouse. She was dressed in a green body warmer over a blouse and tartan skirt. The ensemble was finished off by Dr Martens boots and an eyepatch. She walked with a stick and leaned to her left as she did so.

'Shoo! Shoo, you shower of bastards!' She brandished her stick at the pigs and they scattered amid grunts and squeals of complaint. Shunter got out of his car.

'They associate motor cars with food,' barked the woman, her one eye fixing on him.

'Mrs Tremblett?' said Shunter. 'I hope I've come to the right place. You're a bit out in the sticks here.'

'Miss Tremblett,' said the woman. 'Never married. People call me Connie. You this Munter I'm supposed to see?'

'Shunter. Frank Shunter,' he said, extending his hand.

'I never shake hands,' said Connie. 'You don't know where I've been. Come into the house and I'll get some tea on.'

From the front, Paradise Farmhouse looked like a normal, if substantial, three-storey farmhouse, but over the decades it had been extended, then extended again, and extended a third time to accommodate each new generation of Trembletts. As each new building had been constructed at right angles to the previous one, the farmhouse was now a large hollow square with a central courtyard and kitchen garden. Quite how the Tremblett family funded the building work and, indeed, their lives in general was something of a mystery. None of them seemed to go out to work and the farm itself – in actuality more akin to a giant petting zoo set across a dozen fields – was a farm in name only. 'Paradise' was something of a misnomer too, unless the afterlife was a lot shabbier than most religious texts suggested. Everywhere and everything carried a thick layer of dust and almost every item Shunter saw as he passed through a boot room and into the kitchen was either old or broken, or showed signs of clumsy repair. Things seemed to have been simply left wherever they had ceased to function. Dead televisions and old Bakelite wireless sets proliferated, along with ancient toasters that no longer toasted and vacuum cleaners that would never suck again. Non-functioning barometers hung next to silent cuckoo clocks and every inch of space not taken up with dust or redundant technology was occupied by a cat. On the walls hung oil paintings so dark with old varnish and grime that their subjects were almost indiscernible. There could have been a long-lost Suzie Colebrooke or Simon Thane or Desmond Devries under the muck but no one would ever know. Despite being a keen recycler himself, and an adherent of the idea that old didn't always mean obsolete, Shunter found himself wondering why no one had ever thought to have a clear-out. Cluttered seemed too mild a word to describe Paradise Farmhouse.

'Sit down. But check your seat first,' said Connie. 'Monty likes a warm chair this time of year.'

'Cat?'

'Python,' said Connie. 'How do you take your tea?'

'White, no sugar,' said Shunter, looking around his feet.

'Good. Got no sugar anyway. Mice had it all. Got fat. Then Monty had the mice,' said Connie.

'The circle of life, eh?'

'Death more like. So what do you want? If you'm selling something, I won't buy it.'

'I'm not selling anything,' said Shunter. 'I just want to pick your brains.'

'Won't take long,' said Connie.

'I was wondering if you can clear something up for me.'

'I have all kinds of unguents.'

'That's not quite what I meant,' said Shunter. 'Though I'm told you have something of a reputation when it comes to folk medicine and secret knowledge.'

'We knows what we knows, and we keeps it to ourselves,' said Connie, rolling her eye. 'There's many things as is unexplained in this world and the next. I keeps an open mind. I aren't a believer but I aren't not an unbeliever neither.'

Shunter attempted to disentangle the knot of negatives and gave up.

'The reason I've come to see you is because your father,

Henry, was with the Herewardshire Rifles and was one of the
few who made it home.'

'The Lucky Six? Daft name if ever there was one,' said
Connie.

'Really? Why?'

'Father took the King's shilling at twenty years old. Survived
that show somehow. Then signed up again in 1940 when he
was getting on for fifty. Survived that too. Then he was carried
off by a tumour less than a year after his demob. Don't sound
so lucky to me.'

'Unfortunate, to say the least.'

'Lost my eye when I was twelve. Kicked by a horse. While
I was in the hospital, the house burned down and killed my
two brothers. I'd have died too, no doubt, if it weren't for that
horse. Some people said I was lucky. Others said it was an act
of God. Can't be both, can it?'

'I suppose not.'

'Stuff just happens, I reckon. Because, see, if there is a God,
he has a bloody funny way of going about his business, half-
blinding a little girl to save her while letting her brothers die.
Every morning I tell him what a bastard he is, just in case he is
up there and listening. He never answers, mind.'

'I see,' said Shunter. 'But to come back to the subject of your
father, if I may. You've probably heard that a body has been
found in Black Dog Wood. The police believe it dates from
the 1930s and there's reason to suspect that it might have been
someone who fought in the Great War.'

'Can't be none of our lot. Only six come home. Then three
was carried off by the flu. How lucky was they, eh? To miss
all them bullets and shells and then to get killed by germs. Not
Germans but germs. Other three all died natural, including
Father. All six buried in the ground at St Probyn's. None
missing.'

'Hmm. Maybe a deserter then? Someone who had shell shock and went AWOL?'

'It's possible, I s'pose. Never heard of no one like that though.'

'Someone from another regiment then? Lots of different battalions fought at Ypres,' said Shunter, twirling his moustache. 'Someone who came to visit your father, perhaps?'

'I was born between the wars. Too young to remember visitors. Different story after the second war. I remember lots of old soldiers coming then, when Father took ill.'

'It's the First World War veterans I'm interested in.'

'Then I can't help you,' said Connie. 'Though Father might be able to.'

'Your father? Are you suggesting a séance?'

'Don't talk daft. People may say that I'm some kind of a witch but I aren't into no Ouija boards or table rapping and all that rubbish. I mean Father's correspondence. Him and his soldier friends all wrote to each other and I have his letters in a tin box somewhere. Might be of use, might not. But you'm welcome to have a look.'

'That would be great, thank you,' said Shunter. 'You are aware that there's a massive spider on your shoulder, aren't you?'

'Ah, Boris wouldn't hurt a fly,' said Connie, taking the red-knee tarantula into her hand. 'Prefers a nice fat sugar-fed mouse.'

'You were just meant to follow him,' said McNabb. His sister had phoned him back. 'I never told you to engage with him. I thought this Lorraine person you mentioned was one of the actresses on your books. I didn't realise it was you.'

'Why send someone else when I'm a better judge of

character?' said Ettie. 'I'll know if he's bullshitting me. And I'm sticking to public places. I'm quite safe.'

'So what else did he say?' asked McNabb, tapping his fingers on the steering wheel impatiently. 'Has he said or done anything that implicates him?'

'All he's done is protest his innocence,' reported Ettie. 'And he took a call from someone called Shunter. I have no idea what the conversation was about.'

'And that's it?' said McNabb.

'That's it so far.'

'I need more than that. Can't he be... you know... softened up a bit? Get him drunk or something?'

'I'll see what I can do. But there are limits, Derek. Public places only, I said. He is a bloody murder suspect, after all.'

'Yes, but—'

'No buts. And after this, dear brother, we are quits.'

'Until the next time you need money,' said McNabb.

'Harsh, Derek. Harsh.'

Lorraine returned from her phone call with a smile on her face.

'Good news, I hope,' said Giles.

'My agent, with an audition,' said Lorraine. 'It's only a sofa commercial but it's paid work. We should celebrate with a drink.'

'We should. Fancy some lunch? I know a lovely little brasserie within walking distance of here and their seafood selection is excellent.'

Shunter sat alone in the kitchen of Paradise Farmhouse, nursing the dregs of his tea and looking nervously around him for creatures on the creep, crawl or slither. In the next room, he could hear Connie Tremblett sorting noisily through a pile of boxes and tins, and opening and slamming shut drawers and cupboards. Clouds of dust hovered in the beams of autumn sunlight that shone through the grime-streaked windows.

'Found them,' she announced triumphantly. She bowled into the kitchen and placed a rusty biscuit tin on the table. 'Father's letters. No good to me. Come back and tell me if you find anything useful.'

'I will, thank you,' said Shunter, holding up the biscuit tin.

'I imagine you'll want to be on your way now.'

'Yes, indeed. Things to do,' said Shunter.

'I meant because Monty is climbing up the back of your chair.'

Shunter jumped to his feet, eliciting a guffaw from Connie and a more feminine giggle from a young woman who had walked into the kitchen. Her hair was dyed bright red and she seemed to be wearing far too few clothes for the time of year. She picked up the sluggish python and draped it around her grandmother's neck.

'Hey, mister, you driving over Bowcester way?' she asked.

'Where you'm off to?' asked Connie before Shunter could answer.

'Just meeting some friends,' said Jessie. 'Nothing wrong with that.'

'Hmf. Well, you just be careful.'

'Oh God! Not the condom talk again. I am over twenty-one, you know.'

'I meant because there might be a murderer on the loose.'

'I aren't daft, Gran.'

'I aren't daft? All that fancy private education we paid for and that's what we get? I aren't daft?'

'Stop being such a nag. So, are you going Bowcester way, mister?'

'I'm going as far as Nasely,' said Shunter.

'That'll do me,' said Jessie. 'Can I cadge a lift?'

'Yes, I should think so,' said Shunter.

'Cool.'

'You be back by midnight,' warned Connie.

'Or what? You'll turn me into a pumpkin?'

'No, but I'll cancel your phone tariff. I pay your bills, don't forget. You didn't come home until early this morning and I promised your mother I'd make sure you did tonight.'

'I aren't a— I'm not a child, Gran.'

'My house. My rules. Midnight.'

Jessica Tremblett flounced from the kitchen to wait outside by Shunter's car.

'Kids today, eh?' said Connie. 'Can't live with 'em, can't lock 'em in the attic until they learn to do as they'm bloody told.'

Chapter 23

Professor Gravestock carefully dressed what appeared to be an old log with moss and dead leaves and stood back to check the efficacy of his camouflage work.

'What do you think?' he asked. 'Is that good enough to hide it from passers-by?'

'I don't think you'd spot it unless you were specifically looking for it,' said Pamela Dallimore. She had elected to accompany the professor as he placed his covert camera equipment around the woods and the afternoon had provided her with some decent copy about the life of a paranormal investigator.

'So, tell me a bit about yourself, Pamela,' said Gravestock. 'I understand that you're someone who's not afraid to rock the boat occasionally.'

'I don't court controversy, if that's what you mean. I write to entertain. If people don't like what I have to say, that's their prerogative. You can't please everyone. Especially fanatics like Millies.'

'But you accused Agnes Crabbe of being a lesbian or a bisexual, didn't you?'

'Actually, I did no such thing. If they had read my book

instead of listening to second-hand reporting, they'd have seen that all I did was record suggestions and rumours that came from people who live in the village, including two old biddies who actually met her when they were younger. Crabbe was a bit weird, as you know. A recluse. Tongues wag when you have someone like that living nearby. All I did was repeat the local gossip. It's not my fault if the Millies give it any credence. And it's also not my fault if some people are too dim to sift the wheat from the chaff. I can't accommodate for the stupid.'

'These days, people do tend to believe everything they read in the tabloids or online,' sighed Gravestock. 'It's why my colleagues and I have to spend so much of our time debunking conspiracy theories and other silly nonsense. So, what does Mr Dallimore say about the more vituperative comments aimed at you by Crabbe fans?'

'He's probably loving it. We divorced in 2011 and we didn't part on the best of terms.'

'Ah, sorry.'

Sensing that any further discussion on the subject would be inadvisable, Gravestock returned to his work.

'That was lovely,' said Lorraine, dabbing daintily at her mouth with a napkin. 'I've never had samphire before.'

'Glad you enjoyed it,' said Giles. He smiled contentedly. The brasserie's menu had lived up to his expectations and Lorraine seemed to be genuinely impressed. 'Thank you for today. It's been lovely to forget about my problems for a while. But I will have to go back home and face them tomorrow.'

'Poor you.'

'Yes. I am "half agony, half hope", as Captain Wentworth wrote.'

'Who?'

'Never mind,' said Giles. 'I'm just saying I have faith that the truth will come out.'

'I hope so too,' said Lorraine. 'And we still have the rest of today to cheer you up. If you have nothing else to do, that is.'

'No, nothing,' said Giles, smiling.

'Great. Shall we get another bottle?'

Colin Cheeseman's cottage was the largest in Hope Street and enjoyed a splendid view of the cricket pitch and bowling green. His envious neighbours privately expressed the opinion that Colin was undeserving of it, having spent his entire life doing next to nothing. His parents had made their money in orthopaedic furniture but had died in a motorway pile-up while Colin, a very spoiled only child, was still at university. Finding that he had inherited a house and a modest fortune, he had immediately given up his studies to concentrate on the most important thing in his life: Colin Cheeseman.

Having had his every childhood whim indulged by his doting parents, Colin had been a mollycoddled and unpopular child who wasn't averse to throwing a tantrum when things didn't go the way he wanted them to. The onset of puberty had only made things worse and the spoiled brat had grown into an insufferable adult who believed that the only right way was the Cheeseman way. Consequently, after developing an interest in animal welfare and having been unable to find an organisation to join that was quite right for him, he had formed and funded his own. The number of members recruited to FLAN fluctuated but rarely got above half a dozen. This was partly because there were few jobs available locally that weren't involved with husbandry, slaughter, butchery or meat packaging, which tended to limit the pool of people likely to join an organisation bent on closing the industry down. But mostly it was because there were only so many people who could put up with Colin. But he was perfectly happy to lose dissenting voices; FLAN was his baby, plain and simple, and anyone who didn't like the way he did things could go and form their own gang.

It was with some trepidation, therefore, that he had agreed to Bron's request for an extraordinary meeting at the cottage. Bron was charismatic and very smart, which easily made him the biggest threat to Colin's autocracy. To make matters worse, all of the members of FLAN had made the effort to turn up for the meeting – even Terry and June. Colin rarely managed to get everyone together in one room and the fact that his rival had done so was extremely irritating. At least Maisie had shown no interest in Bron. In fact, she had spent several chaste nights at Colin's and seemed to be growing quite fond of him.

'So, what's so important that you needed us to meet on a Saturday?' asked Terry. 'It's our day off, Colin.'

'Blame Oberon,' said Cheeseman. 'He called the meeting, not me.'

'I did,' said Bron. 'We have a decision to make, a decision that affects us all, so I thought it best to put it to a free vote.'

'Whoa whoa whoa there,' said Colin. 'You didn't say anything about a vote. Members of FLAN don't vote on things until I've decided whether a vote is needed.'

'Are you saying that we can only ever vote on things that you say we can?' said Bron. 'Because that's not how democracy works.'

'I will put things to a vote if I feel that they are suitable activities for FLAN to be involved in,' said Colin.

'Yes, but we should all have a say in what those activities are if we're the ones doing them. We're partners in this, Colin. We're not staff or servants.'

'Yes, but only if I—'

'What is it we'd be voting on anyway?' asked an impatient Onions.

'Willy and I had a recce up at the site this morning and the truth is that we achieved nothing the other night. Absolutely nothing,' explained Bron.

'We made our mark,' protested Cheeseman. 'FLAN has shown itself to be a real forc—'

'No. We didn't,' said Bron. 'The Plash is already more than half drained. Another day and it'll all be over. So, we either need to act tonight or accept that we've failed.'

'We're free tonight,' said Terry, grinning and cracking his knuckles. June frowned at him.

'But the thing is, they're prepared for another protest now,' said Bron. 'They have security lights and there are people working and sleeping on site.'

This fact brought worried murmurs from the group.

'How many people?' asked Onions.

'About the same as current FLAN membership,' said Bron. 'So, if we're going to do this, we need more troops. Now, I've made a few phone calls and we can have thirty, maybe forty protesters here this evening from Coxeter, Hoddenford and Pawley. A few more calls and we could have a small army here to take the pumps down permanently.'

Maisie clapped excitedly, much to Colin's dismay.

'You didn't run any of this past me,' snapped Colin.

'I tried,' said Bron. 'I told you we needed greater numbers but you wouldn't listen.'

'FLAN does not ally itself with other organisations. We are an independent pressure group created to—'

'Created to free lab animals. I know. But once we found that we had no laboratories to protest about, we adapted, Colin. We evolved. Now we need to evolve again. There are animals dying, or are going to die, if we don't stop the emptying of the Plash. That's more important than our pride. FLAN doesn't exist to make us look good. It exists for the animals. We have a golden opportunity here to do something big and brave and worthy.'

Cheeseman looked around the room at the expectant and excited eyes of his followers. Bron was right, of course. If FLAN didn't do something now, when the animals most needed help, its credibility as an organisation would be shattered. Even Maisie's eyes seemed to be pleading him to step up and do the right thing. He sighed.

'Go on, hold your vote.'

At Bowcester Magistrates' Court, Jamie Cordery was the second defendant to enter the dock after lunch, immediately following the appearance of Mrs Patricia Gugge on charges of breach of the peace and actual bodily harm against her husband and PC Dudfoot, who had done his duty in trying to protect him. As she was escorted from the courtroom, Jamie Cordery stepped up to the dock, heard the evidence against him and sheepishly admitted a breach of the peace and agreed to be bound over in the sum of £500.

As he paid his fine Keeley was there to meet him, pleased that he'd got off fairly lightly but also because she hadn't been the one who'd got caught. She had been punished enough, she felt, having endured the worst night of her life – half of it spent naked, shivering with cold and covered in bramble and holly scratches, and the other half lying on the hard floor of a Portakabin and unable to sleep due to the noise of the machinery operating outside. She'd eventually got home by being offered her cab fare by the students, and after a long hot bath and a nap, she'd brought her boyfriend a change of clothes so that he could look smart for his appearance.

They decided to grab a snack before heading home on the bus to Larock and were sitting in a coffee shop, bemoaning the fact that £500 was going to put a sizeable dent in their monthly outgoings, when they were approached by a woman they didn't know.

'Do you mind if I join you?' she said, and sat down before waiting for a reply. 'I have a proposition.'

'Are you a reporter?' asked Cordery. 'Because if you are, we're saying nothing.'

'I don't work for the tabloids, if that's what you mean,' said the woman. 'But I know plenty of reporters who'd be interested to know what sort of people go dogging in Black Dog Wood.'

'Are you trying to blackmail us?' said Cordery. 'Because we haven't got much money.'

'I don't want your money,' said Mrs Dallimore. 'In fact, I want to give you some. I want to buy your story. And take some photos of you.'

'What sort of photos?' said Cordery suspiciously.

'Just some photos in the woods,' said the woman.

'Forget it,' said Cordery.

'You'll be completely unidentifiable, I promise.'

'Not a chance,' said Cordery.

'If you agree, I'll pay you the cost of your court fine and a bit more besides,' said Mrs Dallimore. 'You scratch my back, I'll scratch yours.'

'I've had enough scratches to last me a lifetime,' said Cordery. 'I just want to forget it.'

'How much money are we talking?' asked Keeley.

Pamela Dallimore smiled. The bait had been taken.

Chapter 24

McNabb returned to Bowcester, having spent several fruitless hours following Frank Shunter about in his car. After leaving Paradise Farm, the ex-detective had driven back towards Nasely accompanied by a young woman with red hair. McNabb had wondered if perhaps there might be some kind of naughty extramarital business going on but his hopes were dashed when Shunter dropped her off at a bus stop before driving home. He'd then sat watching the man's cottage for over an hour before deciding that enough was enough and returning to work.

As he walked into the CID office he saw Cliff Jaine at his desk and all his feelings of betrayal bubbled to the surface. It was time to assert his authority and leave his DS in no doubt as to whose side he should be playing on.

'Jaine. My office,' he snapped as he walked past.

Several of Jaine's colleagues mocked him and feigned having their wrists slapped as he followed the inspector into his soulless office and shut the door.

McNabb toyed with a pencil in a way that he hoped would make him look commanding.

'Sit down, Sergeant,' he said. 'How are things progressing with your cold case?'

'Slowly,' said Jaine, remaining standing. 'We think the victim was a First World War veteran and we're following up on some leads. However, I have some—'

'And who exactly is "we"?'

'Eh? Well, there's SOCO Turvey. And I have a couple of people in the intelligence unit checking back through old missing persons' records. But listen, we've found—'

'And no one else?'

'Like who, sir?'

'Like a certain ex-detective.'

'You mean Frank Shunter? Top bloke. Very knowledgeable. He has decades of experience with murders and always has some useful insights. Is there a problem with that?'

'Is there a problem?' snapped McNabb. 'Of course there's a problem! He's working for Luscott-Whorne!'

'Yes, I know.'

'You know?' said McNabb incredulously.

'Yes. But look, we've found something really impor—'

'And you don't think that there's maybe a conflict of interest in consulting with someone who is on the payroll of a murder suspect? My murder suspect?'

'Not really,' said Jaine. 'I'm not investigating your case.'

'What?'

'I'm investigating the body in the woods. And it's a tough one, what with it being nearly a century ago he was buried. Any witnesses are probably dead and the forensics are minimal. So I asked Frank's advice and he came up with some avenues for me to follow. Is that a problem?'

McNabb found himself momentarily stumped for words.

'Or are you suggesting that I'm sharing confidential

information with him or helping him to undermine your case?' said Jaine. He let his words hang in the silence like a bad smell.

'That's not what I said.'

'I hope not,' said Jaine. 'I'd like to think that you see me as more professional than that.'

'Look, Sir Giles is a murder suspect and—'

'And I'm not investigating him. In the meantime, if Shunter turns something up that works either against or in favour of Luscott-Whorne's defence, I'll be in the know,' said Jaine. 'He trusts me. And if I'm in the know, you will be too. That's a good thing, surely?'

'Well, I suppose if you look at it from that point of view—'

'Is that all, sir?'

'Yes. Yes, go. I'm sure you have plenty to be getting on with,' said McNabb.

Jaine left the office, a small smile creeping across his lips. It was rare that he got the opportunity to push back against McNabb's bullying and it was a very good feeling indeed. Plus, the man hadn't given him the opportunity to share the news about the Agnes Crabbe manuscript.

'You can bloody wait now,' he muttered under his breath.

Miss Bultitude finished supervising a class of girls in the drama studio and walked back to the main building and upstairs to her office. Jemima Deak was busy at a computer.

'Any news regarding the fundraiser, Tiggy?'

'I've been checking the message board. It seems that the best date for a meeting is this coming Monday.'

'The day after tomorrow? That's very short notice.'

'I know. But it's the only date on which the majority of members are available. Otherwise, we're looking at early January next year to get a good attendance.'

'January is too far away. The last event was in August and it would mean a gap of nearly six months. Are there really no other suitable dates?'

'Not without inconveniencing many of our top donors.'

'Then it looks like we'll have to go ahead.'

'Monday it is then,' said Miss Deak.

Mrs Shunter wasn't best pleased. Over the course of an hour, her husband had emptied out the contents of Connie Tremblett's biscuit tin onto her dining room table and tiny tumbleweeds of cat hair, dust and small scraps of torn paper covered the carpet.

'I hope you're going to clean this mess up when you've finished, because I'm not,' she warned.

'I will,' said Shunter distractedly as he scanned the address on a yellowed envelope. 'This is amazing stuff, you know. Living history.'

'I can imagine,' said Mrs Shunter. 'Dinner in fifteen minutes. You can tell me all about it then. We'll have to eat in the kitchen, I suppose.'

Shunter nodded and pulled a letter out of the envelope. Over the past hour he'd sorted the contents of Connie's tin into piles and had begun to piece together the relationships that existed between the so-called Lucky Six.

In total, the borough of Bowcester had supplied eighty-four men for the 2nd Battalion Herewardshire Rifles. Of that number, only Henry Tremblett, John Hakesley, Edward Pank, Bernard Craddock, James McFarland and Reginald Quisenbury had come home. Three of them had then died during the 1918 flu pandemic but Tremblett, Hakesley and Pank, despite all contracting the virus, had made it through. Tremblett and Hakesley had been best friends during the war and remained so afterwards, exchanging letters on a frequent basis. But neither of them had maintained any contact with the third survivor and it was easy to see why. Edward Pank had been an unpopular figure even before the war. He had been Sir Rufus Whorne's head gamekeeper and unofficial enforcer, and his reputation for bullying and brutality was unsurpassed. If the stories were true, his punishment of poachers had been particularly savage; one contemporary account claimed that he had once thrashed an emaciated man so badly that his shoulder blades had broken through the skin. When the call to war had come, the gouty and infirm Sir Rufus had served his time in Whitehall but he had insisted that the gamekeeper be assigned to his younger brother, Jolyon, as batman and personal bodyguard. Consequently, Pank had not seen any real action and the fact that he had also been promoted in the field to sergeant soon led to an uncomfortable 'us and them' situation developing between him and the 2nd Battalion. It was even rumoured that he was a kind of *éminence grise* and that Jolyon took his advice on most subjects.

But then had come the disastrous Second Battle of Ypres, during which Jolyon's poor decision-making had caused terrible loss of life among his own troops. The survivors' hatred for both Pank and his master was clear to see in their letters, as was their joy when the Whorne family's fortunes had been reversed.

Like most of the aristocracy, the Whornes had been subjected to taxation at the highest levels after the wars, particularly when it came to inherited wealth. Upon Sir Rufus's explosive death in 1924, his estate and title had passed to Jolyon and, while the newly-widowed Juniper, the dowager Lady Whorne, had tried her best to keep the estate running, even with her brother-in-law's help it had been a losing battle. Juniper knew nothing about business and nor did Jolyon, having spent most of his life sponging off his older brother. To further add to their difficulties, the growth of the middle classes had meant that people were no longer willing to work as servants, while the tenant farmers, whose rents had been the Whornes' primary source of income, had begun demanding a bigger share of the profits from their toil. As a result, the family had been quickly stripped of its wealth. This same story was told all over Britain as many of the great aristocratic dynasties were forced to sell off their houses or to donate them to the National Trust. The wars had heralded the end of Empire and an end to a way of life for the upper classes that had existed for centuries. Certainly, for Jolyon, the fall had been a long one indeed. Juniper had drunkenly drowned herself in Gertie's Plash in 1927, leaving Jolyon with a monstrous bill for death duties. He had consequently suffered a stroke that left him paralysed down his left side, and had then died of a heart attack in 1935, leaving his son, Gawain, to oversee the sale of Harpax Grange, an action that almost certainly contributed to his own premature death in 1946 aged just forty-eight.

The majority of the letters in Connie Tremblett's tin were from John Hakesley but there had also been letters from soldiers from other regiments whom, presumably, Tremblett had fought alongside in both wars. Shunter worked his way methodically through the correspondence, fascinated and saddened in equal measure, but finding little to help in identifying Cliff Jaine's mysterious blindfolded skeleton. He also felt a little guilty spending his time reading letters when he was being paid to investigate the allegations against Sir Giles. But something was telling him that his time wasn't being wasted; some deep instinct assured him that solving one murder would help to reveal the truth about the other. There were simply too many connections to ignore.

Following a trip to the zoo, Giles and Lorraine had enjoyed a night at the theatre. Giles had let her choose what to see and she had picked Agatha Christie's *The Mousetrap*, on the surprising grounds that she'd always wondered whodunit. Giles knew whodunit and was pretty sure that everyone else in the audience knew whodunit too. Despite the theatre's request that patrons keep the play's denouement to themselves, it had been performed twice daily in London's West End for more than sixty years and the secret was well and truly out. But he enjoyed the show regardless and took great delight in watching Lorraine's astonishment when the murderer was revealed. They'd gone on for drinks afterwards at several wine bars and he'd revelled in her exuberance. Her enthusiasm for life was a world away from the cynical and seedy world of politics and from the drab utility of his parochial duties.

'You can't half hold your drink,' said Lorraine. 'I'm so tipsy now.'

'I always could,' said Giles. 'Which is useful at times, but it does mean that I never quite get drunk enough to let my hair down, or what's left of it. At parties I'm always stone cold sober while everyone around me has a much better time than I do.'

'Aww! It's a shame you can't stay in London a bit longer,' said Lorraine. 'I've had a lot of fun these past two days.'

'I have too.'

'Will you be back soon?'

'That all rather depends how things go on Monday,' said Giles.

Lorraine's face grew grave and a little sad. 'How's your wife taking all of this?'

'You know that I'm married?'

'You're wearing a ring.'

'Yes... but... look, it's complicated. And I probably won't

218

be married for much longer,' said Giles. 'And, besides, it's not like we were—'

Lorraine silenced him with a kiss that took him completely by surprise.

'Listen, I know I'm no Einstein,' she slurred. 'But I know a fib when I hear one and I'm a good judge of character. I like you, Giles. I like you a lot. I want you to know that. So, go home, sort out whatever you need to sort out and then, if you feel like it, call me. OK?'

'OK,' said Giles. 'I will.'

Shunter returned to the dining room table and teased a morsel of steak out from between his teeth with a fingernail. Over dinner, Mrs Shunter had asked him how his work for Sir Giles was going and he'd told her the truth, that things were going slowly. But her question had refreshed his feelings of guilt over spending so much time looking into Jaine's case, so he had promised himself that he'd devote no more than a couple more hours to the Tremblett correspondence and then get back on Sir Giles's case in the morning. He took a gulp of tea and returned to the pile once again.

The first item was a letter to Henry Tremblett from John Hakesley dated 1921 in which his former comrade-in-arms described his new home in Gloucestershire and his job as a carpenter and joiner. The second was also from Hakesley and introduced Tremblett to his new bride. The third envelope was postmarked Nieppe, France, and the letter within was dated 11 December 1922. Shunter scanned his way through the contents, which talked mostly about life working on a farm and how someone called Mathilde was still coming to grips with the death of her mother during a mustard gas attack in Armentières four years previously. The letter described the horror of the attack in some detail; the German shelling had apparently been so heavy that liquid mustard had run in the streets and the contamination so strong that enemy troops were unable to enter the town for a fortnight. But the writer and Mathilde had escaped and made a new life for themselves at an abandoned farm that they had been given to renovate and keep as their own. The letter ended with the news that the writer was doing well and was unlikely to return home to Nasely even though the war was now over. He also expressed the wish that Tremblett not share the contents of any of his letters with anyone who might remember him. The letter was signed with the initials TB.

Shunter found himself puzzled. The letter was written by someone who, presumably, had served in the Herewardshire Rifles; there were references to growing up in Nasely and to working as a delivery boy in Sherrinford. There were also mentions of Bernard Craddock's piano playing, of John Hakesley's fine singing voice, and descriptions of what life had been like during the battle of Ypres. Shunter reached for his laptop and did a search for information on the 2nd Battalion. He then followed a link to a website maintained by Colin Tossel of the Nasely Historical Society. On a page dedicated to the Herewardshire Rifles, he found a full list of the conscripts that, annoyingly, Tossel hadn't bothered to alphabetise. It took him a while to check every name but he found only two men who bore the initials TB, and both were recorded as missing in action, presumed dead.

One was called Thomas Brock. The other was Thadeus Bultitude.

Chapter 25

Pamela Dallimore arrived at Black Dog Wood car park and turned off her car's ignition. The clock on her dashboard read 10:21 p.m. She turned around in her seat to smile at Jamie and Keeley.

'Showtime,' she said.

They didn't smile back.

In the garden of Colin Cheeseman's cottage, an extraordinary Extraordinary Meeting of FLAN and its partner protest groups was taking place. An excited energy filled the space, a febrile atmosphere of nervous anticipation. Relegated to a back seat in the proceedings, Colin sulked quietly as Oberon Tremblett outlined his plan to the fifty or so assembled activists. Willy was sulking too because his brother had excluded him from what he was calling his 'Primary Task Force'.

'But the Tertiary Task Force has the most important job, Willy,' he'd explained. 'You're the cavalry. You've got our backs. The cavalry are the people who always save the day.'

'But lookout duty is shit,' said Willy. 'I want some action.'

'A job like this requires subtlety and assertiveness, not brute force,' explained Bron. 'We want to take control of the camp without violence.'

'I wouldn't hurt anyone,' said Willy. 'I just want to smash the machines.'

'But, as I've explained, we don't want them smashed,' said Bron. 'We're going to turn their weapons on them.'

'Yeah, but lookout duty...'

'Look, you're the linchpin in this operation, Willy. We need people we can trust to protect us and I trust you more than I trust anyone. We can't do this without you.'

Willy made a grunting noise that Bron took as grudging acceptance.

The plan was simple. The first priority was to take control of the site and Bron reckoned that a Primary Task Force of thirty protesters would be enough to subdue any kind of spirited defence. Then the Secondary Task Force would move in. Their job would be to deal with the machinery and to use the pumps to refill the Plash with water from the river. Willy's Tertiary Group could then join them and they would all stage a peaceful sit-down protest and refuse to move until the Plash was returned to its former glory and alternative plans for the preservation of Harpax Grange were explored.

And so Oberon and his guerrillas had set off for Harpax in their cars while a disappointed Willy had followed along in a camper van that Onions had borrowed from his parents. Also in the van, and making up the remainder of the Tertiary Task Force, were those protesters most likely to be unpredictable – regular FLAN member Terry and a barrel-bellied biker from Pawley known as 'Revvin' Kevin', who was decorated head to toe in bad tattoos. Both men had taken the news of their assignments as badly as Willy had and the van was full of simmering resentment.

'Why am I dressed as a lion?' asked Cordery.

He presented a strange sight, dressed only in a bath robe borrowed from the new Empire Hotel and wearing an oversized animal costume head. Keeley looked equally bizarre as a sphere-headed panda. They were standing in the dark of a wooded glade, the only light being cast by Pamela Dallimore's torch.

'The fancy-dress shop didn't have any wolves left,' she explained. 'There's been a run on animal costumes, apparently. The important thing is that no one will be able to tell that it's you.'

'Why are we doing this again?' asked Cordery.

Mrs Dallimore took a deep breath and wondered whether her decision to use the haggard-looking couple had been the right one. At first, they'd seemed perfect – nondescript, naturally pale and a little bit pudgy, full of bravado and willing to take a risk for the thrill of public sex. The bramble scratches and bruises they both sported had added an authenticity that would be lacking in hired models. However, they had been through a fairly traumatic experience the night before and they were very tired and grumpy, which was making the shoot a lot more stressful than it otherwise might have been.

'Look, I'm writing a feature about dogging,' explained Mrs Dallimore. 'And all I want is some shots of you two pretending to have sex in the woods. That's it.'

'Pretending is all you'll get. It's too bloody cold for anything else,' moaned Cordery, flapping his arms. 'And, anyway, we don't dress up as animals. That's just bloody weird.'

'And yet last night you were dressed as the Big Bad Wolf. The very big and very bad wolf, judging by the size of that rubber prick you were wearing.'

'That wasn't my fault. Someone put me in that costume.'

'Oh God,' said Keeley. 'We were terrified. People were chasing us.'

'And I got nicked,' sneered Cordery.

'This isn't about you two,' snapped Mrs Dallimore. 'This is about doggers in general, OK? I don't care what you do for kicks. All I want are some photos. The animal heads are there to give you anonymity and to make my article more visual. So, if you could lose the dressing gowns and the attitude and get yourselves into a suitable position, we can crack on. I don't want to be out here any longer than I have to be and I'm sure you don't either.'

'I never want to hear the word dogging again,' grumbled Cordery, disrobing. His girlfriend followed suit.

'At last,' said Mrs Dallimore. 'Now, Keeley... bend over that stump, please.'

Arriving at the car park, Bron noted with some relief that there were only two other vehicles parked there and both were empty. The protesters quickly arranged themselves into their three squads and the Primary Task Force set off along the path to the pump site with the Secondary Task Force, led by Cheeseman and Maisie, following hot on their heels. Three-quarters of the Tertiary Task Force remained in the camper van and opened another six-pack while an agitated Willy paced up and down outside.

'Chill out. Have a drink,' said Kevin from a window.

'We're on lookout duty,' said Willy. 'We have to stay alert.'

'I didn't suggest we get pissed, did I? You can have a beer and still be alert. And we have Onions, our designated driver. He'll be sober.'

'Yeah, lucky me,' said Onions.

'And all we have to do is scare away anyone who comes into the car park,' said Kevin. 'It's not rocket science.'

'Who's going to turn up anyway?' added Terry. 'It's bloody freezing out there.'

'So have a drink,' said Kevin.

'I think I can hear a car,' said Willy. He walked to the entrance of the car park and saw headlights sweeping along the main road towards him. He trotted back to the camper van.

'It's definitely coming this way,' he said. 'I should call Bron. Shit. No phone signal.'

'They're probably just passing by. But if they ain't, scare the fuckers off,' growled Kevin, handing him out a snooker cue through the window. 'That's all we're good for, apparently.'

'That's great! Now kneel down and put your head in his lap,' said Mrs Dallimore, the flash on her camera momentarily lighting up the woods around them.

'I'm freezing my knackers off here,' said Cordery. 'And how can she give me a blowie if she's wearing that giant panda head?'

'Jesus Christ,' said Mrs Dallimore through gritted teeth. 'As I keep explaining to you, you just have to give the impression of having sex. That's all. Now, one more of Keeley on all fours with you behind her and then I've got something to warm you up with.'

Willy waited and nervously handled the snooker cue. It didn't feel at all comfortable in his hands; at least, not in this kind of setting. He was never happier than when smashing up machinery, or cutting through wire fences, or breaking open cages and animal pens, but he had a complete aversion to violence against all living things, including other humans. The purpose of the weapon was to make him look threatening, he realised, and he was under no obligation to actually use it to inflict harm. But he still felt slightly sick at even the thought of doing so.

The approaching vehicle was very close now, and all of a sudden Willy saw that it was a police patrol car. He looked at his phone again, shouted 'Shit!' and then banged on the side of the camper van and shouted 'Police!' before running off into the woods to warn his brother.

'When you said you had something to warm us up with, I expected a nip of Scotch. Or a flask of tea at least,' said Cordery. 'Even soup would be better than this.'

Having watched Professor Gravestock set up his equipment earlier in the day, Pamela Dallimore knew the location and position of many of his hidden trail cameras. She now planned to use them as a resource to get images to accompany her proposed feature. She was sure that she could charm the professor into letting her have copies of the photos.

'I'm only asking you to sprint a few yards, not run the London Marathon,' she said, pointing to an unobtrusive small black box nestling in the crook of a branch. 'That camera is activated by movement. I just need you to trigger it by running past.'

'So why can't I walk past it?' moaned Cordery. 'I've done all the running I want to do this week.'

'Because I want the photos to be a bit ambiguous,' said Dallimore. 'I want them blurry and you have to be moving reasonably quickly to get that effect.'

'But then we're done, right?' said Cordery.

'Yes, then we're done,' sighed Dallimore. 'Thank Christ.'

Oberon and his Primary Task Force arrived at the perimeter of
the pumping site and found that all was quiet. The knowledge
that Sunday would be a busy working day had driven the
students to their sleeping bags. Bron signalled to his troops to
gather round him.

'OK,' he whispered. 'Three to a tent and then, on my
signal...'

PC Dudfoot had drawn the short straw during the night duty
postings.

'I want you to patrol the farms and villages around Nasely,
Harpax, Milverton and Spradbarrow,' his sergeant had
instructed him. 'And pay particular attention to Black Dog
Wood and the Whorne Mausoleum. There's been some weird
shit going on up there this past week. Take young Harbottle
with you. He's keen.'

PC Harbottle was fresh out of basic training and was very
much looking forward to some action. However, PC Dudfoot
was pretty sure that he'd be disappointed. The past couple of
nights had been unusually busy, it was true. However, nothing
usually happened at night in Bowcester or Sherrinford, let
alone anywhere more rural, and an eight-hour shift was
generally spent fighting the constant urge to park up and go
to sleep. Therefore, the officers were simultaneously delighted
and startled to find the mausoleum car park half-full of vehicles.
A camper van was parked closest to the entrance but beyond
that there were seven or eight parked cars, plus Pamela
Dallimore's Peugeot and Jamie Cordery's Vauxhall, which had
been there since the night before. A man with a snooker
cue was caught in the headlight beams, and stared at them
transfixed like a rabbit in a country lane. But then, in an instant,

he was off and running. As the police officers stepped out of their car, two other men tumbled out of the camper van and into the spotlight. PC Dudfoot opened the belt pouch that contained his canister of CS gas spray and gripped the handle of his baton, just in case. PC Harbottle gulped nervously and followed suit.

The students' tents were of the modern pop-up style and their dome-like shapes were created by a pair of flexible crescent-shaped rods that crossed at the apex. At a signal from Oberon, the Primary Task Force flicked the ends of the rods out of their sockets and, within seconds, each tent had collapsed to become a bag full of howling and surprised undergrads. Before the occupants had a chance to escape, the protesters grabbed hold of the sides of the tents where the zippered door flaps were positioned, effectively trapping them inside. Oberon whistled and the Secondary Task Force appeared from among the trees.

'What are you doing here?' asked PC Harbottle. He attempted to keep the nervousness out of his voice as he and his older companion approached the camper van and the two large men standing beside it. They appeared to be quite drunk but, thankfully, were carrying nothing more dangerous than beer cans.

'We're not doing anything,' snarled Kevin. 'There's no law says we can't have a few beers in a car park at night.'

'Are you doggers?' asked Harbottle.

'Fuck off!' said Terry. 'Credit me with more taste than that.' He indicated Kevin, whose face assumed an expression of umbrage. Whether it was the suggestion that he was gay or Terry's critique of his looks that had upset him wasn't clear.

'So why did your friend run off like that if you're doing nothing wrong?'

'He's no friend of ours, the fucking coward,' snarled Terry.

'Perhaps he fancied a jog?' said Kevin.

'Then why did he have that snooker cue?' asked Harbottle.

'Maybe he was jogging to a snooker tournament,' said Kevin.

'Less of your cheek,' snapped PC Dudfoot, pointing his baton at the tattooed drunk. 'Whose cars are these?'

'No idea,' said Terry.

'You don't know much, do you?' said Dudfoot. 'Are you two anything to do with that animal rights lot who broke into the pump site a few nights back?'

'No,' said Kevin, truthfully. 'They're a bunch of wankers.'

'Perhaps we should all take a stroll down to the pond, just in case, eh?' said PC Harbottle, indicating the direction with his baton.

'I have a better idea,' said PC Dudfoot.

'These look fine,' said Pamela Dallimore, looking back over the photos that she'd captured on her DSLR. 'And once I have the photos from the trail cameras, my article will look great. I think we're done here. You can get dressed now.'

'Thank fuck for that,' said Cordery.

'What's that noise?' said Keeley, removing her panda head and pulling on her bathrobe. Some way off, in the direction of Gertie's Plash, could be heard the sound of raised voices. 'Oh God, not again! I can't go through all that again!'

'I can't get this bastard lion head off!' shouted Cordery. The sound emerged as a muffled growl. 'The chin strap has gone right up inside the neck hole and my fingers have gone numb with the cold.'

'Try turning the head around backwards and tackling the strap from behind,' suggested Dallimore.

Cordery rotated the head. 'I can't see a bloody thing now!' he moaned.

Dallimore began fidgeting with the strap just as two police officers came out of the trees, batons in hand.

'Fuck!' said Keeley and she turned and ran, losing her bathrobe as she did so.

With a dramatic flourish, two excitable spinsters from the Boulting Parva Amateur Lepidopterist Society shut down the generator and the pumps ground to a halt. The hoses connected to them lay down and became flaccid, not that anyone could see them. With the generator down, the site had been plunged into darkness. Torches were switched on and Bron smiled in triumph. Colin watched it all with mixed feelings. Part of him was excited that the organisation he'd started had achieved such a great result, but a larger part of him resented sharing the glory with other groups. His annoyance was further magnified by seeing that Bron was getting all the handshakes and high fives. Even though Maisie had hugged him and whispered in his ear that she was probably 'fit for action tonight', he felt undermined and envious. FLAN was his creation, not Bron's. Somehow he needed to reassert his authority and remind people just who was really in charge.

'I know how it looks, officers,' said Mrs Dallimore. 'But I can explain.'

PC Dudfoot looked at the decapitated panda head and then at Jamie Cordery's backwards-facing lion. In the struggle to extricate himself, his bathrobe had come undone and had fallen off his shoulders. His state of undress left nothing to the imagination.

'What's happening?' shouted Cordery.

'I think we've caught ourselves a couple of furries,' said PC Dudfoot.

'Don't you mean doggers?' said PC Harbottle.

'Doggers are people who meet up for public sex,' explained PC Dudfoot. 'Furries are fetishists who dress up as soft toys.'

'We are not furries,' said Dallimore indignantly. 'And we're not doggers either. We're doing a photo shoot for a magazine article.'

'A photo shoot, eh?' said PC Dudfoot, raising an eyebrow.

'It's not what you think.'

'What the fuck is going on?' shouted Cordery. 'Who's out there?'

'Perhaps you should help your friend to get his head off,' said PC Dudfoot. 'And for God's sake, tie up his dressing gown.'

Back in the car park, Onions looked moodily out of the camper van windscreen. The two police officers, upon threatening the use of their CS gas spray, had persuaded the Tertiary Task Force to get back inside the vehicle and stay there before walking off with the keys. Terry and Kevin had immediately resumed their drinking.

'Pigs,' grumbled Kevin. Onions sighed and briefly considered walking home. But what would be the point? The police knew who he was and the camper van was registered to his dad so it wouldn't do him any good. Resigned to circumstances, he opened a can of beer.

'Come on, guys,' pleaded Cordery. 'We've not committed any crimes and we haven't offended anyone. We weren't even having sex. And I was bound over to keep the peace this morning. I could go to prison if I get nicked again.'

'Is this the same bloke you nicked last night?' said PC Harbottle.

'It is. Different costume, mind. Some people never learn,' said PC Dudfoot. 'And you claim you're not a furry?'

'I'm really not,' said Cordery miserably. 'Like I told you, I was put into that costume against my will.'

'And tonight?'

'That's my fault, officer,' said Dallimore. 'I asked them to pose for the photos. You can look at them on my camera if you like. They're not pornographic, just suggestive.'

The older officer looked at some of the images stored on the camera.

'Go on then, hop it,' he said.

'Thank you!' said Cordery and he loped off towards the car park, with Mrs Dallimore following close behind.

'You see, son,' said Dudfoot to his younger colleague. 'Sometimes it's in the public interest to use a bit of common sense. If we'd nicked them, there'd be a court case. And who picks up the tab for that, eh? Us, with our taxes, is who. Is that the best use of public money? Not really.'

'I guess.'

'And besides, what harm were they doing really? Lots of folk have kinks and theirs is pretty harmless.'

'What about the younger woman, though?' asked Harbottle. 'The one who ran off.'

'I'm sure she'll head for the car park to rejoin her bloke and Mrs Dallimore,' said Dudfoot.

'You know her?'

'Oh yes, I recognised her as soon as I saw her. She might be less inclined to write nasty stuff about coppers now. You can't buy that kind of good publicity.'

'So, what do we do with those?' asked Harbottle. He pointed to the lion and panda heads.

'Bring them with us,' said Dudfoot.

'Back to the car?'

'No,' said Dudfoot. 'To the pump site. I don't know whether you've noticed but since we let those two go, it's all gone dark and quiet over there.'

At a signal from Bron, the students were freed from their tents and emerged, nervous and blinking at the torchlight being shone in their faces. They were quickly herded together into a group.

'Are we prisoners?' asked Dougie Fancey.

'Quite the opposite,' explained Bron. 'You're all completely free to go. We have no beef with you. Or you can stay and watch us refill Gertie's Plash if you want to. We don't care either way. But we won't tolerate interference and, as you can see, we outnumber you significantly.'

'We don't want any trouble.'

'Great! Nor do we. So I suggest you and your people get your tents back up, go inside them and try to get some sleep,' said Bron. 'Meanwhile, we're not going anywhere and we have work to do.'

As the students made their way back to their tents, the hoses that had been sucking water out of the Plash were picked up by several of the stronger protesters and transferred to the River Gew. At the same time, the ends of the pipes that had been in the river were placed into what was left of the Plash. Once the hoses were all in position and the pumps had been rotated by 180 degrees, Bron walked over to the generator.

'OK, are we ready?' he asked. With a resounding cheer, the

protesters showed their approval. Bron turned the ignition key and pressed the green start button. 'Let there be light!'

With a gust of black smoke, the generator powered up. The floodlights came back to life in an instant, dazzling everyone on the ground and eliciting another loud cheer. At the same time, water was drawn from the river and along the intake hoses towards the powerful pumps, where it was accelerated and pushed at some force onwards into the outlet hoses that fed into the Plash.

All of a sudden, the protesters' cheers of delight turned to howls of despair. Colin Cheeseman had decided on a course of action that would allow him to stamp his authority on the evening. He had been supervising the groups involved in rotating the pumps but now, as the machines came back online, he lifted the end of one of the heavy hoses out of the pond and aimed it up at the sky. Wouldn't it be a great idea, he thought, to create some kind of spectacle to mark their victory? And, more importantly, wouldn't it be an excellent way to remind people that this was a FLAN victory and that he was the man to whom tonight's success was owed? However, he hadn't anticipated quite how powerful the surge would be. As water thundered out of the pipe at high pressure, he was knocked completely off balance and he slipped and stumbled in the thick mud at the pond's edge as he fought to regain it. In the meantime, the fat hose writhed in his uncertain grasp and a blast of water smashed into the Portakabin, punching in the window and ripping off a portion of the roof. As Colin grappled to tame the hose's wild thrashing, the torrent ploughed up the muddy ground and knocked a handful of protesters off their feet before slamming into the Portaloo, which seemed to explode.

As they entered the site, PCs Dudfoot and Harbottle were suddenly forced to duck as the chunk of Portakabin roof flew towards them like a jagged angular Frisbee and disintegrated loudly against a tree. But before they'd had a chance to regain their composure, the nearby Portaloo burst open and its noxious contents spilled on to the ground. Disgusting though it was, this would have posed little problem to the police officers had Colin been able to bring the hose back under control. However, a jet of water hit the ghastly pool of filth and it rose up, becoming a wave of ordure that broke over the two officers. As the impromptu water cannon moved on to attack more protesters and students hiding in their hastily erected tents, the officers staggered away, tearing off their reeking uniforms as they went. The hose continued along its chaotic course, leaving destruction in its wake, until Colin finally managed to get both arms around it in an attempt to wrestle the flow of water towards the pond. But as he pointed the hose at the ground he suddenly found himself airborne, rising into the air on a jet of high-pressure water. It was at this moment that Bron reached the generator and stabbed at the off button. As darkness suddenly fell once again, the errant hose lay down and died and all was quiet save for the moans of wet and filthy students, and a feeble scream as Colin Cheeseman belly-flopped into the Plash.

PC Dudfoot and PC Harbottle arrived back at their car in a state of undignified undress. Both had stripped to their shirts and underpants, although they had kept their flat caps on just in case anyone mistook them for doggers. The car park, although still full of cars, was thankfully devoid of witnesses other than a hysterical naked woman and the Tertiary Task Force, who were ogling her while restraining a naked man on the ground. Jamie Cordery had returned to the car park, where he'd been captured by Terry and Kevin, who had finally seen the opportunity for some action.

'Please arrest me,' sobbed a tearful Keeley Flosser as the police officers arrived. 'I'll punch one of you if it helps. But I'm not spending another night naked in these fucking woods.'

Chapter 26

Pamela Dallimore awoke in her hotel bed and stared blearily at the print on the wall opposite, a copy of Ernest Wallengren's painting of a can of Simpkin's Cream of Celery Soup. Her night had been short and her sleep minimal due to worry. Had the two police officers told their colleagues back at the station who they had caught in the woods? What if one of them had been hugely unprofessional and had phoned the newspapers, claiming that she was some kind of sex fetishist? She was well-known enough for the story to pique an editor's interest, and 'Bestselling author caught in kinky woodland sex romp' was a headline that any gossip-hungry tabloid would love to run.

Her best form of defence was attack, she realised; she needed to get her story out first or, at least, as soon as possible so that people would understand her involvement as a non-participant. She jumped out of bed, showered and dressed, made some phone calls and then went in search of Professor Gravestock.

Chief Superintendent Edwin Nuton-Atkinson was nothing if not a man of habit. His Sundays charted the same predictable course every week: a modest lie-in was followed by a breakfast of two bacon, one sausage, two eggs, mushrooms, a grilled tomato, two toast and a pot of tea. Then came the reading of the Sunday broadsheet and colour supplements, usually accompanied by *The Archers* omnibus and *Desert Island Discs* on the radio. He would then drift along to his golf club at Milverton to play a few holes and to enjoy drinks and nibbles in the clubhouse, unless the weather was inclement. Finally, he would drive home for a roast dinner with all the trimmings and fall asleep in front of the TV. His routine was so regular that it had come as something of a shock to his system to have it rudely interrupted by events at Black Dog Wood.

He arrived at the pump site at 9 a.m., accompanied by a small phalanx of early shift officers. It being a Sunday, there were very few constables on duty, certainly nowhere near enough to handle this number of protesters if they decided to turn nasty. And with his annual budget already at stretching point, Nuton-Atkinson wasn't about to cancel his officers' day off and land himself with a sizeable overtime bill to settle. Compromise seemed to be the best way forward.

'It's a tricky one, this,' he mused to Dr Pantridge. 'Technically, they're not trespassing as the wood is common land and anyone has free access.'

'But surely they must be doing something illegal?' said Pantridge.

'The chap who damaged your hut and Portaloo has been arrested,' said Nuton-Atkinson. 'But although we have had some complaints about the way the students were treated, they amount to little more than common assault, which, frankly, is a civil matter rather than a police one. Otherwise, the protestors are being well-behaved and we'd like to keep it that way. And they haven't stolen anything or caused any damage to your equipment.'

'They did a few nights ago.'

'Which, as you admit yourself, was minimal and would be difficult to prove.'

'But they are using our equipment. That's theft of diesel, surely?'

'They say the pumps were already running so they're not using fuel that wouldn't have been used anyway. All they've done is redirect the hoses. But even if that were not true, they've also offered to pay for the fuel. So bang goes any intent to permanently deprive you of it and, therefore, any allegation of theft.'

'This is ridiculous. They do not have permission to use our equipment.'

'And they would be happy for you to turn the machines off. In fact, they'd be as happy as Larry if you took possession of the machinery and left altogether.'

'We can't do that and leave the pond in this state. We'd be responsible for killing off the wildlife.'

'They do seem to have an answer for everything, don't they?'

'So you're not going to do anything?'

'Now, I didn't say that,' said Nuton-Atkinson. 'But it is a tricky situation. It's like what happens when travellers turn up and camp on land that they shouldn't. We have no police powers to move them on. It's up to the council and the Woodland Trust to kick the protesters off.'

'That could take weeks.'

'More likely days, sir. And I do sympathise. It must be very frustrating for you,' said Nuton-Atkinson. 'But we don't want to stir up a hornets' nest when things are currently nice and calm, do we? We will establish a police presence here to prevent any further damage being done to your property and to maintain public tranquillity. But that's all we can do at this time, I'm afraid.'

As the Chief Superintendent walked off to supervise his

officers, Ken Arthur smiled wryly. 'Now there's a man skilled in the art of avoiding aggravation,' he said.

'I can't believe it,' said Pantridge. 'We may as well pack up and go home.'

'We could do that,' said Ken Arthur. 'But that still leaves us with the damp problems at Harpax Grange. Perhaps we should start thinking about a Plan B.'

'I'm not very comfortable with the idea of having police officers based here,' said Miss Bultitude. 'It could be very distracting for my girls.'

'All we're asking for is somewhere, maybe an outbuilding, that we can use – somewhere for the lads and lasses to take a break and brew up a cuppa,' explained the early shift inspector. 'And this is the only building anywhere near the pump site.'

'Didn't I see a Portakabin there?'

'You did. But it no longer has a roof and it's full of... well, it's not usable any more, I'm afraid. We promise to be as unobtrusive as possible, Miss Bultitude. Most of the time our officers will be at the Plash and you and your girls won't even see them.'

'Well, I suppose you could use the old sports pavilion,' said Miss Bultitude. 'It's dry and has power. And I'm sure we can rustle up a gas heater.'

'That sounds perfect,' said the inspector.

'Very well,' said Miss Bultitude. 'Let me show you where it is. It'll need to be tidied up a little. We mostly use it for storage at this time of year.'

'Thank you,' said the inspector. 'This is very public-spirited of you.'

'We must all do our bit to help, I suppose.'

Frank Shunter was mopping up the last of his fried egg with a piece of toast when Cliff Jaine phoned.

'I have some good news,' said Jaine. 'Gertie's Plash got invaded by animal rights protesters last night. They've taken control of the site and are using the pumps to refill the pond.'

'How is that good news?' asked Shunter.

'Because the school is providing accommodation for a mobile control room. It means that I now have a legitimate reason to visit the place and snoop around.'

'That is good news,' said Shunter. 'If you can engineer some way to get me an interview with Miss Bultitude without suggesting that she's a murder suspect, I'd be grateful. And, on that subject, I also have some news.'

'Oh yes?'

'I found something interesting among the papers of Connie Tremblett's dad last night. A letter addressed to him dated 1922 from someone who appears to have been a Nasely man, but who wasn't one of the Lucky Six.'

'An extra survivor we didn't know about?'

'It seems so.'

'A deserter?'

'Maybe. His initials were TB and there were only two men with those initials in the battalion. Both were posted as missing in action: Thomas Brock and Thadeus Bultitude.'

'Bultitude? That can't be a coincidence, surely?'

'I'm popping over to Ordon later to return the letters,' said Shunter. 'I'll ask Connie if she knows anything about him. I couldn't find much online other than he was an artist before the war. Royal Academy, no less. I found two exhibition catalogues dated 1912 and 1913 that mention his work.'

'Miss Bultitude did show me a portrait of the school's founder that was painted by her grandfather. Same guy, I guess,' said Jaine. 'There can't have been two Thadeus Bultitudes, surely?'

'It would seem unlikely.'

'Yet another possible connection between the two murders,' said Jaine. 'The plot thickens.'

'You've done what?' said Miss Deak.

'How would it look if I'd said no?' said Miss Bultitude. 'The school doesn't need any bad publicity. And they have promised to be as inconspicuous as possible. It shouldn't cause too much disruption.'

'That's as may be, but I'm not happy with the idea of a lot of men on the premises. And have you forgotten that we've organised a fundraiser for tomorrow night? What will our patrons think if they see police officers everywhere?'

'Oh, hang it all,' said Miss Bultitude. 'I'd forgotten that.'

'Well, it's too late to cancel it now. Some of our benefactors travel from quite a distance. Two from Spain and three from France. They'll already be on their way.'

'Then we'll just have to go ahead. We'll use the drama studio as usual but we'll guide everyone in through the rear car park. That way they won't be alarmed by any police presence. How many are we expecting?'

'Fifty-six, if they all turn up,' said Miss Deak.

'It should be a good evening then,' said Miss Bultitude, smiling.

Frank Shunter parked outside Paradise Farmhouse and waited for the small crowd of pigs he'd attracted to disperse. Now that he'd had the chance to look at them more closely, he noted that their facial features were exaggerated or not quite in the right place, as if they'd been sculpted by a child from modelling clay. Undoubtedly the result of several generations of inbreeding among the small feral population, he thought. Wryly, he wondered if that also explained the eccentricities displayed by the insular Trembletts. Once the pigs had moved on, he stepped out of his car and quickly skipped to the porch and rang the bell, which, as he might have predicted, didn't work. He hammered on the front door instead and it was answered by Jessie.

'Is your grandmother in?' asked Shunter.

'Yeah. Come in.'

'Thanks,' said Shunter, entering the dusty hallway. 'I meant to ask you yesterday – your gran said that you'd had an expensive education. Were you a Harpax girl?'

'Yeah.'

'How was it?'

'OK, I guess. But no boys. And way too many rules. Here you are.'

They had arrived at the kitchen where Constance Tremblett was jointing a chicken with a large, heavy chopper.

'Gran, it's that bloke to see you again,' said Jessica, and disappeared.

Connie looked up from her butchery and scanned Shunter with her good eye.

'Letters any good?' she asked.

'Perhaps. There was one name that interested me, someone your father knew. Thadeus Bultitude?'

'The painter? Got one of his here somewhere. A horrible horse. Hoy, Winnie! Where's that horrible horse painting?'

Winifred looked over from the Aga, where she was stirring a large pan of what smelled like vegetable soup, much to the apparent delight of the small monkey that was on her shoulder.

'It's in Eunice's and Clive's drawing room, I think. Above that bureau with the magic lantern on it. And the stuffed owl.'

'He couldn't do horses,' explained Connie. 'People, yes. He was good at people. But his horses was rubbish. Want me to show you?'

'No, that's not necessary,' said Shunter. 'I'm only asking because your father had several letters from someone with the initials TB. They were all dated from sometime after the war and they were from someone who fought alongside him at Ypres. I thought it might be Thadeus Bultitude as he was listed as missing in action. I think he might have survived.'

'He bloody didn't,' said Connie. 'He stepped on a land mine.'

'He did?'

'Father saw it happen. They couldn't find enough of him to identify, so he had to be listed as missing. But Father knew. Told me his paintings are worth more because of it. Even his rubbish horses.'

'Hmm. So the letter writer must have been the other TB,' said Shunter. 'There was also a Thomas Brock.'

'Thomas Brock, eh? You know who he was, don't you?'

'Should I?

'You should,' said Connie. 'Thomas Brock was Agnes Crabbe's big brother.'

'You want to go and check the cameras already?' said Professor Gravestock over coffee in the hotel restaurant. He raised an eyebrow and smiled a knowing smile. 'It hasn't even been twenty-four hours yet. Or do you know something I don't?'

'There was a lot of activity in the woods last night. You never know your luck,' said Pamela Dallimore innocently. 'Plus, I'm heading back to London this evening.'

'I think you're going to be disappointed.'

'Can we go and take a look anyway?' said Dallimore. 'My car's parked outside.'

Sir Giles placed the last of Phoebe Kingshaw's possessions into a carrier bag and made one final search of his flat to ensure that nothing of hers was left behind. Then he locked up and made his way down to the car park, stopping off at the communal bins and recycling area. He felt terrible disposing of the items in this way but they were just things: cosmetics, a toothbrush, a few clothes. He had his memories and that was enough.

With a heavy heart he set off back to South Herewardshire for what, he mused morbidly, might possibly be the last time for some years. He wondered what the penalty for murder was these days. Fifteen years? Ten? He'd always bemoaned the fact that prison sentences were too short but now, as he faced the reality of being convicted for a crime he hadn't committed, he was thankful that he wouldn't be an old man when he got out. An altogether better scenario would be not being sent to prison at all, of course. He asked the Bentley's hands-free phone connection to call Frank Shunter.

Chapter 27

McNabb rubbed the sides of his head to try to relieve the pressure of the blood thumping in his temples but it didn't help. He'd called his sister to see if 'Lorraine' had managed to extract any kind of confession from Sir Giles, only to be hit by a bombshell.

'Wait. Let me get this straight. You... you like him?' he stuttered.

'He's a gentleman,' said Ettie. 'And you know me, Derek. I'm a very good judge of character.'

'I asked you to spy on him, not get involved!'

'I'm not involved.'

'And does he like you?'

'I think so. Or, at least, he likes the woman he thinks is called Lorraine.'

'So you have nothing for me at all?'

'No. Other than the fact that I'm convinced that he's innocent. I asked him to his face if he killed her and he said no. I believe him.'

'Ettie, I needed you to—'

'I'm sorry, Derek, but it's true. Nature has seen fit to equip me with a built-in lie detector – it's why I'm such a good theatrical agent. People can't bullshit me.'

'I don't believe this.'

'I'm sorry, but I'm convinced you're barking up the wrong tree,' said Ettie. 'He's not your murderer and I think tha—'

'I don't suppose the fact that he's a multi-millionaire has any bearing on matters, does it?'

'Actually, no it does—'

McNabb hung up and looked around for something to throw but his office was still devoid of any clutter. In frustration, he reached for a pencil and broke it in half.

But Ettie was right, he conceded. She did have an unerring ability to spot lies. All of which meant that his case was just about sunk. And he had no other suspect.

The offices of Tremens, Mallord, Hacker and Budge, Solicitors and Commissioners for Oaths, were located in a fine Georgian building called Sibella House that stood opposite Bowcester train station. Upon their arrival, Shunter and Jaine were shown straight into Andrew Tremens's office. Tremens was a slim, dapper man who was always immaculately turned out and who seemed to bathe in cologne. His colleagues joked that his location, as he moved between the firm's various offices, could be tracked by scent alone. He had been intrigued enough by Shunter's text over the weekend to move all of his scheduled appointments for Monday back by half an hour.

'So, who else knows about this?' he asked as he studied the printouts of the manuscript pages with a magnifying glass.

'Other than us three, we're not sure,' said Shunter. He turned to Jaine. 'Did you tell McNabb in the end?'

'I was going to. But with events at the Plash over the

weekend and the fact that he was acting like a complete arse towards me, I never got around to it.'

'This is an amazing find,' said Tremens excitedly. 'Either this was written by Agnes Crabbe or someone got hold of her original typewriter and wrote it, which seems extremely unlikely as it's behind glass at the Crabbe Cottage Museum in Nasely.'

'How can you be so sure?' asked Jaine.

'Look at this upper-case letter P,' said Tremens, handing the detective the magnifying glass. 'The serif on the bottom of the downward stroke is uniquely malformed. It's an absolute giveaway. Agnes only ever owned one typewriter and all of her capital Ps show the same fault.'

'But wouldn't other typewriters have Ps cast from the same mould?'

'It's possible. However, there was also an issue with her number five. The malformed five is here too. The chances of two typewriters having the same two faults are millions to one. The chances of finding both are astronomical.'

'So you reckon it's genuine then?' asked Shunter.

'There's definitely enough evidence to say a tentative yes,' said Tremens. 'If I could see a bit more of the document, to study the vocabulary and syntax, I could absolutely confirm its authenticity. But it looks good to me. You may finally have found *Wallowing in the Mire*. I cannot begin to tell you how much excitement there will be when news gets out to the Millies and Manlies. They'll go positively gaga.'

'Yes, well, that's some way off,' explained Jaine. 'Firstly, because we haven't secured the manuscript yet. And secondly, because if it is real, it might be evidence in a murder enquiry.'

'Do you mean that awful business with Sir Giles Luscott-Whorne? Or do you mean the blindfolded skeleton in Black Dog Wood?'

'Unfortunately, we can't say anything at this time,' said Jaine. 'The waters are a little murky, so we need to keep a lid on things for the moment.'

'My lips are sealed,' said Tremens, clapping his hands. 'But sooo excited!'

'So it looks like it's the real McCoy,' said Jaine as they left the building. 'And I reckon there's enough circumstantial evidence to suggest that it's connected to Phoebe Kingshaw's murder. I'm going to have to tell Kipper now. He needs to know about the manuscript and the hockey stick both possibly being at the school. It's his case, after all.'

'Then let's just hope he does something sensible with the information,' said Shunter. 'Sir Giles called me last night to ask how things are going – he's due to surrender to his bail this evening – and he's panicking that he's going to be charged. I'm hoping that this new evidence might delay matters, which will justify the money he's paying me.'

'I'll go and see Kipper now,' said Jaine reluctantly.

Sir Giles stood on top of Bascombe's Bluff, the highest point in South Herewardshire, and looked out across the pasturelands of his childhood. At a mere 175 feet above sea level, the Bluff was barely higher than most of the rest of South Herewardshire, which was almost uniformly flat, but the hill was a favourite spot for romantics and dog walkers. Giles was neither of those things, but as he stood there beneath the lowering sky, he felt a tear roll down his cheek. It was all over, he realised. His political ambitions. His social climbing. His marriage. Even, perhaps, his liberty. He'd come to this spot many times as a child and he remembered the sense of freedom and elation that he'd experienced when doing so. It had been a blessed escape from the oppressive environment of boarding school and from his father's constant whining about the Whornes' decline in status. Freedom was something that he had taken for granted, just as, he imagined, most people did because they had never experienced the real threat of it being taken away. That threat was what had made millions of men sign up to fight in two world wars and Giles wished there was some similar gesture that he could make to fight for his own liberty. But all he had was the vain hope that Frank Shunter would unearth the evidence he needed to vindicate him. The ex-detective had already found more than the police had, but time was running out.

A gust of cold wind blew past and with it came memories of flying his kite on blustery days and the sudden thought that he too could fly away from all of his troubles if he wanted to. He could grab his passport and board a plane to some country that didn't have an extradition treaty with the UK. It would be so easy to do, but he knew that he never could. Whornes did not run away. They might explode, or be gored to death by giant pigs, or make bad decisions resulting in the deaths of men under their command, but they were not cowards. They faced their enemies and accusers. Besides which, there was a principle at stake here – if he couldn't place his faith in justice and English law, then everything he believed in was a lie. He had to stay the course.

McNabb had spent a harrowing and emotional hour with Phoebe Kingshaw's parents, who had travelled from Hampshire to arrange collection of their daughter's body. The fact that this had come on top of his sister's disappointing news, and a dispiriting phone conversation with the Crown Prosecution Service, had put him in a very bad mood and he was therefore not at all inclined to talk to Cliff Jaine. But the sergeant had insisted that it was urgent so he reluctantly called him into his office once the Kingshaws had left.

'Well?' he said.

'I might have a lead for you, sir,' said Jaine.

'Oh, have you?' said McNabb, folding his arms. 'Something that you and Sir Giles's best buddy Frank Shunter have turned up, I suppose?'

'Yes, as it happens,' said Jaine, rising above the sarcasm. 'In the course of investigating my murder, we turned up some possible information on yours. We think we know what the murder weapon might be.'

McNabb perked up.

'What?'

'There's evidence to suggest that it was a hockey stick bought from Crute's department store by Harpax Grange School,' said Jaine. He quickly explained the circumstances that had led to this conclusion. 'And, as Topsy said that there were particles of beech wood in Kingshaw's head wound, I phoned the manager of the store and he confirmed that the hockey sticks were made of beech.'

For a short while, McNabb simply stared at his sergeant, unable to dispute the evidence being presented to him, circumstantial though it was.

'And we may have uncovered a motive too,' said Jaine. 'We suspect that an unpublished Agnes Crabbe manuscript is in a locked chest in the headmistress's office. We know that Phoebe Kingshaw saw it there because there are photographs of it on her mobile phone. And whoever owns that manuscript will earn millions from it. Maybe Kingshaw was killed because she—'

'We need to search that school now,' snapped McNabb suddenly.

'That may not be—'

But Jaine's words fell on deaf ears. McNabb was already out of his office and barking orders at his staff to drop everything they were doing and to get ready for an operation while he obtained a search warrant. His last chance to redeem himself had unexpectedly appeared and he was not about to squander the opportunity.

'This is uncanny. How did you know?' asked Gravestock.

'Lucky guess?' said Mrs Dallimore.

Gravestock smiled knowingly. Having removed the data cards from his hidden cameras and loaded the contents onto his laptop, he'd found himself in possession of several blurry but intriguing images of a figure running across the camera's field of vision. To Mrs Dallimore's delight, there was nothing that could identify who the individual was.

'And you did say that you were happy for me to have copies?' she said, producing a memory stick.

'Yes, of course,' said Gravestock. 'It's obviously some idiot in a costume and therefore of no interest to me or my area of research. Oh, hang on, this one is a bit different.'

On the screen appeared an image captured by a boulder cam. In contrast to the other images, which showed a naked man wearing an oversized animal head, the blurry image was of a figure covered in coarse, shaggy hair. Pamela Dallimore was genuinely surprised.

'Looks like we both got lucky,' she said.

Shunter pored over a copy of Cowper's *History of the Whorne Family* in Nasely Library and twirled his moustache. Ever since talking to Connie Tremblett, he'd been pondering the subject of Thomas Brock. The name hadn't jumped out at him when he'd first read it, certainly not in the way that the unfortunate

Thadeus Bultitude's had. But then Connie had reminded him that Brock was Agnes Crabbe's maiden name and so they had delved back into the tin of correspondence to reread everything written by 'TB'.

Brock's first letter to Henry Tremblett, dated December 1919, had been a tentative enquiry as to his health, presumably because he hadn't known whether Henry had survived the war or not. But, once he'd received a reply, they had corresponded regularly for seven years. Throughout it all, Brock had insisted that the secret of his survival be kept from anyone who might know him. When Tremblett had enquired why this was, Brock had explained that his face had been disfigured. And besides, technically he was a deserter and he had no intention of giving up his freedom.

The letters were mostly conversational, with Brock describing life in France and reminiscing about their army days. But then there had been Brock's final letter, which had begun: 'Dear Henry. It is with much sadness that I write to you to tell you of the terrible thing that has happened. I have lost both my Mathilde and our child.' The letter had gone on to describe how Mathilde had died during childbirth from 'a heart grievously weakened by tragedy' and because she was 'past the age at which a woman may safely carry'. Shunter knew from previous letters that Brock had escaped the battlefield with terrible injuries and, posing as a deaf and mute peasant, had recuperated for several years at a friary on the French border. He had then moved on to Armentières, where he'd found work in a textiles factory. He had lodged with a co-worker called Mathilde and her elderly mother until the German mustard gas attacks of 1918. Mathilde's mother had been killed but she and Tom had fled into the countryside. The war had ended and Tom had spent several years fixing up an old farm cottage in Nieppe and working the land. Despite

Mathilde being almost twice his age when they'd met, love had blossomed, and Tom had been content with his new life, telling Tremblett that he would never come home. But then tragedy had struck with Mathilde's unplanned pregnancy and death in childbirth. 'There is nothing left for me here any more', the letter had concluded. 'My home is no longer a home. My heart is filled with pain. I care for nothing.' The remainder of the letter placed the blame for everything that had gone wrong in Brock's life firmly at the feet of Jolyon Whorne. 'My miseries began with him and will end with him,' he wrote. 'One day I would see him suffer as I have suffered by his actions.'

The fact that the crime scene in the woods was so strikingly similar to the final scene of *Wallowing in the Mire* had made Shunter wonder if Thomas Brock had travelled back from France to exact revenge on Jolyon Whorne, just as the book's hero, Jack Stillaway, had done to his commanding officer. Had he killed and then buried Jolyon and then confessed to his sister what he'd done? If so, why had she then used it as the plot for her book? Admittedly, the book had never been put forward for publication, but it still seemed a reckless thing to do.

Shunter had naturally assumed that the body in the woods must therefore be that of Jolyon but, annoyingly, a little research had shown that his death had been quite boringly conventional. Unless official records had been falsified, Jolyon had died of a heart attack in 1935 and now occupied a rather grand tomb in the Whorne mausoleum. And, besides, the buried man had suffered shrapnel injuries and Whorne hadn't fought anywhere near the front line with his men.

'Bugger.'

'Sorry?' said a librarian, as she passed by.

'Sorry, Morag,' said Shunter. 'I was just expressing my

frustration at reaching a dead end in my research. A literal dead end.'

'Cowper's, eh?' said the librarian. 'I think you're the first person ever to take it off the shelf who isn't a Whorne. What were you looking for?'

'You know about the body that was found last week in Black Dog Wood? I had a theory that it was Jolyon Whorne.'

'Why?'

'Well, he wasn't exactly popular with his troops, was he?' said Shunter. 'The survivors, I mean. He got a lot of their comrades killed.'

'If he actually did,' said Morag. 'There's a strong school of thought that puts the blame on Edward Pank, his batman.'

'Not a nice man, I understand.'

'He was a bully and a thug. But he had Jolyon's ear and a lot of people reckon that he was relied upon to make all the tough decisions.'

'Like giving the order for the troops to push forward, despite the threat of gas attack?'

'Yes. My great-granddad was one of the survivors,' said Morag. 'James McFarland.'

'Interesting,' said Shunter. 'I had a theory that someone who was recorded as missing in action had actually survived and came back to kill Jolyon out of revenge. Sadly, it doesn't seem very likely now.'

'Sounds like the plot of a novel,' said the librarian.

'You have no idea how right you are,' said Shunter. His phone began to ring and he quickly apologised and stepped outside the library to take the call.

'Hello, Cliff.'

'Kipper has organised a raid on the school for 7 p.m. tonight,' said Jaine. 'And I've got a warrant to search Joan Bultitude's office.'

'That's great. And if the manuscript isn't there?'

'Then I guess the finger points back to Phoebe Kingshaw and Sir Giles,' said Jaine.

'I guess so. Oh, just one more thing – did you order a DNA analysis of your victim?'

'I did. The results should be back by now but I haven't checked them yet. I'm sure Topsy would have called me if there was anything significant. Why?'

'Something I'm ruminating on,' said Shunter. 'It might be worth checking in with him.'

At 7 p.m., Cecily drove her husband to Bowcester Police Station to surrender to his bail. She had insisted on accompanying him as a public show of solidarity. However, there was practicality in the decision too: if Giles was charged with murder, he'd be kept in custody and that would leave his car stranded in Bowcester. At least if she was driving, she could take the Bentley home. These were the sorts of details that she attended to every day while Giles was off dealing with loftier matters of state and business. Perhaps soon, she thought, she might have to take on many more of his responsibilities. It wasn't only Giles's life that would be fundamentally changed if things went against him.

However, upon arrival, they were told that there would be some small delay and that Detective Inspector McNabb was not yet available. Sir Giles's barrister began spitting venom.

'Our appointment clearly states 7:30 p.m.,' he complained. 'I want to know whether or not my client is going to be charged and I want to know now. To delay matters could be construed as a form of mental torture. Where is DI McNabb?'

'He'll be here soon,' explained the custody officer. 'He had to go out on a raid and he's probably been delayed by traffic or something. I'm sure he won't be long.'

'You can be damned sure that his divisional commander will hear about this,' snapped Luscott-Vent. 'And possibly the Chief Superintendent, who is a personal friend of mine.'

'That is your right, of course,' said Custody. 'It's also your right to make an official complaint. I can get the forms if you like.' A very slight smile played across her lips at the thought.

'We will return at eight,' barked the barrister. 'Make sure he is here when we return. If not, have the complaint forms ready for us.'

The party was escorted from the station and the custody officer allowed herself a full smile. She would enjoy watching Kipper grovelling later. Meanwhile, she wondered exactly what the DI was doing that was so important as to risk the wrath of such important and well-connected people.

Chapter 28

The arrival of several marked police vehicles on the school's gravel forecourt caused ripples of excitement and alarm among the group of sixth-formers who were manning the school's reception office. After a short discussion, they had agreed to open the front door.

'We were told not to let anyone in,' explained one of them.

'There must be someone adult in charge, surely?' asked McNabb, after the production of his ID and the search warrant had drawn blank stares from the girls. 'Where are all the teachers? Don't any of them live on site?'

'Just the head and the deputy head,' said Jaine. 'Miss Bultitude lives in the lodge.'

'She won't be there,' said the sixth-former. 'She's at the Millerick Society meeting in the drama studio. So is Miss Deak. It's a fundraiser night. That's why we've been left in charge. We have a number to ring in case of emergencies. Should I call it?'

'No,' snapped McNabb. He glanced at his watch. 'Jaine, go and search the headmistress's office. And make it snappy. I'm due back at Bowcester shortly.'

'Did the Crown Prosecution Service agree to charge Sir Giles then?'

'They'll have someone to charge when I return with the evidence from this raid,' said McNabb.

'Does that mean they didn't then?'

'Just go and search the office!' barked McNabb. The CPS decision not to charge without further evidence was still sticking in his throat and meant that this raid was his next best chance to nail someone for the murder and save face.

Jaine and his small team of officers headed for the stairs.

'Now, you three,' said McNabb. 'Where will I find this drama studio?'

'Round the back of the school,' said one of the sixth-formers. 'But we were told not to disturb them unless it was urgent.'

'You won't be disturbing them. We will,' said McNabb. 'Show me where it is.'

In the trees that skirted the lawns in front of Harpax Grange, Willy Tremblett watched the arrival of the police vehicles. He'd never officially been told that the Tertiary Task Force had been disbanded and, with boredom setting in, he'd taken to roaming the woods to make sure that his friends and colleagues were safe at the Plash. He'd paid particular attention to the school ever since the police had established a presence on site. There were never more than three or four officers on duty at any one time and they operated an hour on/hour off shift pattern that meant there were always at least two at the pump site and two at the school. It had therefore come as a shock to pay one of his regular spying visits and to witness the arrival of several patrol cars, a prisoner van and at least twelve more officers.

'They're planning to raid us,' he growled. 'Fascists.' He made his way back to the Plash as quickly and quietly as he could. He had to warn his people.

'That's an extraordinary piece of furniture,' said Jaine. The photographs on Phoebe Kingshaw's phone hadn't prepared him for the sheer extravagance of decoration on the oak chest.

'I think it might be an ottoman,' said a constable called Chillick, who never missed an episode of *Antiques Roadshow*.

'Well, whatever it is, it's locked,' said Jaine, pulling upwards on the lid. 'Have a look around for a key.'

At the rear of the school building, McNabb found himself looking at an unexpected number of parked cars. The drama studio was a modern, windowless and soundproofed block behind and unconnected to the main school building. It had its own car park and tonight it was full. Many of the vehicles were expensive marques and among them he spotted Jaguars, Bentleys, Aston Martins and several top-of-the-range BMWs, Mercedes and Range Rovers. A quick circuit of the building revealed only two points of entry: a pair of large double doors that were firmly locked shut and a smaller single stage door at the rear. It too was locked and no one seemed to be manning it. From inside the building came the faint, muffled sound of classical music.

'Do we put the door in?' asked a large and enthusiastic officer. He carried a heavy portable battering ram in a holdall.

'This isn't a drugs bust,' said McNabb. 'And you can't flush a hockey stick down the loo.'

He knocked loudly upon the stage door and waited. After a minute he knocked again but there was still no answer. 'The music must be too loud,' he said. 'It looks like we will have to put the door in after all. Go on then.'

The big officer grinned.

'I'm not sure that coming to the pub was a very good idea,' said Sir Giles. 'I mean, how will it look if I turn up at the police station reeking of Scotch?'

The Puppeteers Arms was situated opposite Bowcester Police Station and was popular with police officers who fancied a quick pint after a tough shift. Judging by his fellow drinkers' short haircuts, and the way they seemed to be studying him whenever they thought he wasn't looking, Sir Giles assumed that there were a few in this evening.

'We'll get you some mints or something if it bothers you that much,' said Luscott-Vent. 'Listen, old boy, that ginger weasel is out to get you and if he charges you, it's the last decent tipple you'll taste in a while. I should savour it if I were you.'

'You make it sound like it's a done deal,' said Giles gloomily.

'It most certainly is not,' said the barrister. 'Even if he does charge you this evening, which is by no means definite, we're still some way away from a trial and who knows what evidence may turn up before then? So, even if you do end up temporarily in the clink, that's no reason to give up the fight. One more for the road, eh?'

As the wood splintered around the lock and the door slammed open, the officer holding the ram barged through and into a small, dark hallway, closely followed by two other colleagues and McNabb bringing up the rear. A halo of light surrounded a closed door at the far end of the hallway and they made towards it. The classical music was much louder now and was recognisable as Offenbach's 'Can-Can'. At McNabb's signal, the officers opened the second door and stepped through.

They found themselves at the back of a small theatre, at the front of which was a brightly lit stage upon which eight people were performing the famous dance. They were clumsy and uncoordinated but McNabb barely noticed the quality of the choreography. What had arrested his complete attention was that the Can-Can dancers were all wearing costume animal heads, were all undeniably male, and none of them had bothered with underwear.

'Are you sure they're planning to raid us?' said Oberon. He looked at his watch. 'It's been half an hour since you told us they were coming.'

'I don't know how long it takes to organise these things,' said Willy.

'We must assume the worst, I suppose,' said Bron. 'Perhaps it's time to cut our losses and go.'

'We're packing up?' said Willy.

'You're welcome to wait around for the cops if you want to but the engineers and archaeologists have packed up and gone, and the Plash is restored to ninety per cent of its former glory. I reckon it's a good time to scarper.'

'But they could come back and start emptying the Plash again.'

'I doubt that,' said Bron. 'They know that we'd come back and in larger numbers. Trust me, it's over, Willy. FLAN has finally done something worthwhile. Shame Colin's not here to see it.'

The Can-Can dancers' heavy footfall thundered through the theatre as they galumphed around the stage to the music. Their cute cartoony heads boasted vacant smiles, big watery eyes and exaggerated lashes, and below their flouncy dresses and clouds of petticoats, the troupe's gender was quite clearly on display. Every time they kicked up their legs, the audience was treated to a full-frontal view and, as his mind slowly came to terms with what he was seeing, McNabb turned to look at the audience to assuage his feelings of revulsion. However, there was no respite to be found there. Like a scene from a surrealist art film, the members of the audience were also dressed as animals: baby blue teddy bears jostled with pastel pink rabbits, and lime green hippos snuggled up to indeterminate horned creatures covered in soft downy fur. And to add to his growing sense of unreality, he could see that their costumes were mutilated or had been adapted in some way. Some had holes cut in them to reveal the most intimate parts of the wearer's anatomy. Others were augmented with sex toys or saucy underwear.

'What the f—' was all he managed to say.

Onstage, the music was reaching a crescendo and the dance troupe kicked furiously before performing a reverse bow and showing their naked buttocks – and in the case of two of them, butt plugs with tails attached – to the audience, who applauded wildly and whooped with delight. Their appreciation was eerily quiet, muffled as it was by their furry gloved hands and costumed heads. Suddenly, a unicorn screamed softly and pointed at the police officers. As one, the audience turned and McNabb found himself the main focus of an army of insanely smiling giant soft toys. He tried to find the words he needed to say – 'This is a police raid. Everyone stay in your seats' – but they stuck in his throat. Several of the theatregoers were now on their feet. One bizarre creature – McNabb assumed it to be a hedgehog although it was covered with pricks of a very different kind to those found on its woodland cousins – buzzed menacingly, in contrast to its incongruously rosy-apple-cheeked smile, and made a run for the door. McNabb finally found his voice.

'Stay where you are! We are police officers!'

The audience, rather than stay where they were, followed the hedgehog's lead and stampeded for the double doors, only to find them locked. In the centre of the mass of panicking furry bodies, a large tiger, adorable in every aspect except for its giant rubber penis, tried to force its way through to the door, a key held high above its costumed head. But it was no use; the press of bodies was just too great. McNabb reached for his radio.

'All units employed on Operation St Trinians – I repeat, all units employed on Operation St Trinians – make your way to the drama studio at the rear of the school now! And I mean now! Stop anyone from leaving the building!'

Realising they were caught like rats, or piglets, or ducklings, or even plush lobsters, in a trap, the audience began to wail and moan. Several seemed to faint but most just fell to the floor in a dejected heap or retook their seats. The dancers climbed down off the stage and joined their furry friends.

'Who's in charge here?' demanded McNabb.

The tiger walked forward, pulling off its head as it came near.

'That would be me, officer,' said Joan Bultitude.

'You should be celebrating, Colin,' said Bron, clapping Cheeseman on the back as they left Bowcester Police Station. Following his exploits with the hose, the leader of FLAN had been charged with criminal damage and assaulting two police officers in the execution of their duty and had been bailed to appear at court in a week's time.

'The Plash is saved, FLAN has finally proved its worth, and you've got yourself a cracking girlfriend into the bargain,' continued Bron. 'So why do you look like a man who's taken a dump with his trousers on?'

'I am pleased, really I am,' said Cheeseman unconvincingly.

'Come on then, let's go and celebrate,' said Bron. 'And as you're the one with money, the first round is on you.'

They walked into the Puppeteers Arms to find all of the members of FLAN waiting, plus a few representatives from other animal rights groups. As they burst into a rousing chorus of 'For he's a jolly good fellow', Maisie rushed forward and hugged Colin.

He looked around the faces of the people gathered and genuinely smiled for the first time in what felt like days. Meanwhile, the other pub-goers frowned at the noise.

'Loutish rabble,' grunted Luscott-Vent.

'They look familiar for some reason,' said Cecily.

'I've seen some bloody sights in my time but this takes the biscuit,' said McNabb. 'What on God's earth was going on in there?'

Miss Bultitude, still dressed in her tiger outfit and towering over the diminutive detective inspector, was unrepentant. 'It's just a gathering of friends with similar interests,' she said. 'We're not committing any crime. If anything, we're providing a public service.'

'A public service?'

'Yes. A safe place where men who want to be punished can meet women who want to punish them.'

'But this is a bloody girls' school!'

'We are very careful,' said Miss Bultitude. 'We'd never do anything that might affect the girls. They don't have a clue what goes on at our fundraisers and nor do the other teachers, for that matter. We operate in complete secrecy. Or, at least, we did.'

'But there are minors on the premises!'

'At the school, yes. But not in here. The Millerick Society has been holding meetings like these for over a decade and it's never been a problem.'

'Sooner or later, word would have got out.'

'I doubt that, Inspector. Our members pay for absolute discretion, which is understandable considering that many of them hold important or influential roles in society. So who among them would ever tell? My deputy and I are the only people who know who the society members are. And they have to wear costumes that disguise them. Strict anonymity is paramount and it is a club rule that no one is allowed to give their name or reveal their face to any other member.'

'So no one has any idea with whom they're having the pleasure?' said Jaine. He had arrived during the conversation, along with two burly detective constables who were carrying the heavy oak chest between them.

'What's that for?' asked McNabb.

'We couldn't find a key,' said Jaine.

'I'm not sure that it has one,' said Miss Bultitude. 'It came with the school and has never been opened as far as I know.'

'Are you saying that you've never been tempted to call in a locksmith to have a look inside?' asked Jaine.

'It's crossed my mind a few times but life is so busy here at the school that I never seemed to get round to it.'

'Phoebe Kingshaw got it open.'

'Did she?' said Miss Bultitude sadly. 'She really was a very smart girl.'

'Shame you killed her, then,' said McNabb.

Miss Bultitude looked genuinely startled. 'What on earth makes you think that I killed her?'

'Because of the manuscript,' said Jaine.

'Manuscript? What manuscript?' asked Miss Bultitude.

'Joan Bultitude, I am arresting you on suspicion of the murder of Phoebe Kingshaw,' said McNabb and he proceeded to caution her.

'But I haven't murdered anyone, Inspector.'

'Just get in the van,' said McNabb, looking with some disgust at Miss Bultitude's costume. 'Impressionable young ladies are watching.'

'Yes, of course,' said Miss Bultitude. Over McNabb's shoulder she could see girlish faces pressed up against the school's brightly lit windows. 'I assume someone is coming to take charge of my girls?'

'There are some women police officers coming over from Coxeter,' said Jaine.

'And can someone look after my dogs? Though I should warn you, they can be a little excitable.'

'I'll call the local RSPCA guy,' said Jaine.

'Excuse me, sir,' said PC Chillick. He arrived puffing and panting, his face beaming with pride. 'I found this in the deputy head's rooms.'

He held up a hockey stick, its club end wrapped in a clear plastic evidence bag. Even through the plastic, McNabb could see rusty brown stains.

'Oh, Tiggy... what have you done?' said Miss Bultitude.

'Go and see if she's among that lot we're interviewing in the drama studio,' said McNabb.

'She's dressed as a hedgehog,' said Miss Bultitude. 'But whatever she's done, I had no part in it.'

'I guess this means that Sir Giles is off the hook,' said Jaine. 'Speaking of which, shouldn't you be at Bowcester now?'

McNabb looked at his watch.

'Shit!' he shouted.

'Manners,' said Miss Bultitude, automatically.

McNabb stared at her and at the monstrous dildo stapled to her costume.

'Really?' he said.

'Oh, fuck it,' said Miss Bultitude.

Chapter 29

The storms that had been threatening for the first half of the month arrived in the third week of October, bringing buffeting cold winds and rain that turned to hail. But all was warm and snug in the saloon bar of the Happy Onion. It was very busy – festival busy – which was just how Vic Sallow liked it, even if it was just for the one night. A fire blazed in the hearth, the pub smelled of woodsmoke and good ale, and the barflies were discussing the extraordinary events of the past fortnight, prior to attending a press conference being staged in the village hall.

'I bet she got the idea from the Diabolical Club,' said Charlie Barnfather. 'Sir Redvers and his lot liked staging orgies and things like that.'

'But at a girls' school?' said Len Youlden. 'It's disgusting.'

'The girls were never at risk,' said Shunter. 'The Millerick Society was only interested in punishing and degrading men. I spoke to Jessie Tremblett – she's a former Harpax girl and as broad-minded as any young woman I've ever met, and—'

'That's an understatement,' snorted Youlden. 'I hear she's one of that lot who go dogging in Black Dog Wood.'

'But that's my point,' said Shunter. 'If anyone would know

about a secret sex club, it would be her. But when I asked her about it, she knew nothing, nothing at all, even though she was at Harpax Grange for eight years, right up until she was eighteen. She seemed quite annoyed, to be honest.'

'I still think it's a bloody disgrace,' said Youlden.

'No one is arguing with that, Len. But while I can't defend their actions in any way, you have to admit that Bultitude and Deak ran a slick operation. The girls didn't ever find out that the club was there, right under their noses, and nor did any of the other teachers.'

'That's their story.'

'They seemed genuinely shocked and most of them have resigned,' said Shunter. 'And there were no other teachers among the partygoers.'

'They wouldn't have been able to afford it even if they'd known,' added Jaine. 'The membership fees were extortionate. No wonder the school was so well off.'

'Exactly. It was the perfect set-up for sadists and masochists who want to remain anonymous. That's what made it so popular. It had over three hundred members.'

'Hell of a membership list, too,' said Jaine. 'There are going to be some very red faces in some very high places. Including police HQ, now we know about Nuton-Atkinson's penchant for dressing up as a koala and having his arse whipped raw. I know he wasn't technically doing anything illegal but our dear Chief Superintendent's credibility is shot to hell. I can't imagine him staying in the job.'

'Grown men letting a bunch of women do… things to them. And paying for the privilege,' said Youlden. 'You wouldn't credit it.'

'It's nothing new,' said Gerry Waxleigh. 'Aristotle's mistress used to insist on riding him like a horse before she'd allow him to ride her.'

'So what happened to Miss Bultitude?' asked Vic, joining the conversation. 'I know that Deak was charged with murder.'

'Are you not coming over for the press conference?' asked Jaine. 'You'll hear the full story then.'

'Too busy,' said Vic. 'You can tell me all about it afterwards.'

'She didn't know about what Miss Deak had done so she was only charged with operating a brothel,' explained Jaine. 'And she would have got away with that if she hadn't charged a membership fee. Fundraisers is what she called their meetings.'

'And she did very well from it, too,' added Shunter. 'She wouldn't have needed to sell the Crabbe manuscript, even if she'd known she had it.'

'Amazing to think it was locked in that chest for seventy-odd years and she had no idea,' said Vic.

'And we were completely wrong-footed by it,' said Shunter. 'We were so focused on the idea that Phoebe Kingshaw was murdered over the manuscript that we missed what had really happened – that Miss Deak had overheard her phone call to Sir Giles and had wrongly assumed that "something dynamite" meant she'd discovered the truth about the Millerick Society. She killed Phoebe Kingshaw for completely the wrong reason, tragically.'

'Turns out Deak was a proper sadist and a very strange lady,' said Jaine. 'She got off on inflicting pain, and she hated men. She wrote a lot of dark poetry too, mostly about death and torture. The club was her idea and at the time the school desperately needed the money, so Miss Bultitude went along with it as she's no great lover of the patriarchy either. And it's been going on ever since.'

'Hadn't you better get going?' said Vic, glancing at his watch. 'The talk starts in a quarter of an hour.'

Cliff Jaine and Frank Shunter downed their pints and headed for the door.

'You not going, Barry?' asked Vic.

'I don't really feel like it,' said Chetwynd. He sighed deeply.

'Cheer up. Might never happen,' said Waxleigh.

'It already has,' said the butcher miserably.

The village hall was full to bursting. The majority of the audience was made up of intense middle-aged Agnes Crabbe fans and they had turned out in force. Constance Tremblett was also there with her grandson Oberon, as was SOCO Turvey and local historian Colin Tossel, who looked most aggrieved at not having been invited to contribute. At front and centre sat the Luscott-Whornes, looking remarkably happy and relieved. Jenny Highnote sat next to Cecily; a very recent shift in the domestic arrangements at Proutt House meant she was no longer expected to keep a low profile. Reporters had come from many of the major newspapers and from TV, radio and internet news outlets. Among them all, local pressman Mr Levinshulme and Mr Wyngarde the verger snoozed peacefully. A warm round of applause greeted Andrew Tremens and Frank Shunter as they appeared at the front of the room and took their seats behind a table. From the back of the hall, Cliff Jaine gave them the thumbs up.

'Good evening, ladies and gentlemen,' began Tremens. 'And welcome. I'm Andrew Tremens, legal custodian of the Agnes Crabbe Archive, and I'm joined by my friend, retired police detective Frank Shunter. We have some tremendously exciting news to share with you tonight.'

The room was filled with anticipatory whispers and the sound of digital cameras.

'Firstly, let me lay any rumours and nay-saying to rest,' continued Tremens. 'Agnes Crabbe's long-suspected-lost novel, *Wallowing in the Mire*, has indeed been found, thanks, in no small part, to the diligence and investigatory skills of my colleague here.'

He indicated Shunter and the audience broke into polite, spontaneous applause. Shunter looked mildly embarrassed. Tremens waited for the noise to die down before continuing.

'The manuscript has been authenticated and is currently being prepared for publication in time for the Agnes Crabbe Murder-Mystery Festival in May – and yes, we know that the next six months will feel like an eternity for all true fans. That's why we've decided to hold tonight's event to tell you the story of how the manuscript came to be found. I must warn you, however, that there will be spoilers. We would have preferred to keep the plot of the novel under wraps but, unfortunately, it is inextricably linked to the story of how the manuscript was discovered and it's going to become public knowledge whether we like it or not. I would therefore suggest that if you really don't want to know what the book is about, you leave now.'

'And spend the next six months living like a hermit, like Agnes Crabbe,' added Shunter.

There was a murmur of gentle laughter but no signs of anyone leaving.

'Very well. The book, and our story, both begin in 1914,' said Tremens. 'Frank?'

'As war broke out in Europe, millions of able-bodied men volunteered for active service,' said Shunter. 'Among the many who signed up for the 2nd Battalion Herewardshire Rifles were Agnes Crabbe's father, John Brock, her brother, Tom, and her husband, Daniel. After basic training in the early months of 1915, the battalion was allowed one brief trip home to say goodbye to loved ones before being shipped out to western Belgium to fight for control of the strategically placed Flemish town of Ypres. On the twenty-fourth of May, the battalion took part in the battle for Bellewaarde Ridge, a four-mile-long front near the village of Hooge. It did not go well for our boys. The Germans unleashed their latest weapon – chlorine gas – and half of the battalion fell. Their commanding officer, Lieutenant Colonel Jolyon Whorne, ordered the survivors to launch a counter-offensive. It proved to be equally disastrous. By the end of what became known as the Second Battle of Ypres, more than fifty thousand soldiers had been killed, wounded or were missing in action. And among them were Daniel Crabbe, and John and Thomas Brock.'

'For more than a century, it's been believed that Tom Brock died in that battle,' explained Tremens. 'However, what Frank has discovered, with help from the Tremblett family, is that he not only survived but he probably returned to Nasely in the 1930s.'

In the silence that greeted Andrew Tremens's revelation, Constance Tremblett blew off noisily, much to the amusement of those not sitting close to her.

'Gas warfare,' said Gerry Waxleigh. 'I had no idea we were going to watch a reconstruction.'

'Tom wrote regularly to his sister and to his fiancée, Iris Gobbelin, until April 1915, when all correspondence suddenly stopped,' continued Tremens. 'This was shortly before he was listed by the War Office as missing, presumed dead. However, Frank has discovered letters that he wrote to his best friend, fellow survivor Henry Tremblett, that begin in 1919, some four years after his supposed death. After reading them, and the manuscript, it quickly became clear to us that *Wallowing in the Mire* is not a work of pure fiction.'

This news was met with much excited murmuring among the audience.

'I should explain something before we go any further. *Wallowing in the Mire* does not feature any of Crabbe's regular characters such as Miss Cutter, Colonel Borwick or Inspector Raffo. Nor is it a murder mystery. It's a stand-alone novel that follows the adventures of a soldier called Jack Stillaway both during and after the First World War. And his story appears, in part, to be a fictionalised version of what really happened to Tom Brock. For example, both men fought at the Second Battle of Ypres and their respective battalions suffered heavy losses. And, like Brock, Stillaway was posted as missing in action but he survived and made it off the battlefield.'

'We know from Tom's letters that he wound up in Armentières,' said Shunter, picking up the story. 'But when the town was bombarded with mustard gas in 1918, he and a co-worker called Mathilde fled the city and ended up working on a farm. They lived there contentedly for nearly a decade. And it was from there that he first contacted Henry Tremblett.'

A silence had settled on the hall as the audience drank in the story. The only sounds came from the reporters, and contributors to the many Agnes Crabbe blogs and fanzines, who were scribbling furiously in their notebooks or tapping on tablet screens.

'Then, in 1927, Mathilde unexpectedly fell pregnant,' continued Shunter. 'She was somewhat older than Tom, nearly twenty years older in fact, and, tragically, both she and the baby died during childbirth. Tom was naturally devastated and was still suffering from shell shock, or what we'd now call PTSD. He seems to have had some kind of breakdown after her death. In his final letter to Henry Tremblett, he wrote that he blamed Jolyon Whorne for all of his misfortunes and wished nothing but pain and suffering for him. However, he may have gone further than just wishing.'

'We don't have any real documentary evidence for what happened next,' said Tremens. 'But in the book, Stillaway becomes fixated upon revenge against his former commanding officer, Sir Charles Alyface. He slowly works his way across France by taking on farm work and earning enough money for each stage of his journey, finally arriving in England in late 1929. He intends to return to Little Hogley, but he is tormented by his demons and plagued by doubts. It takes him over three years to work up the courage to return home but he finally does so in the winter of 1933, four years after leaving France. He then builds himself a shelter in Hogley Wood, where he waits for his moment.'

'If we assume that Tom did the same and returned to Nasely, this was when he might have made contact with Agnes and told her his story,' said Shunter. 'He might even have stayed with her at her cottage.'

'Another good reason for her to be so reclusive,' added Tremens.

'Or maybe, as suggested by the novel, he used his army skills to live rough,' said Shunter. 'Perhaps in Black Dog Wood, thereby causing the rash of Shaggy Beast sightings between 1933 and 1934. We know from his letters that he had suffered some kind of facial disfigurement during the war and maybe that, combined with his unkempt hair and a beard, made people think that they'd seen a monster.'

'But now we come to the final part of the story, and it's the part that we know least about,' said Tremens. 'In the book, Stillaway confronts Sir Charles and drags him off into the woods. He blindfolds him to make him understand how his tear-gassed soldiers had felt on the battlefield. Then he tells him that he's going to die. But Sir Charles's own terror is what kills him and he dies of a heart attack. Stillaway buries him where he falls and walks away.'

There was a sharp intake of breath from the audience.

'*Wallowing in the Mire* is a dark tale of revenge,' he continued. 'And quite unlike anything Agnes wrote before or after.'

'The body of a man was found buried in the local woods a few weeks ago,' said Shunter. 'What you may not know is that the body dates from around the time that Agnes wrote *Wallowing in the Mire*, and that the crime scene exactly matches her description of the death of Sir Charles Alyface.'

The room was suddenly full of noisy whispers.

'I therefore imagine that you are now putting two and two together and guessing that the body in the woods must therefore be that of Jolyon Whorne,' continued Shunter. 'But you'd be wrong.'

The whispers turned to excited mutters.

'We'll take a short comfort break,' said Andrew Tremens. 'Any questions so far?'

A roomful of hands were suddenly raised in unison.

In his office above the butcher's shop, Barry Chetwynd read through a feature in the latest copy of scandal rag *The Naked Truth* and cursed the name that appeared in the byline. Pamela Dallimore's exclusive about South Herewardshire's hotbed of sexy shenanigans had appeared, to her good fortune, at exactly the right time. The revelation that a prestigious girls' school had been used for a discreet and exclusive sex club, where the anonymous participants dressed up as animals, had led to her eye-witness accounts being very much in demand. As a result, she had also sold articles to *Hot Bits*, *The Goss* and any number of other similar supermarket magazines where reader titillation was the goal. She had also made frequent TV and radio appearances and bidding among publishers for *The Secret Queen of Crime's Biggest Secret* had become fierce and lucrative. But for Barry Chetwynd, every single article felt like a nail being driven into the coffin of his aspirations. In Dallimore's defence, he conceded that she had only mentioned the legend of the Shaggy Beast in passing and as a rather predictable way to include a pun on the word 'shag'. But there was little doubt in his mind that, barring a miracle, the legend of the Shaggy Beast had been irreparably damaged. He sighed deeply, tore the article from the magazine and tucked the page into his scrapbook, where it nestled with the others that he'd bought. Even though the stories had probably done more harm than good, he couldn't quite break the habit of collecting anything connected to the legend. He'd been doing it his whole life.

He stood up, ducking his head to avoid a sloping beam, and was about to walk downstairs when a resounding ping from his laptop told him that he had a new email. He considered ignoring it but then decided to check, just in case it was from one of his suppliers. To his surprise, it was from Pamela Dallimore and it said, simply, 'A present for you. Partner'. Attached to the email was a photograph, a slightly fuzzy boulder-cam photograph of a human-like figure covered in shaggy fur.

Chetwynd smiled. Perhaps he'd pop back to the pub for one more drink before going home.

'So what's next for you?' asked Shunter.

'Politics is a dead duck,' said Sir Giles. 'Shit sticks, I'm afraid, and even though I've been exonerated, it's unlikely I'd ever land a senior post again.'

He had joined Frank Shunter, Cliff Jaine and Andrew Tremens for a post-gig drink in a packed Happy Onion. Cecily and Jenny had elected to go on to Proutt House.

'To be honest, I'm actually not that bothered any more,' he continued. 'I suspect that this government is going to shoot itself in the foot fairly soon anyway. There was a time when politicians were people who'd seen a bit of life before setting their sights on Westminster. This current generation has gone from prep school to Eton or Harrow, then on to Oxbridge and straight into the party without ever getting their hands dirty. They all have trust funds or Daddy's money to live on, and they have absolutely no idea how normal people live. You can't represent people whose lives you don't understand. So I'm resigning after the election, and then I think I may just take a year off. My companies run themselves anyway, so maybe it's time I enjoyed spending some of the money I've worked so hard for. I really fancy an African safari. Or seeing the Northern Lights. Of course, none of this would have been possible without you two.'

'Just doing what I was paid to do,' said Shunter.

'Me too. Though not paid as well,' said Jaine. 'Who'd be a public servant, eh?'

'There are jobs for both of you, well-paid jobs, working for me if you want them,' said Sir Giles. 'It's the least I can do.'

'I might take you up on that,' said Jaine. 'With all the cutbacks and pay freezes and endless bureaucracy, policing isn't what it used to be.'

'I'm retired,' said Shunter. 'But thanks for the offer. And for making the Whorne family records available to me.'

'You're welcome,' said Sir Giles. 'Having been through what I've been through recently, I have every sympathy with people falsely accused, so I'm keen to find out if my great-grandfather really was the bastard that everyone seems to think he was. Considering where Brock was buried, I have to admit the possibility.'

'It was definitely Tom Brock buried in the woods then?' asked Vic, from behind the bar.

'Definitely,' said Shunter. 'The DNA match was close enough to Brenda Crabbe, his closest living relative, to verify his identity.'

'But was Jolyon directly involved in his death or did his staff do the deed without his knowledge?' said Sir Giles.

'We may never know that for sure, but if I were a betting man, my money would be on Edward Pank, the gamekeeper,' said Shunter. 'I reckon Brock did everything that Stillaway does in the book and Jolyon died of a heart attack. But then I think Pank caught Brock in the act and killed him as an act of revenge.'

'Brock's skeleton has a few broken bones, which suggests a struggle, but not enough to have killed him,' said Jaine. 'And the soil around the bones didn't contain toxins or any indication of excessive blood loss. So we don't know exactly how Brock died. Perhaps he had a heart attack too? Or was asphyxiated in some way that didn't leave any evidence of neck trauma? We'll probably never know for sure.'

'But that doesn't explain why Agnes wrote it all down as a book or how the manuscript ended up at Harpax Grange,' said Sir Giles.

'I have a theory about that,' said Tremens. 'We know that Agnes used her writing as a form of therapy. She slew her personal demons by nailing them to the page, like she did when she wrote about giving her daughter away in *Swords into Ploughshares*, for example. I think that Tom went to Harpax to confront Jolyon but when he didn't return, Agnes guessed that he'd been caught and wrote down his story to keep him alive in the fantasy world inside her head. After all, she never intended it for publication in her lifetime.'

'That doesn't explain how the manuscript ended up at Harpax, though,' said Shunter.

'I suppose Pank and his heavies might have seized it. The timing coincides with some pages that were torn out of Agnes's diary. They could have contained incriminating information.'

'But how would he have learned about the manuscript?' asked Jaine.

'Perhaps he learned about it from Iris?' said Tremens. 'We're pretty sure that Agnes loaned her the manuscript to read. And you know how quickly gossip travels in small villages.'

'We may never know,' said Shunter. 'But I'm going to see if I can discover the truth. And I'll keep digging until I run out of places to dig.'

Epilogue

It was the week before the Agnes Crabbe Murder-Mystery Festival weekend and Nasely was preparing itself, as it did every year, by dressing for the occasion. Clever use of props had transformed the High Street into a facsimile of Crabbe's fictitious Little Hogley and the excitement was building. The event was being used to launch the publication of *Wallowing in the Mire* and fans were coming from all over the world to get a festival special first edition. Ownership of the manuscript had been a tricky subject to resolve but it had eventually been assigned to Andrew Tremens and the Agnes Crabbe Trust. The publishing rights had then been sold for an unspecified amount believed to be in six figures, but Tremens refused to be drawn on the subject. Instead, he had focused everyone's attention on the book's release and had done all he could to make the edition a very special thing indeed, with high production values, a leather slipcase and gold embossing. He had also suggested that it be dedicated to Thomas Brock and to Phoebe Kingshaw. After all, she had found the book after decades of it being lost and she had paid the ultimate price for her discovery. It seemed only right, he argued, that she be recognised. The gesture had delighted her grieving parents, who had also approved the use of some of the advance money to set up the Kingshaw Prize, an award for aspiring new crime fiction authors.

At St Probyn's church, a small congregation had gathered to witness the second and final interment of Tom Brock. The investigation into his murder had been put into storage pending further evidence coming to light, but his remains could provide no more forensic material and had therefore been released for burial. Among those who were braving the warm rain were Brock's great-niece, Brenda Crabbe, Andrew Tremens and a small gang of ardent Millies.

The Reverend Tirbett, sheltering under a quivering umbrella held by the verger, began the final words of blessing.

'And in the certain hope of the resurrection to eternal life through our Lord Jesus Christ, we commend to Almighty God our brother Thomas, and we commit his body to the ground; earth to earth, ashes to ashes, dust to dust. The Lord bless him and keep him, the Lord make his face toaaaarrgh—'

The Reverend Tirbett suddenly yelled and clutched at his eye, having been unexpectedly stabbed by the end of one of the umbrella's ribs. He staggered sideways, dropping his Book of Common Prayer, and as he stepped on it and the pages slid under his foot, he lost his balance and fell backwards into a heavily pregnant Milly, who then fell on to her backside and immediately announced that her waters had broken.

'Oh dear,' said Mr Wyngarde. Ambling forward to render assistance, he slipped on the same open book and, in an effort to regain his balance, grabbed at the nearest person to him, who happened to be Brenda Crabbe. She, in turn, reached out for Andrew Tremens's arm. As all three of them fell into the open grave with a resounding thump, Gerry Waxleigh, who was watching the service from over the outer wall of the graveyard, smiled and patted his companion on the shoulder.

'That's possibly the new Number One, Len,' he said. 'Fancy a pint?'

'No time,' said Youlden. 'I've got a tourist party coming on my Shaggy Beast tour in ten minutes.'

'Then how about we go and take one last look at Gladys Brockhole's cock? They're painting over it today. It feels like saying goodbye to an old friend.'

As they made their way along the busy High Street, they watched the decoration of the shops and ruminated upon recent events.

'Don't seem the same without Harpax girls coming into town, does it?' said Youlden. 'I used to like seeing them around.'

'You wouldn't remember what to do with one if you caught her,' said Waxleigh.

'I don't mean it like that,' said Youlden. 'I mean that the village just seems… older now they're gone.'

'Chin up,' said Waxleigh. 'Cecily Luscott owns Harpax now, and with her and that wife of hers turning it into a drama school, there'll be lots of pretty young things in the village again soon enough.'

'The damp problem's all sorted now?'

'So I understand. Perhaps they'll start work on fixing Miss Shelmerdine next?'

'Miss Bultitude selling her the Grange like that must have stuck in Sir Giles's throat,' said Youlden. 'He'd been after it for years. And on top of a divorce settlement too.'

'Ah, he has plenty more money. And he says he's lost interest now. As I understand it, he's pretty keen to divorce himself from his family's past. And he's happy enough, travelling the world with his new woman.'

'I'll tell you what I never figured out,' said Youlden. 'Why did Miss Bultitude spend her evenings wandering around the woods in that wolf costume?'

'To scare away the doggers, that's why,' said Waxleigh. 'The last thing she wanted was regular police visits to the area. Nothing more guaranteed to frighten her clientele away.'

A small crowd of tourists was waiting outside what had once been Witton's Florists, closed ever since Mrs Witton had discovered that Mr Witton had been a member of the Millerick Society and had a fetish for displaying flowers using one of his bodily orifices as a vase. It now bore a sign that said 'Shaggy Beast Museum and Gift Shop'. Outside the door stood a tall fibreglass werewolf that people were posing with while taking selfies.

'Is that your tour party?' asked Waxleigh.

'That's today's beer money,' said Youlden with a gap-toothed smile. As he approached the tourists, he launched into his patter.

'Let me tell you all about the legend of the Shaggy Beast... It all began with Sir Veryard Whorne. He had a prize hunting hound, you see. A big black monster of a brute it was...'

Waxleigh smiled and made his way towards the Happy Onion.

Inside the new museum, Barry Chetwynd made the final adjustments to his displays. It was his first festival as proprietor and he was hoping to do a roaring trade with the hundreds of Agnes Crabbe fans soon to arrive. He'd commissioned all manner of touristy gifts for people to take away as mementos of Nasely's local monster. Shaggy Beast postcards, snow globes, tea towels and key rings; he had it all. There was even a set of Russian-style nested dolls; a *matryoshka* in which Colonel

Trayhorn Borwick sat inside Miss Cutter who sat inside Agnes Crabbe who sat inside the Shaggy Beast. Even though there was no real link between the great author and the Beast, Chetwynd was keen to make one, and on display inside the Whorne family's ottoman was a facsimile of the manuscript to *Wallowing in the Mire* along with the outsize dog collar that had been found with it. No one knew why it had been in the trunk, nor to what animal it had belonged, but that didn't matter to Barry Chetwynd. It was now labelled as the collar once worn by Shax, Sir Veryard Whorne's great black hunting hound, whose death had given birth to the legend. The ottoman sat underneath the stuffed head of the Boar King, which, like the ottoman, had been kindly donated to the museum by Cecily – she'd never liked the thing anyway. And hanging behind the cash desk was a blow-up of the mysterious photograph captured by Professor Gravestock's cameras of a man-sized hairy figure. No one had yet come up with a good explanation for it. It wasn't a photo of Miss Bultitude, as her costume had been in the police property store ever since Jamie Cordery had been arrested wearing it. And it wasn't one of the Millerick Society members. The photo was the subject of much discussion among cryptozoologists and had formed the centrepiece of Pamela Dallimore's three-part TV series *Monsters Walk Among Us*. Barry Chetwynd was delighted, as his many interviews and TV appearances had given him the cash boost he'd needed to set up his museum.

'Where should I put this box of T-shirts?' asked Jessie Tremblett.

'In the store room, on the shelf above the wolf masks,' said Chetwynd with a smile. He knew that local people looked upon them as an odd couple and that some even saw him as some kind of cradle-snatcher. But Jessie was twenty-three, had always had a mature head on her shoulders and she much preferred older men. They'd met quite by accident in Black Dog Wood one evening while he'd been prowling about recording video for a podcast and she'd been looking for some excitement. One thing had led to another and they had been together ever since. They still thoroughly enjoyed the occasional bout of al fresco sex in the woods, even if some of the time Barry insisted that they did so in werewolf costumes for the sake of the tourist trade.

The Land Rover came to a halt and the driver handed Sir Giles a pair of binoculars. He pointed towards a dark shape some distance away. Giles peered through the lenses.

'That's fantastic,' said Giles. 'Take a look, Ett.'

Ettie McNabb took the binoculars and aimed them at where Giles had indicated. A large rhinoceros lugubriously munched on a mouthful of dry grass, unaware that it was being spied on.

'Wow. I hadn't realised they were so big,' she said. 'What an amazing creature. How can anyone kill one of them just for its horn?'

'Greed,' said Giles. 'People get paid a lot more to kill rhinos than to protect them. That's why I made such made a big donation to the charity; to help fund the anti-poaching staff. Rhinos need all the friends they can get.'

'You're a good man, Giles,' said Ettie. She snuggled into him as the Land Rover moved off. He wrapped a protective arm around her as the vehicle bucked and bounced its way over the grass towards a dirt track road. 'So, is this better than the Northern Lights?'

'Not better. Different. But just as amazing,' said Ettie. She snuggled even closer, despite the heat of the day. 'I love you, Giles Whorne.'

'And I love you too, Lorraine Butler,' said Giles.

'You're never going to let me forget that, are you, Gerry?'

'Touché,' said Giles. He smiled. 'I didn't think I'd ever get to say that to anyone, you know.'

'What?'

'I love you.'

'Not even to Phoebe?' said Ettie. 'You said that she loved you.'

'I suppose I might have one day. I was very fond of her.'

'That's sad. It means she died never knowing if you loved her back.'

'I know. I was a different man back then – a selfish and not very nice man,' said Giles. 'I'd lost sight of the important things. You fixed me.'

'I guess you could say that the Butler did it,' said Ettie.

At Gertie's Plash, a Nagle's red-headed merganser came in to land and skidded to a halt on the surface. It shook the water drops from its wings as it was closely followed by its mate. They were one of three pairs that had been spotted nesting among the reeds and bulrushes in recent months, to the delight of local twitchers. One nest reportedly had seven eggs in it already, which was very good news. Colin Cheeseman ticked the double sighting off his checklist and cross-referenced it to wherever his sightings book demanded and then showed Maisie how to do the same. It wasn't the easiest of books to complete but it was exactly how Colin wanted it, which was the important thing. No other local birdwatching group had a system as complex or as comprehensive as his. That was why he and Maisie – who had introduced him to the joys of birdwatching – had co-founded the Bowcester and District Ornithologists Society. At least, together, they could ensure that things were done the right way.

'Lunch?' said Maisie.

'Good idea. Where shall we go? There's a pub in Ordon that does really nice veggie burgers.'

'You choose,' said Maisie. 'Oh, hello, Bron, Willy.'

The Tremblett twins had appeared.

'Did you see the mergansers?' asked Willy excitedly.

'Actually, we were the first to see them,' gloated Colin. 'It'll mean a fourth nest if they stay.'

'That's great news,' said Bron.

'Still taking water samples for the university?' asked Maisie.

'Yeah. The draining churned up a lot of muck at the bottom of the pond so they're monitoring it, just in case. And you'll be pleased to hear that FLAN has stayed active since you left. We're keeping up the protests at the abattoir.'

'Glad to hear it,' said Colin sniffily. 'Be seeing you.'

As he walked away, Bron sidled up to Maisie. 'Tell me,' he said. 'What do you see in him?'

'I'm hugely OCD,' said Maisie. 'And he's a control freak. We keep each other's lives in order. I need someone like that. And I think he does too.'

'Then I'm happy you're happy,' said Bron. 'Just do your best to make him less of a twat, will you?'

As Maisie went off to join her boyfriend, Bron joined Willy at the pond to take their samples. Some of the effects of Colin's hose incident were still evident seven months on in the form of two trenches that the force of the water had cut into the muddy shore. Bron smiled as he remembered that moment. And then he spotted something glinting in the shallow water at the very edge of the pond. He reached in and lifted it out. It was a gold signet ring inset with a large blue stone which itself was inset with the gold initials RW. It was obviously very old and possibly quite valuable. Without a second thought, Bron threw it out into the middle of the pond.

Frank Shunter locked his shed and looked proudly at his garden, which was wonderfully in bloom. His months of hard work were showing in the colourful borders, flower-filled beds and neatly cropped lawns. All was well with the world once again; the house was finished and Mrs Shunter was happy. They were even looking forward to their first overseas holiday in years and had deliberately booked it to coincide with the Agnes Crabbe Murder-Mystery Festival. It was likely to be an even busier affair than usual because of the book launch, and Shunter planned to be a long way away when the first copies went on sale.

His mobile phone rang. It was Cliff Jaine, now head of security at the abattoir and meat-packing factory.

'So, how's the new job suiting you?' asked Shunter.

'Great,' said Jaine. 'Half the hassle, double the wages and all the free sausages I can scoff. Sir Giles has done me proud. The toughest it gets is keeping an eye on light-fingered staff and monitoring the protesters outside the slaughterhouse.'

'They're still there?'

'Every day. But they're no problem really. There's only about five of them and the worst thing they've ever done is draw a cock and balls on a wall.'

'Excellent. So what can I do for you?'

'Just thought I'd let you know that you'll be getting a new DI at Bowcester soon. I'm told by my ex-colleagues that McNabb is being transferred to HQ at Uttercombe.'

'Out of harm's way, eh? Smart move.'

'He got a good result with the Harpax Grange case but he's not Chief Inspector material so they can't promote him.'

'He's reached his level of incompetence.'

'Ha! That's about right. They're putting him in charge of an HQ department – parking or pub licensing or something equally non-threatening like that – so that he feels like he's being rewarded, even if he isn't.'

'Perfect.'

'Well, have a great holiday, Frank. We'll have a beer in the Onion when you get back.'

'Cheers, Cliff. Don't eat too many pork pies.'

Shunter hung up and realised that his ancient radio had fallen silent during his phone call. Or he assumed that it had. How long ago it had actually stopped working he didn't know; its crackly sound had only ever been background noise to accompany him while he worked. He shook it a few times and considered changing the batteries but he knew it would be a useless gesture. The radio had had its day, as everything eventually did. But that was fine. That was the way of things; the new eventually replaced the old and he promised himself that he would buy a new radio the next time he went shopping in Bowcester. He had been paid quite handsomely by Sir Giles for his services and his bank account was looking unusually healthy. He could afford it.

Or perhaps he'd buy himself a sports car.

We hope you enjoyed your visit to South Herewardshire.
Please come again soon for Stevyn Colgan's next novel:
Cockerings.

Visit here at:
unbound.com/books/cockerings

Acknowledgements

This book was written at home in South Buckinghamshire, but also on trains to Birmingham, Bristol, Cardiff, Edinburgh, Folkestone, Gravesend, Oxford, Stoke-on-Trent and York; in tea shops in Fitzrovia and Covent Garden; in the Coal Hole in Charing Cross; in the Pillars of Hercules and the French House in Soho; at the extraordinary Barscobe House in Balmaclellan, Kirkcudbrightshire, and the equally fantastic Cluer Cottage on the island of Harris; at the ITV London Studios and BBC Broadcasting House; in the Wellcome Library and the café at Foyles bookshop, Charing Cross Road; on flights to and from Berlin and Aberdeen; and the final two chapters were written at the St Regis Hotel, Kuala Lumpur.

It's been quite a year.

In the book that preceded this one, *A Murder to Die For*, I planted anagrams of ten Agatha Christie book titles as character names and invited readers to find them if they felt like it. If you were one of those readers and you want to know the answers, please go to:

> https://amurdertodiefor.blogspot.com/2016/05/putting-
> you-out-of-your-misery.html

I haven't put any sneaky anagrams into *The Diabolical Club* but I have paid homage to some of my favourite books, films, TV and radio shows – mostly comedies or murder mysteries – by liberally sprinkling references throughout the text. For example, in Chapter 26, when Mrs Dallimore sees a copy of 'Ernest Wallengren's painting of a can of Simpkin's Cream of Celery Soup', I'm referencing three episodes of the TV show *Diagnosis Murder*; specifically, a Season 2 two-parter called *The Last Laugh* and a Season 5 episode called *Obsession* in which the painting appears. And in Chapter 6, the village of Tingwell is named for Charles 'Bud' Tingwell who played Inspector Craddock in all four of the Margaret Rutherford *Miss Marple* films (there's also a character called Craddock in Chapter 24).

I wonder how many you'll spot? You'll find a full list of them here:

https://amurdertodiefor.blogspot.com/2016/05/putting-you-out-of-your-misery-part-ii.html

Now, on with the thanks.

This book only exists because of the genius of those that went before. I therefore want to take this opportunity to say 'thank you' to the late Douglas Adams, Kingsley Amis, Beryl Bainbridge, Ronnie Barker, H. E. Bates, Michael Bentine, W. E. Bowman, Eddie Braben, Anthony Buckeridge, Graham Chapman, T. E. B. 'Tibby' Clarke, Peter Cook, Alan Coren, Richmal Crompton, Roald Dahl, Les Dawson, Mary Dunn, Marty Feldman, George MacDonald Fraser, Ray Galton and Alan Simpson, Stella Gibbons, George and Weedon Grossmith, Alan Hackney, Harry Harrison, Joseph Heller, Jerome K. Jerome, Carla Lane, Compton Mackenzie, J. P. Martin, Spike Milligan, Eric Morecambe, John Mortimer, Neil Munro, David Nobbs, Dennis Norden and Frank Muir, Flann

O'Brien, Michael Pertwee, Stephen Potter, Terry Pratchett, Frank Richards, Talbot Rothwell, Willie Rushton, W. C. Sellar and R. J. Yeatman, Tom Sharpe, Ned Sherrin, Larry Stevens, Eric Sykes, Leslie Thomas, Barry Took, Keith Waterhouse, Evelyn Waugh, Leonard Wibberley, Geoffrey Willans and Ronald Searle, Kenneth Williams, P. G. Wodehouse, Victoria Wood... and so many others whose loss to the world of comic writing is incalculable. They taught me that words are funnier than pictures, and this book would not exist without their inspiration. There are far too few humorous novels being published these days and far too many risk-averse publishers. I hope that *The Diabolical Club* does its small bit to rectify that.

And so, on to the personal thanks, starting with my excellently named literary agent, Piers Blofeld, my speaking agent Bruce Hood, and my unimpeachable gaggle of close friends and critical readers: Terry Bergin, Jo Haseltine, Steve Hills, Andrew Hodge, Sarah Libman, Erica McAlister, Linda Nagle, Morgan Phillips, Phil Speechley, Janice Staines, Mark Vent and Huw Williams. Thanks also to Michael Dillon at Gerry's Club, to Sam and Briege at Jazz After Dark, to m'chum Dr Ciarán O'Keefe for tea, banter and paranormal investigator stuff, and to Andy Aliffe, Eddie Brazil and David Kidd-Hewitt for sharing their storehouse of local folklore and knowledge about secret societies and demon dogs. Additional thanks to Helen Saxton and Charaderie (who organise the best murder-mystery parties) and to the staff of the Hell-Fire Club Caves and Dashwood Estate in West Wycombe.

On the production side of things, I need to thank Xander Cansell, Mathew Clayton, Sara Magness, Josephine Salverda and Simon Spanton for taking on and steering *The Diabolical Club* through to publication, Ilona Chavasse, Catherine Emery and Caitlin Harvey who tirelessly organise things behind the scenes, and Mark Bowsher and Elena Lopez-Brea Sanchez of Rabbit Island Productions who braved fog, drizzle and cold to make my promotional video. My amazing editors were Bill Massey and Jenni Davis and my proofreader was Lottie Fyfe. The book was designed by the incomparable Mark Ecob and the cover painted by the legend that is Neil Gower. Big thanks also go to Aimee Hogston and Catherine Thompson of Isis Publishing and the divine Rula Lenska for their brilliant audiobook production of *A Murder to Die For*.

I must also thank the authors who populate the Unbound authors' private Facebook group. Never has there been gathered together a more understanding, supportive, inspiring and energising group of writers. They are amazing.

But, as always, my biggest thanks go to my family and to all of those wonderful people who saw my book on the Unbound website and pledged their hard-earned or ill-gotten money to ensure that it got published. There's a list of them on the next few pages. As long as there are kind, generous, open-minded people like these, new books will continue to appear that aren't all TV tie-ins, or the ghost-written 'autobiographies' of ephemeral celebs.

Thank you lovely patrons. You are the best.

Unbound is the world's first crowdfunding publisher, established in 2011.

We believe that wonderful things can happen when you clear a path for people who share a passion. That's why we've built a platform that brings together readers and authors to crowdfund books they believe in – and give fresh ideas that don't fit the traditional mould the chance they deserve.

This book is in your hands because readers made it possible. Everyone who pledged their support is listed below. Join them by visiting unbound.com and supporting a book today.

Meagan Cihlar
Sue Clark
Jenny Clarke
Theo Clarke
Michael Cmar
Dane Cobain
Bill Colegrave
Liam Colgan
Gina R. Collia
Thomas Collier
Debra Collis
Louis Constandinos
John Crawford
Heather Culpin
Ruth Curtis
Trisha D'Hoker
Steve Dabner
Andy Davey
Nicholas James Davey
E R Andrew Davis
Amanda de Grey
John Dexter
Miranda Dickinson
Chris Dingley
Jenny Doughty
Allan Douglas
Helen Ducker
Robert Eardley
Cherise Elizabeth
Sean Ellis
Ptolemy Elrington
Grahame Elson
Chris Emerson
Clare England
Tony Evans
Jane Farmery
Liam Flanagan
Terence Flanagan
Piers Fletcher
Lizzy Fone
Matthew Fox
CM Franklyn
Kevin Friery
Caroline Gale
Alison Garner
Sharon Garratt

Andrew George
Alex Gilbert
Robin Gluckman
Heide Goody
John Goonan
Heather Govier
Tony Greengrass
Eamonn Griffin
Paul Groom
Stephanie Grootenhuis
Geoff Haederle
Dave Hall
Pat Harkin
Michael Harris
A.F. Harrold
harryfiddler
Jo Haseltine
Maximilian Hawker
Liz Hayward
Tony & Maria Hearne
Katherine Heathcote
David Hester
Kathryn Hill
Matt Hill
Steve Hills
Peter Hobbins
Andrew Hodge
Ivonne Hoeger
Paul Holbrook
Rachael Hulbert
Andy Hunter
Julian Hynd
Oli Jacobs
Crispian Jago
Cliff Jaine
Neil Jeffery
Alexander Jegtnes
Paul Jenkins
Marjorie Johns
Kitty Johnson
Al Johnston
Joyce Jones
Laura Jordan-Rowell
Michelle K
Peter Kelly
Sian Kelly

Adam Kennedy
Ella Kennedy
Andrew Keogh
Dan Kieran
Patrick Kincaid
Shona Kinsella
Doreen Knight
Ian Knight
Mit Lahiri
Terry Lander
David Lars Chamberlain
Iszi Lawrence
Ewan Lawrie
Robert Loch
Amy Lord
Angela Lord
Tim Lund Jørgensen
Rhona Macfarlane
Alistair Mackie
Alisdair Maclean
Cait MacPhee
Rebecca Major
Philippa Manasseh
Sarah K. Marr
Victoria Mather
Trevor Mathers
Bartolome Mayol
Pamela McCarthy
Carol McCollough
Audrey McDade
Mo McFarland
John A C McGowan
Alan McHenry
Gavin McKeown
Liane McNeil
Jesper Meisner
Andrew Merritt
Barry Miller
Pauline Millward
John Mitchinson
Virginia Moffatt
Louise Moore
Gareth Morgan
Cara Morris
Lauren Mulville
Jessica Myles

Carlo Navato
Chris Neale
John New
Marie-Jose Nieuwkoop
Jenny Noakes
Vaun earl Norman
Jan O'Malley
Lev Parikian
Samantha Parnell
Rebecca Pascoe
Isobel Payne
David Perez
Melanie Perry
Morgan Phillips
Derek and Dave Philpott
Kim Pike
Jane Pink
Justin Pollard
Beki Pope
Daniel Pope
Lawrence Pretty
Trevor Prinn
Paul Rawcliffe
Rebecca Read
Colette Reap
Simon Reap
Val Reid
Natalie Reis
Christopher Richardson
Deborah Rivers
Kate Roberts
Paul Robinson
David Roche
Angella and Alan Rodgers
Sid Rodrigues
Kenn W Roessler
Bernie Sammon
Helen Saxton @Charaderie
Neil Sayer
Danny Scheerlinck
Richard Selwyn
Sue Sharpe
Keith Sherratt
Rebecca Sickinger
Mark Skinner
Andrew Sleight

Keith Sleight
Neil Sleight
Peter Sleight
Toni Smerdon
Jennie Smith
Jenny Smith
Peter Smith
Lili Soh
Elizabeth Stahlmann
Janice Staines
Karen Staines
Roy and Lynn Staines
Ruth Staines
Terry and Sue Staines
John Stares
Malcolm Stein
Ros Stern
Kathryn Stevenson
Tom Stone
Tanya Stratton
Rory Sutherland
Christine Taylor
Jillian Tees
Mike Scott Thomson
Dougald Tidswell
Solitaire Townsend
Kelly Townshend
Dan Trudgian
David G Tubby
Cara Usher

Sue Valentine
Mark Vent
Jose Vizcaino
Tabatha Von Spanksalot
Damon L. Wakes
Lauren Walker
Steve Walker
Michael Wallbanks
Nick Walpole
Breda Walton
Julie Warren
Paul Waters
Pete Watt
Andy Wears
Lucy White
Chris Whittle
Carol Whitton
Geoff Williams
Julian Williams
Sean Williams
Iris B. Willinger
Alexa Wilson
Derek Wilson
Elizabeth Wilson
Gavin Wilson
Stacey Woods
Liz Wooldridge
Wendalynn Wordsmith
Colin and Rachel Wright
Lucien Young